I0691988

SAGA OF A NEUROSURGEON SERIES, BOOK III

HEAVEN

AND

HELL

*Garven Wilsonhulme takes on all comers
in the jungle of modern competition*

Carl Douglass

Neurosurgeon Turned Author Writes with Gripping Realism

PO Box 221974 Anchorage, Alaska 99522-1974
books@publicationconsultants.com—www.publicationconsultants.com

ISBN 978-1-59433-351-4
eISBN: 978-1-59433-352-1
Library of Congress Catalog Card Number: 2013930990

Manufactured in the United States of America.

Disclaimer

"This is a story, a fiction, where all but a very few names have been changed to protect the people deserving of great respect and are, in all cases, cast in a deservedly positive light. They are minor characters in the book and its story. Other characters and the part they play in the *Saga* are loosely based on real people, including the author, whose names are changed; the places they work in the book are fictitious or different from where they were actually encountered by the present author. Some of the experiences described and the characters depicted are amalgamations of persons, places, and actions, and some diluted and altered autobiographical remembrances. There are healthy dollops of whimsy running throughout even the autobiographical hints.

The world of Garven Wilsonhulme is indeed fiction, but while not exactly real, it is faithful to an era of neurosurgical training and experience that is almost entirely a thing of the past. The independence and cowboy experience of being trained in a blood and guts trauma hospital in that era is not an exaggeration. There are some of those old men (and women) out there who will smile as they read and remember. If nothing else, the experiences of those semi-pioneers are the stuff of legend, humor, and pathos that invite endlessly fascinating yarns by all those consummate raconteurs.

The world of medicine and surgery is far more sophisticated and genteel now, far more of a closely controlled corporate money and legalistically driven environment. No longer can residents work 120 hours a week by federal and state law. It is all but unthinkable for a trainee to act with cavalier unsupervised independence in the closely monitored environment of the programs of the twenty-first century. A Garven Wilsonhulme would never make it into or through the training or the vicissitudes of neurosurgical practice in today's world without a very considerable amount of refinement and bowing to the ethical, moral, legal, and scientific standards of the present day. But then, neurosurgeons are eminently tough and adaptable. Maybe even Garven could make his way in the new paradigm as he did in the era of forty and fifty years ago when this *Saga* took place. The author would like to think he could.

Dedication

The series of books is dedicated to those giants upon whose shoulders I stood, including: Harvey Birsner, M.D., my partner and friend; Shelly Chou, M.D., PhD., my great mentor; Kemp Clark, M.D., The Chief; Stephen David Durrant, PhD., professor of biology/evolution/comparative anatomy, a curmudgeon, humorist, inspiration, and friend; Lyle A. French, M.D., PhD.; the grand master at Minnesota; William Wallace Newby, PhD., Professor of biology/embryology, my greatest friend and help; Lito Porto, M.D., The Indian; J. Charles Rich, M.D., my worthy opponent in premed and the consummate neurosurgeon and contributor to the neurosurgical community; Theodore Roberts, M.D., my start; Duke Samson, M.D., the great builder of neurosurgery and foremost of brain vascular surgeons; Charles Sternbergh, M.D., the rock of integrity; Clark C. Watts, M.D. J.D., my friend and support during the lean years.

Acknowledgments

The author acknowledges with appreciation the direct contributions to the books of Harvey Birsner, M.D., Keith Hooker, M.D., Kim Oliver, M.D., Brent Pratley, M.D., Charles Stewart, M.D., and all of the general surgery and neurosurgery interns, residents and professors in California, Utah, Minnesota, Texas, Virginia, and the men and women of the navy who served with me.

"It was Prof. Newly's announced opinion and intention that no student ever deserved a 100 percent score on one of his tests, and Garven Wilsonhulme made it one of his lifetime goals to achieve a perfect paper, as much for the sporting aspect of it as anything. He had done very well, demonstrating a real aptitude for the advanced zoology subjects. On the midterm, Garven found the test to be a combination of old test questions which he had meticulously written out and memorized in advance. He was delighted at the opportunity to excel, and painstakingly recreated his mental notes about the previously answered questions. The material was as clear in his mind as if he had held an open book in front of him, and when the time was up in the test, Garven knew that he had handed in a perfect test, blue books full of detailed and accurate argument and description.

Dr. Newly was correct about his tests, even on this one. Garven read his score on the written segment—99 percent. At first, he was angry; the old man was just being contrary and arbitrary. Then he read the red pencil note explaining why he had lost a point on his perfect paper:

"Your answer was too long."

Garven burst out laughing and caught Dr. Newly's eye. The professor had been watching him to see his reaction. There was a brief bond between teacher and student; Garven stifled his protest.

"Formerly, when religion was strong and science weak, men mistook magic for medicine; now, when science is strong and religion weak, men mistake medicine for magic."

-Thomas Szasz, *The Second Sin (1973)*
"Science and Scientism"

CHAPTER
One

Lyle's apartment house was not difficult to find; it was in the rundown section of Phoenix, across from the Union Pacific Motor Freight depot. It was tricky to find the specific apartment because the numbers on most of the rooms had long since fallen off. By counting and a judicious guess, Garven selected the correct door and entered. The door was unlocked—there was no lock. He knew it was the right apartment because he found a hand-scrawled note from his old friend:

June 3, 1951

Garv -
Had to go back up to Cipher, my dad's sick. Left Wed. be back
Sunday. Meet the others (I did tell you about them, right?) and
I'll see you then. Take the empty back bedroom bed. I have the
one by the door.

Lyle

He would have known anyway by the degree of litter in the apartment. Nobody but Lyle could make such a mess without hiring the job done. Garven relaxed and threw his things on the dirty mattress, making an effort not to look at it closely.

Lyle's note gave him a small inspiration. He wrote his own note to corroborate his story that he had left Stanford the day before Dr. Simpkins' accident.

June 3, 1951

Lyle,

Thanks. I got your note when I came in from Calif. late Wed. night. I had to go up to Emmett to see my dad. See you Sun.

Garven

Garven knew that Dr. Wilsonhulme was on a European tour, his 'last fling', as he termed it, and would not be back for three weeks. He could say that he had made the trip to Emmett, and no one would be the wiser. He placed both notes in the empty drawer of the only chest of drawers in the two-room apartment. He presumed the space had been left for him. The lie in his note obligated him to be gone until Sunday, two days away, since he was likely to run into the other two roommates when they came home from work, and they could poke a hole in his story if it ever came to that. Garven was a belt and suspenders pragmatist unwilling to take chances; so, he checked into a no-tell motel on the opposite side of town and paid cash. The motel had the luxury of having a pool, and Garven spent two days basking in the sun and slipping in and out of the pool, draining away the enervation accumulated from the past quarter's grind, and the ennui that had settled in on his psyche after the initial sustained adrenaline charge from the terrible meeting with Dr. Simpkins had worn off.

The two Neanderthals were on their beds asleep when Garven walked back into the apartment mid Sunday afternoon. His unpacking and bed making waked them up. The place and the two roommates made Garven think of Halloween at the Elk's club.

"Hey, you must be Garden," said the smaller, thinner of the two.

"Hey, Garden," called the other in a slow, tired voice.

"It's Garven with a 'v', not 'Garden' like in vegetable," Garven corrected hopefully.

"Hey, right," the smaller man said semi-apologetically. "I'm Ray. Ray Hubbard."

"Bill Robert Taylor," said the larger young man. "Everybody calls me 'Bubba'. I'm from Arkansas originally. More'n half of all the men I know are called 'Bubba'."

"Ray, Bubba, glad to meet you. I guess you guys work with Lyle for UPR, huh?"

"Yep."

"Lyle, he's went back home for a coupla days. Expect him in tonight."

"I got his note."

"You hired on official, yet, Garven?"

"Nope, what do I have to do?"

"We'll go in early tomorrow and see old Holespeach; he's the foreman. Lyle said he fixed it up already. You just have to sign a few papers and all. Simple. Start work tomorra, I 'magine."

The four young men, including Lyle, who had come back to the apartment during the night, were on the loading ramp at seven-thirty the next morning. Garven stood out from the others by his small stature, but more because of his new bib overalls, steel-toed shoes, and mule skin gray gloves. There was no one else on the dock.

Leonard Holespeach strode rapidly to his office door, opened it with one of the Sladge keys from the huge ring hanging from a retractable chain on his belt, and gestured for the workers to come in. He was a florid faced, bluff man with bushy eyebrows and a mustache that matched them exactly. It looked as if he had started out with three eyebrows, and one of them had slipped.

"This the new man, Lyle?" he asked.

"Garven Carmichael," Lyle answered.

"It's Wilsonhulme now, Lyle," Garven interjected.

"You the college boy?" Holespeach asked, turning his attention to Garven finally.

"Yes, Sir."

"I presume you can lift boxes. Can you drive a truck?"

"Yes, Sir."

"You have to have a chauffeur's license to drive a UP truck, you got one?"

"Yes, Sir."

He was glad Lyle had forewarned him. He had gotten the required license in California during Spring Quarter—in his copious free time.

"You want to start today?"

Holespeach looked at his watch—still plenty of time before shift start at eight o'clock.

"I'm ready."

"Okay, fill out these here papers. They're the application forms, the swearing that you aren't a convicted criminal or a mental patient or anything, and the union sign-up sheet."

Garven quickly filled out the forms, except the union sign-up sheet to join the Teamsters and handed them back to Holespeach, who was busy making out the work assignments for the day.

"You don't have the union sign-up sheet filled in. Got to do that."

"Well, Mr. Holespeach, I don't really want to join the union. Arizona is a right-to-work state, right? And I am just not much for joining organizations."

"No union, no job. Simple as that. You are the new boy here. Let me tell you the way it is. If I let you work on this dock or get into one of those trucks out there without bein' in the Teamsters, they would find you and me in a ditch somewheres before the end of the week. So, it's Holespeach's rule, the company rule, and the union rule—no union, no job here. Any other dumb questions or comments?"

Garven did not feel like any kind of crusader for individual rights, even his own. He filled out the forms and signed them. There was a separate line to sign guaranteeing payment of initiation dues up front and monthly union dues. For his convenience, the dues could come right out of his check unless he signed the next line refusing to have the deduction. He was content to have the union pick his pocket before he ever saw the money, he guessed; so, he left that line blank.

"Your first check will be a little short, what with the union initiation fee and first month's dues. Be glad you got a job that pays union scale; can't beat a buck an hour these days."

They shook hands, and Garven turned to leave to find out where to go to work.

Holespeach called him back for a minute. "Look Garven. It's first names around here. We try to get along. Come to me if you have any trouble. Otherwise, I will keep out of your hair as long as you do the work. And I'm servin' notice right now. You are through at the end of September. That's because you got a chance to be somethin', somethin' more than these bums here. I ain't goin' to let you stay here thinkin' you are makin' so much money that you even hesitate about shuckin' your education. You understand me?"

"I do, and thanks."

"Thanks, Leonard," the foreman said and smiled.

"Leonard," Garven said.

Garven worked for two weeks before he had any trouble. Everyday he came to work on time and watched the guys who had been around for a while, including Ray and Bubba, find hiding places on the freight cars to lie down and rest most of the day while he patiently loaded the trucks on the opposite side of the dock with Lyle. It was particularly commodious for the other guys because some of the main things hauled by the railroad through Phoenix were mattresses. He figured it was none of his business. Leonard Holespeach never came out onto the docks except to bring a bill of lading or a loading authorization to one of the leadmen. Those guys had an uncanny sense of when Leonard would be coming and were always up and working when he arrived.

Lyle clued Garven in about how to load the boxes onto the trucks—sixty to seventy percent of the load in the front and twenty-five percent of the remaining over the rear axle; heavy boxes on the bottom, light on top; stack the boxes right to the ceiling of the truck in the front and taper off to the rear, unless the boxes were of uniform size, and there were enough of them. The big fellow patiently showed Garven how to drive the truck; despite possessing a chauffeur's license—Garven had never actually driven one— and where the main delivery sites were in the city.

One of the freight car loaders got badly hurt in the spring rodeo in Apache Junction and was out of work indefinitely. Lyle got the cowboy's job and a little raise; and he, too, went off to find a place to lie down during work hours.

Lyle had only one complaint, "I don't see why they don't just mail out the checks and save everybody the bother of showing up here every day."

A malcontent who had some way run afoul of the local Teamsters boss was to be punished by having to leave the cushy job on the railroad cars to come out onto the dock and to partner up with Garven to load the trucks—a job whose main drawback was that it was done in the open where the foreman could see them for the most part. The malcontent's punishment was that, in addition to coming to the job every day, now he might have to work, too.

Harvey Bitdorf, Garven's new partner, was stupid and lazy to begin with and generally of bad temper. Now, he had been made to suffer an injustice. The Teamsters' boss did not talk nice to him, not nice at all; and he had had to take it without opening his yap. Bigshot Holespeach had acted pleased as could be that he could make Harvey get back onto the dock to load trucks. He had had to take that, too. But he did not have to take any lip or anything of the new guy, the college kid. Think's he's so smart. Who's he think he is anyway?

Harvey had little to say. He stood by just inside the truck freight compartment and watched Garven work when he was not watching for Holespeach to sneak out on the dock to spy on him. Garven decided it was none of his business if the ugly, mongrel-looking moron wouldn't work, but it still bugged him some. The only time the two of them spoke was when Garven carried in a heavy box, and the moron was in the way of where the box had to be transported or had to be set down.

Then the conversation was "Move, please," and "Don't have to."

Harvey usually did move without causing undue impediment to Garven's work; so, Garven did not let himself get upset. Not for two weeks. The trouble started when Garven finished loading a truck with newsprint bound for the

Arizona Republic; and because there was only one guy loading, the shipment was behind schedule; and Leonard got on his and Harvey's butts about it.

Garven knew the chewing out was deserved, at least on dumb Harvey's part; and he was disinclined to say anything about how lazy the brute was. He was tempted just a little to break his rule about snitching, but he controlled himself. Harvey got in his way as Garven rushed around to get into the driver's seat of the truck.

"Gotta move faster, college boy, or old Holespeach is gonna take off another chunk. I guess you are just gonna have to work harder or get reported to the union, little man," the larger worker—using the term loosely—said in his dull and taunting voice.

Harvey was mad at being chewed out and had decided to take it out on the soft little city boy-college boy who couldn't fight back. The college boy was worried about his job, so he wouldn't fight back—last hired, first fired. Harvey knew that firm dictum. Besides, he was big, and the kid was little.

Garven was the model of patience. He walked around the big jerk having to walk sideways to avoid rubbing against the beer belly. He made a beeline for the truck door. Harvey moved with him, interfering with his line of motion.

Harvey said, "I'm drivin'. I got more seniority that you anyways."

Leonard Holespeach had given specific instructions that Garven was to do the driving. He had implied that it was because Harvey did not do such a hot job, but maybe it was just part of dumb and lazy Harvey's punishment. Whichever the case, the ruling had made Harvey even madder at Garven. Now, Garven was getting mad. He did not like to be interfered with. The big dummy had been egging him on for the past two weeks, Garven knew that. He just hoped he could get the job done without having to have a fight. He did not particularly want to be drinking buddies with Harvey and his Neanderthal friends, but he had hoped to get along without trouble, especially since he was so new on the job. He needed the job.

"Look, Harvey," Garven said in a very reasonable voice, "you know as well as I do that Leonard wants me to drive the truck. If you don't like it, take it up with him or with the union, or with anybody else you want, but right now we're late, and you're getting in my way."

"I'm drivin'"

Garven sighed.

Harvey misinterpreted Garven's exhalation as capitulation. He was big enough that little guys usually did what he wanted even without him having to punch them. This was good. He pushed Garven on his chest to move him aside.

Garven's face changed. His eyes bored into the dull, stone eyes of the larger man. Harvey reminded Garven of Lenny in the Tennessee Williams' play, *Of Mice and Men.*

He said to Harvey/Lenny, "Don't put your hands on me. I don't let anybody put their hands on me."

Harvey made the best facial expression of a taunting sneer he could manage without actually sticking out his tongue. He reached out to brush Garven aside once and for all. Garven took a quick look around. Seeing no one in that rapid view from his peripheral vision, Garven smiled at Harvey without taking his eyes off those of the big fellow. Harvey was discombobulated by the smile. Harvey was fairly easily discombobulated.

Garven whammed a rock–hard, full-force fist up from his knees and into Harvey's gut. Harvey grunted and gasped, totally discombobulated now. The response was completely unexpected. Little guys never did such things. Garven followed up with a right cross into Harvey's teeth and a pair of left jabs into his nose. Then, he stepped back. Harvey put both hands to his face and slowly kneeled down, trying to get his breath, trying to figure it out. Then, it was Garven's turn to be surprised. Harvey started to cry. Garven looked at him in total disdain and walked around the kneeling, sniveling, completely reduced bully and got into the cab of the truck.

When he got back two and a half hours later, Harvey was standing on the dock waiting for him. He was holding a baseball bat.

"Uh-oh," Garven said to himself.

He could see Holespeach looking at Harvey, and then at him from his office window. The loaders in the freight cars had roused themselves to look on as well. Garven knew the test of his right to work there was about to take place. He had the alternatives of walking off, of reporting to Holespeach, or of walking right into dumb Harvey and probably getting his head whacked off.

It took him a portion of a second to make up his mind. His decision was characteristic. He quickened his step and walked straight for Harvey who raised his bat. Right then, two more desert rat-looking clods stepped out of the relative cool of their freight cars and began to walk menacingly towards Garven. They, too, were carrying clubs, one a piece of Ree bar, and the other a broken broom handle. Holespeach had left his office and was watching closely.

Lyle, Bubba, and Ray came walking out of their resting places and, moving faster, came up to stand beside Garven before he could reach Harvey and his bat or the two desert rat teamsters could come within striking distance of Garven. The four stood eye to eye with the three. The three had clubs, and the four did not. Holespeach walked down the dock towards the gathering. The tension was enough that there was nearly a smell of ozone arcing between the two sides. Eight eyes stared across at six eyes for a long couple of minutes. Nothing was said. Then, the six eyes blinked. The three club wielders stepped back, and the smell of ozone dissipated.

Holespeach walked up to the men and said, "Not enough work for you, boys? I think I can find some more, if you have so much time on your hands."

He turned to the four men without clubs and asked, "Some kind of problem here?"

The four shook their heads. The foreman then looked at the three club wielders with the same, this time implicit, question. Three heads shook negatively, somewhat reluctantly.

"Then put that stuff in the trash and find some brooms and clean up if you're done loading the cars. Let's get back to work."

Harvey went over to the truck and actually picked up a box for Holespeach's benefit. The five men returned to their hiding places in the freight cars, not making much of an effort at concealment of their feather-bedding. Garven turned toward his work.

"Handled yourself okay, Garv. Don't think you'll have anymore trouble," Leonard said as Garven passed him on the way back across the loading dock to the truck.

He was right.

Garven went home to Cipher for the first time that summer after two weeks in Phoenix. He felt a little ashamed as his car kicked up a column of dust behind him. He looked away from the Burma Shave signs, catching only the one about the bearded devil. Cipher was a small source of embarrassment to him. Rachel was waiting on the front steps as he knew she would be. Garven wondered how she could stand to stay there.

"Welcome home, son; welcome home!" she said fervently.

He could feel a tear on her cheek as she put her face against hers.

"It's great to be here, Mom. I had to get to work right away, or I would have been here sooner. You haven't changed a bit."

"Well, you have. You look older, bigger...," she looked at his nose and his thickened ear, "and tougher."

Garven blushed. Only his mother could make him blush, it seemed.

"Wrestling. It got kind of rough at times."

"So I read. And thanks for taking time out of your busy schedule to write your poor old mother."

She was smiling.

"Oh, Mom," Garven said sheepishly.

"No, I mean it. You wrote three letters this quarter—a world record. And congratulations. Congratulations on winning the Pacific Coast championship. Who'd ever thought that a little old hick from Cipher, Arizona, could win the wrestling championship clear out in California. I told everybody. Just about took out an ad in the paper. Let me show you something!"

Rachel led Garven to the chest of drawers in her bedroom. She opened the top middle drawer and drew out a handsome black photograph album and opened it to the last page. He saw a clipping of a local newspaper article with his picture (at age sixteen) with the caption, "Local boy California University Wrestling Champ."

"Oh, Mom, you shouldn't have. It's embarrassing."

But she could see the pleasure and pride in his eyes.

"This is your baby book," she said, and turned over a few pages at random.

"Oh, for crying out loud! This is really embarrassing! What if somebody saw this?"

He was blushing, but he did not look embarrassed or angry. He did not take his eyes away from the keepsake album until he had looked at every page. There was an expression of unconceivable pleasure on his face.

Rachel waited; then, when he closed the book, she tugged at his arm and said, "Come on into the living room and sit down while I finish up lunch. Hope you're hungry. I have lots of good stuff. I'll get your mail so you can read it while you wait."

Garven had forgotten what it was like to be in an impeccably clean house, to see flowers on the tables, to smell the enticing aromas of his mother's home cooking, to be served like he was somebody important, somebody that somebody cared about. He relished the feeling.

The mail included a rolled up *Stanford Chronicle* newspaper and an envelope from the university. He opened the envelope first, sure it would be his grades. He was right. His first scanning look showed all 'A's. He looked more carefully and saw the 'C' in trig. It could have been worse; he had thought it was going to be a 'C-'. He looked very carefully at psych. An 'A'. A big handsome well deserved 'A'. He took a big breath of relief. His GPA had been computed for the end of his sophomore year—3.99. He muttered a small curse on trig, but he could not work up much anger.

Garven slit open the wrapper around the college paper. It had been folded backwards with the classifieds outermost. His eye caught several of the ads for some reason, probably to avoid looking at the front page.

LOST AND FOUND

Stupid near-sighted old lady has lost her glasses. If found, return to Mabel Jennings in the admin office at Florence Moore Hall. Reward.

PERSONALS

Will the person—you know who—that gazed soulfully into my eyes at the Madera dance the night before dead week please be brave enough to give me a call? C.J. at 4867 on campus.

WANTED

Man to work long hours at backbreaking job for low pay and no thanks. Must be able to work all day in the cold with minimal air, to endure frostbite, chilblains, and monotonous food. And to share in real glory. Contact K-2 Climb Expedition at 3245 before June 1. Only one opening.

Garven made himself open to the front page. The article was there as he knew it would be, full headline, and top left first column.

PROFESSOR DIES IN FALL

Professor Dr. Johnathon Paternost Simpkins fell to his death from the fourth floor of the Hildebrand Psychology Building in a tragic accident that occurred late on June 3 or early June 4 according to campus police who discovered the body. "There was no evidence of foul play," Chief O'Brien told the *Chronicle*. The police investigation concluded that the professor had backed out of his office in the dark and tripped over the low railing on the fourth floor balcony. Campus Building Maintenance was contacted, and they have indicated that plans have been submitted to the administration for construction of more protective barriers.

President Cheevers spoke for the entire campus community when he said, "The death of the Head of Psychology, Professor Simpkins, was not only a shock to us all but is a profound loss to the academic world. Dr. Simpkins, a former student of Sigmund Freud, was a major contributor to the psychology literature in his own right, a much admired teacher, and a friend of all who knew him. It is a very great personal loss."

Dr. Simpkins came to the university....

His eyes hurriedly scanned the remainder of the article. The usual obituary stuff—where he was from, where he trained, his academic degrees and something about his publications and the learned societies he headed or to which he belonged. No mention of anything out of the ordinary; just a fall, an accident. No apparent witnesses. Nothing to worry about. Garven let out a long low sigh of relief. Although Garven knew that he had skipped the class on guilt and repentance in Sunday school and harbored no remorse; he was not cut out for this clandestine or fugitive feeling or whatever it was he had felt. His appetite returned with gusto, and he enjoyed the first meal he could remember since the professor had fallen. He learned something about himself; he felt neither sympathy or guilt. In the ever-present struggle of the desert, he, like the coyote, had prevailed and had lived to see another day. He could forget the whole thing now.

CHAPTER
Two

The following weekend, while Lyle, Bubba, and Ray borrowed Ray's uncle's boat and went on a "drunk on the water", Garven made the long drive up to Emmett to welcome home Dr. Wilsonhulme. Peter Wilsonhulme had aged appreciably since Garven had seen him last. His health was worse instead of better from the European trip. After greetings and a restaurant supper at the Emmett Pass Cafe, Peter told his adopted son all about the Grand Tour that he had tried to copy in as much detail as possible from the old travel annals that had so enthralled him in his youth. Garven was most impressed with the details of the expense and thought that his dad must have spent the bulk of his retirement money on that one excursion. As the doctor recounted his travels, Garven worried that the older man must know more about his own health than he was telling which would account for his cavalier spending.

Seated back home in the comfortable overstuffed chairs in Dr. Wilsonhulme's large den, Peter asked his adopted son, "What about you? Tell me about the quarter. How's school? I want to know about your wrestling championship."

The room was quiet, and its light subdued. The colors were soft old greasy and browns conducive to restfulness and confidence. The furniture and accouterments were circa 1930 and had not changed in twenty years lending a calm and deliberate ambiance, an atmosphere of permanence. Garven felt the need to talk, to confide, to feel the security of having a protector and father. He had determined never to speak of the final incident with Dr. Simpkins, but wanted to discuss his schooling and some considerations about his education with his dad. The time was perfect.

"Dad, school was fine. I have a 3.99 average; I won the PAC wrestling championship in my weight. All in all school this year was good. I'll give you the details in a bit. But first there is something I would like to get your advice on, though. I have been thinking long and hard about getting into medical school, and what is the best way to get in, and where is the best place to apply."

"Places, and aren't you a bit premature?" Dr. Wilsonhulme asked, drawing on his pipe, the one vice still vouchsafed him with his self-imposed regimen for his atherosclerotic heart.

"I'll apply several places, all right; but still, you need to finagle the odds in your favor. It's different than it was in your day, Dad."

"You mean back in aught-six."

"You know what I mean. You wouldn't believe the competition to get into medical school now. Last year there were two applicants for every seat in Stanford's med school. They had more than 250 men apply. They have been talking about opening up more of those seats for women for some reason, modern stuff. That will make it even harder. But at the Arizona Faculty of Medicine, an Arizona citizen has a real good chance to get in—something like 90 percent. They only take three out-of-staters total."

"Logical, since we fund the school."

"Right. And I want to take advantage of that fact. I am nothing of a gambler. If I do my third year of pre-med at the U. of Arizona, my chances for getting in are almost perfect. I am thinking very strongly of transferring to the U. What do you think?"

Peter puffed on his pipe thoughtfully. It went out, as always, and he fussed with it, getting it relit. Garven thought he would go nuts if he had to fiddle with a pipe. He could never see how otherwise sensible men put up with the habit.

"Well, Garven, on the plus side of the ledger, there is a real advantage for me. Two, actually. First of all, and most important, you would be nearer to home. I am not well, and the opportunity to see you more frequently is very appealing. I hope it is for you as well."

Garven nodded in agreement.

"Secondly, it is lots less expensive all the way around—tuition, housing, travel, everything. Stanford is a fancy and costly place, not that I'm complaining; but it is something to consider."

"There is the third factor, Dad. As far as I can determine, my chances to get into medical school are better at Arizona than Stanford. I'm sure of that."

"I think your chances are excellent in any case. You have become a worry wart, but I do recognize your point. I happen to have an additional serious advantage for you at Arizona. Two of my oldest and dearest friends are on the faculty at the university and are directly involved in the admissions process. If you are serious about switching, I will arrange a dinner for the four of us. The extra connection should cinch it. Never underestimate the value of the old boy route. In fact, you ought to be sure to cultivate your own set of 'old boys' even now."

"I know that, Dad. I do pay attention to that idea. The main thing I have gotten out of my expensive schooling to this point, besides the education itself, is the level of friends I have made. I am sure they will stand me in good stead just like yours have."

"You have to make an effort, even after you get out of school. Keep those friends, Garven. They will be invaluable in time."

Garven nodded.

"So, are you sure about this? You sound like your mind is about made up already."

"Pretty much."

"Do I detect something else? Is there something I should know about Stanford, something you've done? Eh, Garven?"

"No, dad. My trouble days are over. Like you told me before last quarter, I had to grow up."

Garven sounded convincing but could detect a little hesitation in his own voice. He hoped his dad would miss the hint of pause and would not speculate on its origin.

Peter smiled. He liked the maturity he saw in his son.

"When I was a child, I thought as a child, I spake as a child; but now that I am a man, I have put away childish things, or words to that effect, eh?"

"Um hummh."

Garven was neither a believer nor a prayer, but he said a little private prayer then just to hedge his bets that the Simpkins affair would remain buried with the man.

Peter had tried to arrange the dinner with the university professors, his old friends, in Phoenix for their convenience. They were aware of the failing state of his health, and both insisted that they would like to get out of the crowded city and get out into the hinterlands. If it was not too much trouble, they would rather have a home-cooked meal in Emmett. Peter had never been much of a cook, and was not inclined to work on an important dinner now. He made arrangements with the local Mormon ladies' Relief Society to prepare a dinner and to get their young girls' group to cater it. The local ward of the church was in a fever of fund raising to build a new chapel, and the women were happy to oblige.

Harold Newly and William Durham had been friends of Peter Wilsonhulme's from their college days at Stanford. Harold and Peter had known each other in Pennsylvania where they both grew up. They had all remained close even after Harold and William, who had been called "Bull" when he was young but let that old nickname die of attrition since he regarded it as obvious and trite, had gone on to get their doctorates in zoology, and Peter had gone off to Cornell to medical school. Harold—nobody-calls-him-Hal—was the long-time professor of embryology and one time Biology Department chairman at the U, and William—friends-call-me-William—taught comparative anatomy and evolution. Together, they were the most important faculty members for determining who did and who did not get into the Arizona Faculty of Medicine School. Two generations of pre-medders had loved and feared them, suffered agonies trying to get through their classes with high grades which were few and far between, and had learned the folly of trying to curry artificial favor. Peter apprised Garven of those salient facts before the dinner.

"Come on in!" greeted Peter.

He was excited and obviously very pleased and flattered that the two men would drive all the way to Emmett for his dinner.

"Wait 'till we shake off the dust, Peter. The place hasn't changed much. Still all the red dust you could want in a lifetime here," William said in mock distress.

Their car was coated with a fine pink dust so complete and homogeneous that its underlying color could not be recognized with certainty.

"It's not as bad as all that. Come on in. I presume your throats are parched from the desert passage. I'll get you something serious."

"Bourbon and branch water for me," said Harold.

"Sarsaparilla for me," said William.

He was the only person in America who pronounced the name of the flavorful root correctly and could spell it. He took an eccentric pride in being correct in such obscure and arcane details.

"Doctor's orders. Something about my liver. Too much booze during my checkered career."

Peter poured him a generous helping of Cutty Sark on the rocks and said, "Sarsaparilla."

"Right, and thanks," said William savoring the aromatic liquor. "I have really gotten to like sarsaparilla," as if he had ever tasted root beer.

Garven was standing off to one side feeling very much the fifth wheel, the interloper. Peter made sure the two men had their drinks in hand then guided them to where Garven was waiting.

"This is my son, Garven," he said.

"The son of your old age, Abraham," commented Harold with a warm and understanding smile.

Garven liked him instinctively.

"And my pride and joy," answered Peter.

"Garven Wilsonhulme, I have the pleasure to present professors, Dr. Newly and Dr. Durham. Harold and William, this is my boy, Garven."

"How do you do?" said Garven formally and extended his hand to each man in turn.

The two professors liked the forthright face and earnest, respectful, but confident, uncowed eyes.

The dinner was a success. The local girls did a splendid job carefully supervised by their leaders. Garven remembered one of them—Sarah something. Their fetching innocence and unspoiled enthusiasm was refreshing. The food was of similar honest quality—hearty slabs of lamb roast, creamed potatoes and peas, steamed zucchini, homemade whole wheat bread with sweet home churned butter, and a huge whip cream covered apple cobbler. The girls set out large foamy glasses of cold milk and looked askance at the men's cocktails. The girls' leader whispered to Peter that they would have to decline respectfully to serve coffee or the wine he had set out, she hoped he would understand. William recognized the dynamics and suppressed a chuckle.

By apparent pre-arrangement after dessert, Dr. Newly asked Garven, "How about you and William and I going for a walk. You can show us the metropolis of Emmett, and you can have a chance to probe us with your questions."

Garven said, "Great."

His dad nodded, indicating his part in the small conspiracy and that he would stay behind and deal with the church women.

"Peter told me that you were thinking of transferring to the U," said Harold Newly after the three had gotten underway along the broken and neglected sidewalk.

The east-west streets were unpaved and a fine dust eddied in the light wind that ameliorated the otherwise baking heat of the late June day.

"That's right. I'm still not altogether sure what's the best thing to do. I think my chances for getting into med school are better if I come back to the U. Is that true?"

"Yes. Statistically, that's true, and individually your good record and your experience at Stanford should be helpful. You really have a 3.99 GPA?"

"That's right."

"You will probably be okay to get into Stanford or UCLA or one of those good west coast schools with that academic record. That you are a Westerner will count against you at the eastern medical establishments. They still see us folks west of the Mississippi as primitives and treat our applicants pretty much as if they were only semi-literate. There is a lot of snobbishness in this business of getting into medical school," Dr. Newly said.

Dr. Durham added, "Another consideration is that many of the major medical school admission committees are getting more liberal. They want well-rounded students, whatever that is. They look for guys that speak other languages, who have interesting talents and hobbies, who have degrees or experience in other fields, that sort of thing. The State of Arizona University is still pretty much meat and potatoes. They go by merit: good grades and good recommendations are more likely to get you in than your ability to play the tenor sax or to juggle knives and hatchets."

"I certainly fit the 'meat and potato' category," Garven said.

"When you get right down to it, I think you fit the Arizona category. The medical school is only five years old and the head honchos up there would rather build their reputations on solid citizens than on the idea of getting exciting and imaginative students. Those kind of students are likely to become flamboyant doctors, and the country already has enough of those, thanks. Stanford might think twice about a solid worker like you, but the U will welcome you with open arms, I predict," Dr. Newly told Garven.

"What are the advantages of coming to the U for my last year, if any?"

"The people who count get to know you. You get familiar with the way things are done here, make the right contacts, show you can do the work here," Dr. Newly answered without hesitation.

"You need to realize that universities are jealous and prideful. Every institution thinks it is better than every other one. They are all suspicious about the credits from the other university. The main advantage of coming back to finish up at the U is to demonstrate that you can handle the work here, that your good record at that party school was not just a fluke," Dr. Durham said with a little mischief in his smile.

Garven had hardly thought of Stanford as a 'party school'. It was a learning experience to find out that his own point of view and slant on things was not a universal opinion. By the end of his conversation with the two professors, Garven had made up his mind. By the end of the month he had completed the application process for transfer; and on the first of September, he was a matriculated student at the State of Arizona University in Phoenix.

CHAPTER
Three

After the freshman year, the University of Arizona students were free to live off campus; and since he was coming in as a junior, Garven stayed in the dump with Lyle, Bubba, and Ray. It was bigger, if dirtier, than the on-campus dorms and most of the apartments in close proximity to the sprawling desert campus. It was considerably less expensive. The local landlords knew they had a captive clientele of renters, and they exploited the students gleefully. The drive was not unreasonable especially since most of the time Garven would be going in at off hours from the rush. Phoenix was losing its little town character as its population and the diversity of inhabitants was increasing. There was starting to be enough traffic for the long-time residents to complain about. Garven thought it was pretty funny that they griped about their traffic. They should go to San Francisco or LA.

Garven's credits all transferred straight across from Stanford, to his relief. He had to get in a few more liberal arts group filler classes and his physics series, genetics, and of course, Dr. Newly's embryo course, and Dr. Durham's comparative anatomy class. It did not promise to be as heavy a schedule as he had had at Stanford. He was hopeful that the competition would not be as tough.

PHYSICS 101, the sign over the lecture hall announced. Unlike the sloping amphitheater lecture hall at Stanford, this one was no more than a large classroom. The seats were all separate, and some of them had folding desk trays on them, others were simple folding chairs. The room was utilitarian and sparse. There were no Nobel laureates on the faculty, but that was not of any great moment to Garven. At Stanford he had considered himself lucky to be lectured to by a real faculty member instead of the ubiquitous Dr. Staff grad students. Stanford was a post-graduate school—Arizona, an undergrad school. For Garven's purposes, that factor was probably going to be a positive one, he thought.

"I am Dr. Henry Eitling, Head of Physics. I will present the lectures, and my staff will conduct the labs, the testing, and any necessary tutoring or counseling you may need. Graduate students will assist in several areas, but we at Arizona are of the opinion that you pay good money to get a good education, and we will not give you less than our best."

That sounded encouraging to Garven. It was the first time in his recollection that a teacher had actually indicated a desire to give him a good education. Who knows, he might even learn something about physics.

"This is Physics 101, the general course. We do not include calculus in this three quarter course. Pre-meds and those of you who are just filling your science group for graduation stay here. Physics and math majors, and engineers, you should check out today and get into the Physics 200 series. There is plenty of room. I have found out over a few decades of teaching that there is always plenty of room in classes where calculus is taught."

There was a small ripple of agreeing laughter.

"I love physics. I like teaching it. Sometimes I feel guilty about taking money to do this. Just sometimes," Dr. Eitling added quickly. "Classically physics is the science of physical matter and how matter is acted upon by energy. That is mostly what we will deal with in this introductory course. There is a tendency now to think of physics as a science of questions concerning reality. Is the real world made of matter or of energy or both? Einstein's $E=mC2$ is now an established part of our lives and of the understanding of the universe. We will not ignore the controversies, but we expect to turn out people well founded in the physical sciences to make use of what they learn by contributing to society as doctors, engineers, architects, bridge builders, developers and the like. The theoretical physics thinkers will not be in the majority here in this practical institution. I suggest that you pay strong attention to the mundane solid basis of physics that I will present here. You can leave the worries over whether light bends because it is a wave or because it is a particulate material to the Einsteins, the Bohrs, and the Eitlings. Voltaire characterized the ultimate religious argument as being about how many angels can dance on the head of a pin. Some of the physics questions are about as meaningful.

"Our physics this year will be about things and how they move—about mechanics, if you will. The current theoretical physics makes most people nervous because it even questions whether there are things, more like metaphysics than physics sometimes. For our practical purposes we will still believe in measurements and explanations that can be verified by experimentation and observation rather than sinking into the morass of murky thought that holds that there are no objective properties of matter or energy but only statistical approximations. That is in the realm of the existentialists and the theoretical quantum mechanics physicists.

"At our level, the measurements are valid and can be subjected to mathematical analysis and to understandable and verifiable laws. At the extremes of subatomic particles or the breadth of the universe, perhaps the questioning, ever questioning, is pertinent, but not on our level. We will agree with Erwin Schrödinger who told us, 'If you cannot, in the long run, tell everyone what you have been doing, your doing has been worthless.' We are not going to worry about how many angels can stand on the head of the pin. We will look at the pin and the forces that act on it.

"Granted, the 'new physics' of quantum mechanics has been around for a while. Max Planck proposed a theory of 'quanta' as early as 1900 and Einstein introduced the special theory of relativity back in 1905. We will have to cope with Isaac Newton and gravity that has been around much longer and has been subjected to much more scrutiny. Quantum mechanics is a peculiar twentieth century religion. Classical physics is a firm foundation in science."

Garven's head was swimming. Physics had to be the dullest field of intellectual pursuit ever invented. He was sure that the only purpose of the discipline was to add one more bit of hazing for pre-med pledges trying to get into medical school. The only saving grace of the entire lecture that day was a mathematical proof carefully written out by the professor:

"And God said:

$$\frac{mv^2}{r} = \frac{Ze^2}{r^2}$$

$$mvr = n\frac{h}{2\pi}$$

$$r = \frac{r^2 h^2}{(2\pi)^2 mZe^2}$$

$$E = \tfrac{1}{2}mv^2 - \frac{Ze^2}{r}$$

$$E = \frac{2\pi^2 mZ^2 e^4}{n^2 h^2} = R$$

And there was light.

True to his firmly held belief that Garven and the students like him who had a promising future should not be allowed to stay on in the teamster's job lest they be seduced, Leonard Holespeach laid Garven off as soon as school started. He would not even let him work part time despite telling Garven he liked his work. Garven had set aside five hundred dollars from his summer's work after rent and food. That would be enough for tuition and books, and probably food, provided he had the appetite and social life of a Buddhist bonze, but not enough for rent and his car. Garven had gotten to like the feeling of independence he got from making his own money; so, he would not have to feel beholden to anyone, even his dad. Dr. Wilsonhulme had been making allusions to a decline in his holdings in recent conversations, and Garven thought it prudent to get some personal security.

The initial tremendous demand on the economy's limited job supply occasioned by the returning war vets had settled down, and there were more part time and summer jobs opening up all the time. On June twenty-fifth that year, the North Korean communists invaded South Korea, and the Phoenix national guard unit was called up to join the United Nations defense force. The fictions that this was not a war but a 'police action' and that this was not a United States military action, but rather a 'United Nations' one were considered jokes on campus, in the city, and in the country. The people of Phoenix were alarmed by the prospect of another war, which was what they knew it was, whatever Truman said. Garven was safe in his school deferment and mostly thought it was not his business. The departure of the national guard unit opened up a number of decent jobs, and Garven decided that the 'police action' was not all bad.

He got a part time job at a car parts store taking the place of Jake Engle, a man who had been with the company for twenty years, interrupted by five years of WW II service. Jake was furious at having to go again; the store owners were upset at the loss of their man who knew the parts business inside and out; and the customers were dubious about the new little guy hired on to take Jake Engle's place.

Garven convinced the two bosses, Manny Chipioni and Dezi Klug, that he was a real expert on cars, that he lived and breathed for them, and that they would not be sorry to hire him on. It did not occur to Manny or Dezi to give Garven a test, and they were not very observant about the fact that the smallish young man had clean hands. In truth, Garven did not know the first thing about cars, or engines, or parts; but he needed the job; he was a good reader and a quick study; and he knew he could count on his house mates, who were out-and-out car nuts, to bring him up to speed. After all, how much could there be to it? It was an age of rampant self-confidence for Garven.

As the fall quarter at State U. progressed, Garven decided that he liked Arizona better than Stanford. For reasons he could not clearly define, he felt more at ease, more assured. Part of that, he had to admit was the fact that he no longer had that academic sword of Damocles, trigonometry, hanging over his head; and another part of that feeling of security came from the diminishing, now nearly absent fear of exposure and trouble over the catapult and water balloons affair and Dr. Simpkins' fall off the building. The classes did seem easier also, at least genetics did.

The concepts of genetics, starting with Mendel's work and conclusions that were first published in 1866, and progressing to the modern era seemed pretty understandable to Garven. He liked the teacher, a Zuni Indian with the somehow appropriate name of Sunflower. Dr. Naomi Sunflower.

"Your term paper assignment is to take one major review article from the past six months of *The Journal of Genetics*, the red journal, *Heredity*, or from the *Journal of the Society of Geneticists*, and follow through the bibliography and come up with a cogent argument for, and a counter argument against the major thesis of the review article. The paper will be due no later than the day of the midterm. A word to the wise: get it done early because you will have all you can do to master the material for the midterm by the time it rolls around.

"Okay. Today's lecture. We reviewed Gregor Mendel's experiments with pea plants during the past two weeks and learned not only his results but the terminology and fundamental concepts that govern heredity even today. He established the first step as the parental cross or 'P' generation whose offspring constitute the first filial or F1 generation. When the offspring of F1 interbreed and reproduce, they produce the second filial or F2 generation. In that generation we see dominant traits, or those which prevent the expression of other traits, and recessive traits—the characteristic that is not seen in the F1 generation. In classical Mendelian genetics the F2 generation displays a 3:1 production of the dominant to the recessive trait.

"The beauty of the pea plant experiment is the simplicity of the traits being separated and studied. Mendel assumed that the stamen to pistil transfer of pollen was analogous to the transfer of sperm to the egg and each contained governing factors or characters, which we now term genes. He indicated that the recessive trait only appeared when two pure recessives were mated—in his experiment that was the wrinkly pea seeds—based on the fundamental and crucial presumption that each parent had only one half, called a gamete, of the final combination required to establish the zygote which becomes the offspring and to determine its trait or traits.

"Your work books explain the Punnett square charts. I expect you to do the exercises and to be prepared to demonstrate your understanding in front of the class by the time we next meet. That will be Wednesday. I will ask some lucky person to explain the law of segregation, and I don't want to hear any nonsense about South African apartheid or 'separate but equal' policies in the American south. I expect you to speak in terms of alleles, genotypes, phenotypes, dominants, recessives, homozygous, and heterozygous, statistical product rule, genotypic and phenotypic ratios, incomplete dominance, and law of independent assortment. Do the problems and memorize the definitions, and you will be all right. Or you could take a chance and not study. If I call on you and you cannot demonstrate your knowledge, your letter grade for the course will drop by one grade for the quarter. Consider that fair warning."

Five days a week, Garven attended either a lecture or had a lab in embryology, both taught by Dr. Newly. From the first day of class, Dr. Newly was friendly to Garven, but showed him no detectable favoritism. On the contrary, it seemed to Garven as if his dad's old friend singled him out for tough questions and criticism. It was noticeable enough that some of the other members of the class laughed when another of those kind of questions was asked, knowing that it would fall on Garven's head, more likely than not. If it was indeed a method, it seemed to work because Garven toughened to the challenge of the hard questions and of being put on the spot. Often he could not answer the questions, but he got better and better at figuring out what the professor wanted. He also found himself learning the early embryology of the chicken and the pig quite thoroughly.

Dr. Newly had a monotonous voice that proved to be hypnotic. The real trick in embryology was less to cope with the rigorous academic discipline than it was to stay awake long enough to hear it. The room was quiet and dark. The students were quiet and serious. The professor's voice was quiet and matter-of-fact, free of major changes of pitch or tone. The worst thing about the class was the constant lulling hum of the slide projector. Professor Newly regularly referred to his collection of thin-slice slides of chicken and pig embryos to illustrate his points. Garven knew the class material was all important, but on balance it was more somnificant than anything.

The professor smiled in the semi-light as he watched the students struggling to keep awake. He gave the same lecture today that he had given for nearly twenty-five years; a lecture he could have given in his sleep.

"To illustrate my point about the practicality of selecting the embryology of the pig to study as a vehicle to learn human ontogeny, compare these slides. I have the 2 millimeter fetal pig along side the same stage human fetus, and I would defy you to find a verifiable difference. Why are they so much alike, you may inquire? Much as we like to flatter ourselves about our noble evolution from monkeys, we have to admit that humans and pigs are related."

There was a titter of laughter.

"That was not necessarily an observation from sociology; try not to take offense," he said and paused for effect. "But if the shoe fits…"

He appreciated the hearty response of laughter from his students that this well executed humorist remark always produced.

"Nevertheless, it is a well-accepted theorem that the more alike are embryos and their pattern of development the more closely related are the two organisms in evolution. The closeness of embryonic similarity indicates not only that the two organisms share a common ancestor, but gives an indication of how far back in time that commonalty may have occurred. Stages of embryonic development are quite similar in a number of closely related animals including the shark, the chicken, the pig and the chimpanzee, to cite but a few pertinent examples. Only in the later stages of development of the fetus do the individual species become easily recognizable. Ontogeny recapitulates phylogeny—a worthwhile dictum to remember."

Garven forced himself to rouse to take down a note and to put an asterisk by it.

"It may seem demeaning, but the earthworm, pig, dog, chimp, and the human have common ancestors somewhere in the mists of time. When you get to the section in Dr. Durham's course on comparative anatomy dealing with comparative embryology, you will get a much fuller description of the changes and branches in our family tree. For now, we will concentrate on the common factors.

"We have seen the gametes, sperm and egg, in our early lectures. Suffice it for our purposes that the union of those two entities to form the zygote is the critical event, not the method of introduction of the two, contrary to the self-delusions of the more randy of you young men."

A ripple of laughter.

"It matters not that humans and pigs employ coitus."

Somehow that does not conjure up a very romantic view," thought Garven.

"Or that lady fish deposit their eggs on the sand and gentlemen fish come along afterwards and spread their milt over those eggs—hence the expression, 'poor fish'."

More laughter.

"What really matters is that the membrane of the egg gets penetrated and gamete meets gamete thereby starting the chain reaction that results in the cleavage, multiplying, twisting, folding, elongating, and changing that forms the blastomere, the morula and the blastocyst that eventuates in the newborn infant possessing all of the inherent characteristics of its species.

"Now there are those of you who have a religious bent. We always have a Mormon or a Catholic or a Born-Again or two that take offense at the evolution concept. Let's not argue; try and consider that this was the way God did it; and just try to learn the process. If there is a soul sent by God, it is in that activated zygote the instant of conception because everything that comes out in the end as an adult organism was there at that instant. We are here to learn what went on in that marvelous process; we will leave the metaphysical and the religious considerations to different departments. For my own part, having gone to Catholic school, I take comfort in the statement of religious belief of George Santayana's, 'There is no God, and Mary is His mother'."

CHAPTER
Four

After watching Garven operate for a couple of weeks, his boss, Dezi Klug, found the bit of blue collar theater amusing. He was perceptive, a good businessman in a tough racket, and not half as dumb as he looked. It was obvious from the first day that Garven did not know a thing about cars or car parts. He had pointed that fact out to his partner, the humorless Italian, Manny Chipioni. Manny was for firing the pretender on the spot, but Dezi convinced him to hold off. He accepted responsibility for the young college student's certain-to-be-made mistakes, and then sat back figuratively, at least, to watch the show.

Garven put on a pretty good show all of the time, and was able to accommodate the customers accurately most of the time. Dezi saw that Garven listened very closely to what the other parts men and the customers said and mimicked the lingo early on. Using what he heard, Garven found the parts in the huge parts books and located the desired item in the storage shelves or arranged to send out for any part not in stock. That was simple, and constituted most of what the regular old-line parts men did for the majority of their work day. Dezi felt vindicated when he saw that Garven came early and stayed late to read any and everything on cars and parts until he was beginning to get a feel for the job. What was amusing was the performance put on by the young man when a customer came in to chat about the relative performance and preferability of one car over another with the in-store expert. Garven seemed to have a photographic memory and devoured *Popular Mechanics,*

Car and Motor, Motor Trend and trade publications which he then rattled off verbatim when the customer twanged the right chord.

"Hey, Mack. I gotta prob with my forty-eight Ford. Maybe you can help," one greasy customer started.

"Usual thing?" Garven had said sympathetically. "Every time you open the window, the door falls off?"

"Somethin' like that," laughed the customer warming to the parts guy who had obviously been around an engine or two and had the same love-hate relationship with Fords that he felt.

Garven was listening to the man as if nothing else mattered.

"What my heap does is knocks and makes a real bangin' noise when I stop, and the engine keeps goin' after I turn it off. I done everythin', but it keeps on a doin' it."

"Then the doors fall off?" asked Garven seriously, betraying no smile.

The guy laughed.

"That'll be the next thing. Anyway, got any ideas? I was thinkin' that the head gasket was old or loose; you think that could be it?"

"Never think that anything that is so much work to fix is the problem until you have to," Garven said sagely.

The customer shook his head in agreement.

"Sounds to me like either your timing is off or your carburetor intake manifold is sticky. '38 and '39 coupes and all the '48's have carburetor problems. The company puts in cheap ones, and sticks the poor schmuck who buys it with the cost of getting a decent one from an honest parts store like Manny and Dezi's."

"I changed the plugs and points and set the timing. Must be the carburetor, right."

"What did you set the timing for?"

"Since it was missing so much, I opened it way up. Come to think of it, the problem has been worse. Got any idees?"

"You came to the right place. First of all, you have got to be professional about this, and you look like a pro to me. Get this set of spark adaptors and this Acme Timing Light, best in the business, and set it for four thousand feet elevation. That's the usual advice. In my experience though, you ought to make the settings a little tighter because of the heat here in the desert. I tell you what. You might as well get a new carburetor now, a genuine Ace Parts model, and save yourself another trip. Fords are notorious."

"Think that'll do it."

"Yeah, but take some Carbo-Lube and stick a can of it in your tank every time you fill up. Costs eighty-nine cents, but will save you a bundle on repairs, guaranteed. Cheaper than having to put in a new carburetor every 2000 miles, right?"

"Sure is. Hey, thanks. I'm Jimmy Jenkins. I'll ask for you next time."

"Name's Garven. Just ask for me. We'll get your old clunk going if it kills us, or you have to take out a loan to cover the cost of parts what with all you're saving by doing your own labor."

"Ain't that the truth," Jimmy laughed. "Cars is the work of the devil, I sometimes think."

Garven looked at him seriously, then said, "You know, I learned at the U that cars are just another example of the first law of physics."

"What's that?"

"The Principle of the General Pernicious Nature of Inanimate Objects."

Jimmy was bemused.

"Best known as Murphey's Law."

"Ain't that the truth."

Jimmy mused to himself that this guy was all right. He didn't try to sell you a bunch of useless junk, and he had a sense of humor about cars. You had to have that if you were going to be able to work with them. Especially Fords.

"Sure I can't sell you a new set of floorboards or running boards?" Garven asked innocently.

Jimmy laughed again. It was kinda fun coming to Manny and Dezi's. Women could never really appreciate why men liked cars so much. This Garven guy, with all his experience, really understood.

Dezi watched as Garven found the parts, the tools, and the lubricants. Garven's customer was hanging on the parts dealer's words as if he were visiting his doctor.

"And look, if you still have trouble, come on back in, and we will go over it again until we have this thing solved."

Dezi liked that 'we' business and told the rest of the parts men to use the same line.

Garven kept Dezi laughing in the background by singing one ditty or another. Whenever he made a sale, Garven quietly went about singing:

> My mother makes counterfeit money.
> My father makes synthetic gin.
> My sister sells kisses to sailors.
> My, how the money rolls in.

CHORUS

Rolls in, rolls in,
my, how the money rolls in, rolls in
Rolls in, rolls in,
my, how the money rolls in.

My brother is a slum missionary.
He saves fallen women from sin
He'll save you a blond for a shilling
My, how the money rolls in.

CHORUS

My grandma's a boarding house lady.
She takes poor working girls in.
Then, she puts a red light in the window
Oh, how the money rolls in.

CHORUS

After Garven had been on the job for a month, he had sold Jimmy Jenkins a new head gasket, a set of socket wrenches, four Phillips Head screw drivers of varying sizes, a new set of hot points, a long lasting battery, a hygrometer to test radiator water for its ability to resist freezing (the last freeze in Phoenix occurred in '32, and the one before that was sometime along about '20 or 21, when there was a freak snow storm), a set of seat covers and padded floor rugs, salt and water resistant paste wax, and a new hydraulic jack. Jimmy was the first man in Phoenix to have his own hydraulic jack in his trunk.

Garven had accumulated thirty or forty personal customers, and everyone of them not only swore by the little guy that made them laugh by making disparaging jokes about their pride and joy cars and pickups, but they all spent more money and had more fun doing it than any of them could remember. Even Manny had to admit that Garven was worth his pay and considerably more. Dezi and Manny personally inaugurated a crash course in the concepts of auto mechanics and parts distribution on the hypothesis that if the kid could sell as much as he did without knowing anything, just imagine what he could do if he had a bigger vocabulary about parts.

Before he started the quarter at the U., Garven had found out everything he could about the two main classes he had to get through, Vertebrate Embryology, and Comparative Vertebrate Anatomy. Through his persistence, he found two medical school bound juniors from Emmett who knew and respected his dad, and were willing and eager to pass on their hard won pearls about how to get through the two make-or-break classes. They gave him a large pile of old tests, including not only their own, but some from years back from a firmly established network of successful pre-medders at the U. who had gotten into medical school. They spent several hours helping Garven understand the special ins and outs of the two classes. Garven studied the old tests and learned that there were no more than ten recurring essay questions in Embryology, and about two hundred in Anatomy. Garven spent nearly as much time getting together perfect answers to the questions from the old tests as he did in the actual study of the class material. He did know how the student profession worked, if he had learned nothing else in college.

The two juniors had carefully warned Garven that he had to spend the bulk of his time before the first midterm in Durham's bone room that Garven found to be a bewildering, unlabeled assortment of the strangest pieces of bone he could have imagined. Whenever he could, Garven cornered Dr. Durham or one of his lab assistants to ask the name of a given bone, or from what animal or bird it had originated, or what did they call that articular surface or bony prominence.

He was careful not to be too annoying, but he was persistent enough to make William Durham laugh and comment, "Looks like you are either a budding orthopedist, or somebody clued you in on how important bones are on the first test. Think you can beat me? Think I can't find something strange enough that you will miss it?"

"I'm sure there's no contest, but if you stick to the specimens in the bone room or to our lab cats, and fish, and rats, I'll give you a good go," Garven responded making a serious effort to sound friendly and confident, but not cocky.

"You're on," Dr. Durham laughed good-naturedly.

Garven wondered why it was that he felt that the professor had more questions than Garven had answers, and about what tricks that devious old rascal kept hidden.

The bone room had separate bones, partially and fully articulated limbs, and spines, and whole skeletons of a mind-boggling variety of creatures. There were bones and parts of pigeons, snakes, rats, mice, domestic animals, great cats, alley cats, dogs, elephants, whales, bony fish, bats, porpoises, a giraffe cervical spine, and a larger than necessary for an adequate education collection of walrus penile bones. A huge fat disc-like bone intrigued Garven.

"That's an elephant patella," the grad student told him.

Garven marveled at the encyclopedic memory of the lab instructor. He figured he would have to be in that bone room for more than a decade to get all of those peculiar specimens clearly in mind.

Garven's hard work paid off. In the 'bone test', as the first midterm was affectionately known although it covered the evolution of the swim bladder, the lung, and the forelimbs as well, he achieved an unheard of 98 percent on the practical. There were two points for each of fifty specimens, and Garven missed one. He had even guessed right on a tiny sea lion penis bone. The specimen he had guessed wrong on had been the huge fat disc of bone. He had remembered that it was an elephant's patella; he was sure that he was correct in his memory of what the friendly grad student lab instructor had told him. It was hard to understand that red check mark by his answer.

After the test, Garven waited to talk to Dr. Durham until a cluster of desperate students who had bombed on the exam were finished pleading their cases.

When it was his turn, Garven asked simply, "I distinctly remember that that big flying saucer bone was an elephant patella. Isn't that right.?"

His face was serious, quizzical, earnest.

Dr. Durham had a serious professorial look on his face—for about half a minute; then, he started to laugh. Garven did not feel like he was in on the joke. In fact, he was pretty sure from the spontaneous character of the outburst, that he *was* the joke.

"No, Mr. Wilsonhulme, that is not an elephant kneecap; that is the dorsal vertebral body of the humpback whale."

He laughed some more.

"How did you get that imaginative idea that it was an elephant patella?"

"And how come I have this thought that I've been had? Some little birdie told me it was an elephant patella, a lab assistant birdie. I remember quite distinctly."

Garven's face could not maintain a serious scowl, and he was beginning to laugh at himself. He knew he had been had.

"Sound's pretty imaginative to me," were Dr. Durham's parting words.

He seemed to be having a good time that day.

"Don't take yourself too seriously," he imparted as Garven walked away shaking his head good-humoredly.

He caught the eye of the lab assistant who had suckered him.

"I'll know who not to trust next time," he said smiling at the grad student who had a Cheshire Cat expression on his amused face.

The lab assistant made a gesture of *non mea culpa* and said, "I just works here. I just does what the massa tells me."

Both young men laughed heartily.

William Durham was known for his puckish sense of humor in his classroom and in his life. He chose to look on life as a source of humor and dealt with problems that way. He tried to teach his students, predominately over-anxious, self-centered, narrow-scoped pre-medicine aspirants to accept life and themselves as something less than ultimately serious. He told them anecdotes from his life history to illustrate.

He had born in Salt Lake City, Utah, the son of a Mormon bishop. When he became nineteen years old, like all of his friends, he left on a foreign proselytizing mission for his church. He was sent to Paris where he learned the French language, found limitless sources of amusement much to the fretting annoyance of his ecclesiastical superiors in the otherwise very disciplined missionary group, discovered women quite unlike the decorous and seemly Christians of his youth resulting in a forbidden *affaire de coeur*, and lost his religion. In an unheard of act of profligate individualism, instead of attending the disciplinary church court held in his honor, he simply packed his bags and went on a tour of the romantic country and had a marvelous time. In later years William described himself not as a religionist, an agnostic, or as an atheist, but as an *amicus humani generis*; and most of his students agreed with his self-assessment.

Dr. Durham gave hope to generations of struggling potential doctors, both the clinical medicine and the strictly scholarly types. He recounted with self-deprecating amusement his trials before being awarded his doctorate in zoology. He worked for eleven years on pocket gophers, demonstrating the differences in the little rodents that occurred as a result of the isolation of their colonies, much as Charles Darwin had done with his finches on the Galapagos Islands, and made a carefully reasoned argument for the Darwinian theory of evolution. When he presented his dissertation, it was rejected, to his consternation, because another graduate student in another university had that very year earned his doctorate with a nearly identical thesis. With characteristic good humor, he set out for another eight years to write the most cogent biography of Darwin yet in the literature. He always concluded his story by stressing that the doctoral board awarded him his Ph.D. more out of pity or to be rid of him than for any recognition of his scholarship.

Garven found that the spark of hope offered by the professor and his stories helped him to keep up his relentless work-load with faith in himself despite the ephemeral specter of possible rejection and failure that dogged his and his classmates' heels.

In October Garven wrote requests for application forms from twenty medical schools at an average cost of twenty-five dollars each, making a sizable hole in his budget. He investigated every aspect of the applications process before making his final choices. He applied at Stanford because of his attendance and good record at the university. He selected the University of Utah and George Washington University because he had heard that they had a strong preference for Mormons, and on those applications he was a Mormon. Pursuing that reasoning ploy, at Maharry and Albert Einstein he told them of his Jewish mother. He did not think a similar stratagem would work at Howard University, but if he could have successfully altered his application photograph, he would probably have tried it.

He obtained half a dozen more letters of recommendation than the applications called for.

Dr. Wilsonhulme suggested that idea citing the old dictum of pharmacology, "If a little is good, a lot is better."

Garven went to considerable effort to include the most influential Arizonians he could muster up for his application to the State Faculty of Medicine of Arizona. His extracurricular activities, as recorded on the applications, were descriptive of a man with the idealism of Saint Ignacius of Loyola, the athletic pursuits of Jim Thorpe, the intellectual pursuits of the Renaissance genius, Leonardo da Vinci, and medical research enthusiasm that would have inspired Ambrose Paré, Sir William Ostler, and the Johns Hopkins research committee.

That year a matching program for students and medical schools had been instituted across the country to alleviate the yearly chaos of students being accepted at several schools and nobody knowing which accepted student would end up at which medical school when. The applications deadline was now to be the end of December, and the response from the medical school had to be in the hands of the student and the national clearinghouse by the middle of April. The student then had fourteen days to commit to the medical school of his choice before any offer of acceptance could be withdrawn. The students who were not accepted in the first round then had another six weeks of communication and interviews or re-applications to fill in the remaining available freshman class seats.

The reform of applications procedures came as an updated result of the sweeping reforms of the nation's medical schools starting in 1940 with the modern applications of the 1910 Abraham Flexner Report. Proprietary schools, that is, schools that were mere extensions of private hospitals, began to disappear. A nationally standardized set of criteria for medical school curricula with wide latitude for the independence of the institutions was attempted with some degree of success, and a set of nonbinding guidelines for state licensure were suggested. The uniform applications process was considered experimental. A Medical College Aptitude Test patterned after the fairly widely accepted Scholastic Aptitude Test for undergraduate universities was established and was going through a period of alterations and refinements. The Med CAT was not binding or even considered in some cases and for most it was considered only an adjunct to the better methods of the personal interview, letters of recommendation from trusted professors, or simple reliance on undergraduate grades. The sciences grades were the most important determining factor and always the final arbiter.

Garven took the MCAT in December and got a well-above average score despite having not yet completed his physics and biology series. He attached a note, an addendum, to each of his applications indicating that he planned to take the MCAT again in the spring after he had completed his courses and hoped that the schools would bear in mind the fact that he needed the opportunity to finish those classes in order to best display his capabilities. About half of the applicants affixed a similar codicil.

By the end of the fall quarter, Garven's applications were off in the mail with the test scores to be sent separately by the scoring company. Now, all he could do was wait and hope. He had to keep up his grades. That was an obvious corollary requirement. Garven and thousands of other hopefuls sweated.

Manny and Dezi, not having the compunctions of Leonard Holespeach from the UP Motor Freight Company about interfering with a promising young man's education, particularly in such a noble field of study, offered Garven a serious inducement to come and work for them full time in the auto parts store. $800 a month for a fifty hour work week, a week's paid vacation a year after three years, health insurance through Blue Cross, and he would not even have to put up with the limitations of the Blue Shield system.

Garven told the two men that he would think very seriously about their offer. He had no intention of considering a move from his education into business, even for such a tempting offer. He only waited and appeared to be vacillating as a bit of theater; so, he would not hurt the two men's feelings and maybe compromise his job standing. Garven Wilsonhulme had a steely singleness of purpose that could not be turned aside for any inducement, principle, cause, creed, or career preference. He was not even completely sure that he knew what it was that a doctor did, but he knew one absolute certainty—Garven Wilsonhulme was going to be a doctor and nothing else.

"Thanks Dezi, but I can't stop my medical career now. I have to see this thing through. Maybe I won't get accepted; if that happens, then I will jump at the chance to work full time."

Garven knew that was untrue. If he did not get into the freshman medical school class in 1952, he would just finish another year and get a bachelor's degree and apply again. If he could not get into an American medical school, he would get into a foreign one. If he had to, he would change his name, or fake his accomplishments, forge his transcripts, make up letters of recommendation, or figure out a way to bribe or blackmail somebody somewhere on an admissions committee. Garven Wilsonhulme was going to be a doctor.

"We decided to leave the best news until last. You done good while you have worked here. Business come up real good. We was thinking about askin' youse to come into the business with us; you know, buy into a partnership over time," Manny said, making his ultimate offer, one that put small scars on his heart.

Garven learned that what the juniors from Emmett had told him about the horrors of Newly's tests, especially his lab tests, had been vastly understated. Garven had slaved over his microscope identifying every germ layer, every segment of differentiating cells, following every change in a region or a tissue from the morula to the 5 millimeter fetus. He knew the material cold. But he was unprepared for the picayune precision required in identification or the difficulty in differentiating one layer from another on slide preparations he had never seen. The colors were different; the angles were unusual; the emphasis was skewed away from everything he had determined was important. The method of grading alone made the lab examination the test from hell.

The tests were so notorious and such a source of apprehension for decades of students that Dr. Newly instructed the students to sit quietly in their seats for a full two minutes before receiving their test materials. The professor was an atheist; but before each lab test, he required every student to participate in two minutes of silent prayer.

It had a calming effect on the mental maelstroms, "can't hurt," he routinely said, "might help."

Dr. Newly told everyone that he was firm believer in prayer. Garven was no more religious than his professor; but he, too, was inclined to like the prayer sessions.

Dr. Newly and the lab assistants had set up twenty microscopes with slides under them accompanied by a single question. The questions were on the order of "identify the structure", "name the germinal layer from which this structure originated", "what will this region become?", "describe a congenital anomaly associated with this structure", "point to the layer of endodermal origin in the slide under the microscope."

The twenty questions were so structured that the student got two chances on each. He was to point to the structure or write the answer, then call Dr. Newly or the lab instructor over to pass judgment. If the answer was wrong the first time, a red slash was placed by the number of the question. If the question was answered incorrectly a second time, a second slash appeared converting the red mark into an 'X'. The student was treated to the suffering and ignominy of watching his grade erode gradually away as the test progressed. It was as much a test of nerves as it was of knowledge of the material.

Dr. Newly took genuine delight in being able to announce on the first try of a hapless student that, "Your pointer is one cell layer off!"

The effect was Dantesque. The poor student had to make the fateful decision of which cell to move the pointer to next, the horns of a dilemma with his career in medicine hanging in jeopardy. Dr. Newly seemed to raise his voice unnecessarily when it was Garven's turn to be off by one cell.

The tests were the Arizona proving ground for would-be medical students. Some men decided that it was not worth it after getting into the class and facing one of those nightmare tests. Some learned that their nerves could not take the pressure, and no one had to tell them that medical school and medical practice were only going to be worse. One hopeful, whose father had decreed from before conception that his son was going to be a doctor and had pressed and driven the sensitive artistic boy from his earliest conscious period in that direction, had stopped in the middle of a test and had begun to rock back and forth in his chair humming childhood lullabies. He was still doing so a day later, Garven found out via the grapevine.

The attrition was staggering and frightening. Half of the hopeful pre-med students were gone before the quarter was over. Some failed the work; some failed the implicit psychological test; some learned the error of their choice. Medicine is plain and simply too hard a discipline; and some were told by the professor that they should seek new avenues when they themselves were unable to recognize the obvious. Garven never let down his guard, refused to let the test method intimidate him, and found that as the ranks of fellow students diminished, his capacity to remain awake even when the lights went out in the slide lectures, increased inversely. He was coming to grips with what it meant to be a doctor.

It was Prof. Newly's announced opinion and intention that no student ever deserved a 100 percent score on one of his tests, and Garven Wilsonhulme made it one of his lifetime goals to achieve a perfect paper as much for the sporting aspect of it as anything. He had done very well, demonstrating a real aptitude for the advanced zoology subjects. On the midterm, Garven found the test to be a combination of old test questions which he had meticulously written out and memorized in advance. He was delighted at the opportunity to excel, and painstakingly recreated his mental notes about the previously answered questions. The material was as clear in his mind as if he had held an open book in front of him; and when the time was up in the test, Garven knew that he had handed in a perfect test, blue books full of detailed and accurate argument and description.

Dr. Newly was correct about his tests, even on this one. Garven read his score on the written segment - 99 percent. At first he was angry; the old man was just being contrary and arbitrary. Then he read the red pencil note explaining why he had lost a point on his perfect paper:

"Your answer was too long."

Garven burst out laughing and caught Dr. Newly's eye. The professor had been watching him to see his reaction. There was a brief bond between teacher and student; Garven stifled his protest.

CHAPTER
Five

Garven's house mates were not finicky about messes and smells, and they were understanding about the things Garven had to do to get through his biology courses. This good combination of traits was strained to the maximum by the requirement that he bring home his formalinized cat to work on during the winter quarter cat anatomy section. At first they were interested, almost fascinated, rather awed, when Garven showed them the muscles, ligaments, tendons, nerves, veins, and arteries. It was a revelation to them when he rattled off the names and functions of the myriad of stringy structures. He could have made up every name or used Swahili equivalents, and they would never have known. It was impressive that those gray-brown preserved muscles looked so human.

Ray said, "I seen a skinned bear once. My uncles nailed its arms to the side of a barn and skinned it out. It was creepy. Looked like a man. Like somebody had been crucified. I never felt much like bear huntin' after that. I don't mind lookin' at this little thing. It don't look so real."

"Kinda looks like roast beef, don't it?" offered Bubba.

Lyle did not appreciate the comparison to his favorite food and asked them not to talk about it any more.

Their enthusiasm did not extend as far as a willingness to do anything but take a cursory sickly look at the internal viscera.

"Slimy lookin', ain't it?" observed Bubba after his careful study.

"Creepy," said Lyle.

"I don't think I was cut out to be a doctor myself," said Ray. "You know, cuttin' on people's guts, stuff like that. Seein' a cow have a calf about freaked me out. I don't especially like blood and runny stuff. Guess somebody's got to do it, though. We should be glad there's guys as smart as Garven around. Guys that can handle that kinda stuff."

Although they would not have been considered fastidious by most experts in the field, Garven's three roommates finally balked at the growing ring of gray-brown formalin that dripped from the cat to the floor. Garven kept the cat on a tray on the top of his chest of drawers. One dissected paw hung over the edge and dripped a few drops of the pungent liquid onto the floor every day. The spot steadily grew bit by bit, and the smell became semi-permanent, persisting even when the cat was not there. Bubba was the most sensitive to such things and began to have nightmares about ghouls and zombies.

Garven made the mistake of not taking Bubba and the others' concerns about the desecrated cat and the images it conjured seriously enough. He even teased them with oblique references to "walking dead" and "the time the cats invaded the town in California and massacred the people." He put up a sign over his bed quoting the old Scottish invocation,

From Ghoulies and Ghosties, and long legged Beasties and Things that go bump in the night, Good Lord deliver us.

It was too macabre for those Union Pacific Motor Freight dock workers. The cat had to go. By a democratic vote of three to one, Garven had to sanitize the formalin spot that by the time of its removal had assumed an aura of being possessed in the susceptible minds of the young men. The cat, now in several pieces, had to be relegated to the trunk of Garven's car.

A domino effect of the cat anatomy class and the overwrought reaction of the house mates was that Garven lost his girl friend, the nearest he had come to having a girl friend thus far in his life. He dated Sarah Marie Luke several times until she could not tolerate the smell of the formalin wafting from the trunk of the car where he was obliged to keep the partially dismembered feline. Sarah Marie loved cats; and although she thought of herself as a sophisticated college co-ed, she could not adjust to the image of that mutilated cat in the trunk she had had to look at more than once. She found a new boyfriend, an elementary education major.

The third week of April, 1952 brought four or five letters for Garven every day of the week. He had not received a letter at that apartment before that period; and the import of the official envelopes was unmistakable. The first letter was a rejection from the University of Pennsylvania; then came a rejection from Cornell, his dad's alma mater. Not to worry; they were eastern schools. Garven felt panicked but not discouraged. It had never occurred to his imagined scheme of his life that he would fail to get into medical school. His panic centered on which school. Panic was inappropriate, but that is what he felt anyway. When he discussed his feelings with Dr. Wilsonhulme, the older man assured him that pre-med and medical students always felt panicked; it was an endemic part of their world.

The University of Utah rejected him also. The letter informed him that they considered him qualified and would be happy to have him as a student, but there were too many qualified state citizens applying that year. George Washington University informed Garven that they would consider him for their alternate group. All of this hovered in Garven's mind.

On Wednesday the envelopes from Stanford, and Maharry were waiting for him. There was serious expectation in the Stanford envelope. He could not, at first, force himself to open it. He knew it was silly; but he had too much invested. He decided to get someone for whom the findings would not be important to open it. His roommates fit that description. Garven waited until Lyle got home because he was not certain Ray or Bubba could read. Lyle opened the envelope without the slightest hesitation just because Garven asked him to do that favor and read the letter with all the fervor of a postal clerk. Garven had him read the whole letter again, then the first paragraph one more time before he dared to look for himself. He was accepted to Stanford!

"I'm going to medical school!" he shouted.

His roommates looked up from their comic books somewhat startled. His excitement was contagious.

"Let's party!" said Ray.

"Hey, Garven, congratulations!" said Bubba. "Nobody in my family ever even went to college, let alone to doctor school. Jeez, it's great! I guess you're the smartest guy I ever knew!"

"Thanks Bubba!" Garven said.

He shook hands all around and could not get the grin off his face.

"Let's go out and eat at someplace fancy. It's my celebration. I'll pay. You guys can eat escargot and crepes suzettes, and calamari, and drink champagne!"

"What's es-car-go?" asked Ray carefully.

He did not eat strange things and was a little suspicious of Garven who had been out of state for a while and might have gotten into some peculiar stuff.

"Snails," Garven said laughing.

"Jeez. I don't even eat mushroom burgers," declared Ray.

"I'll take you up on the champagne," said Lyle. "I never tasted it before. That stuff costs ten times as much as Midnight and Revel. I like them; so, I oughta love champagne."

The boys compromised on steak and found a great place uptown. The next day he took cigars to Dezi and Manny who made the expected comments about him having a baby, but the two good hearted men were genuinely pleased for their college boy. They even sprang for the bill at another dinner— this time the best Italian food in the city, Mama Louisa's.

Maharry rejected him. Albert Einstein accepted him. Like Stanford, the tuition was eight thousand dollars a year. Garven did not know where such a king's ransom was supposed to come from. He was pretty sure that Peter Wilsonhulme did not have an extra forty thousand for the whole four years; Garven certainly didn't. He was looking for his real hope for a medical education in the Faculty of Arizona Medical School envelope. It did not come that week, and it was not there by the week before winter quarter finals.

The competition at Arizona was not quite as great as it had been at Stanford. The courses seemed as hard to Garven, and the finals were every bit as taxing.

In Comparative Anatomy, he was asked to answer and to explain:

> Which came first, the chicken or the egg?
> In the recently fertilized human zygote, where is the soul?
> Why don't cats have five legs?

In Vertebrate Embryology, he was required to discuss:

> The mesodermal origin and development of the notochord and spinal column versus the ectodermal origin of the spinal cord.
> The origin, histogenesis, and morphogenesis of the central nervous system
> The transition from the original two endothelial tubes to the at-term fetal heart, including a description of the changes from the in-utero state to the normal extra-uterine heart.

In Genetics, Garven wrote on:

> The discoveries by Thomas Hunt Morgan using Drosophila melanogaster regarding chromosomes, particularly the dif-

ferentiation of autosomes and sex chromosomes, and sex-linked recessives.

The phenomena of chromosomal nondisjunction of Bridges, gene linkage, and crossing-over.

A short description of Sickle-cell Anemia, Galactosemia, Phenolketonuria, Hemophilia, and Tay-Sachs Disease.

The Physics final asked:

Discuss Galileo's principle that, since a sphere rises to its original height regardless of the slope of its incline, motion along a horizontal plane ought to be perpetual.

How is it that light can be shown in conclusive experiments to be a wave and in other conclusive experiments to be particulate? Describe two experiments by which you could determine the speed of light and state the nonsense about the speed of light in a vacuum in terms of relativity theory.

Garven scored well; he got a four point for the quarter. He repeated the MCAT and raised his average by fifty-one points. Before that data could be considered in any of his applications, he received the envelope from the Arizona Faculty of Medicine. His future was in that envelope. He made Lyle open the letter. He felt like his teeth were chattering.

> April 7, 1952
>
> Dear Mr. Wilsonhulme,
> I have the distinct pleasure of informing you that you have been accepted as a first year student in the Arizona Faculty of Medicine beginning fall quarter, 1952. Congratulations. You are to be commended on the fine record that led the board of admissions to select you. We trust that you will be as fine a medical student as you were in your undergraduate work, and that you will represent our school of medicine as a superb physician.
>
> Yours truly,
> John Taft Bledsoe, MD
> Dean of the Medical School

CHAPTER
Six

Garven spent the first two weeks of the summer between completion of his three year pre-med program and the start of medical school visiting *the* family, in which he considered himself to be the pretender, the Wilsonhulmes of Providence, Rhode Island. They were pleasant, more than simply correct, but distant. They were old money, and he was not even *nouveau riche*. Every slightly raised eyebrow at his western accent, particularly his occasional homespun colloquialisms, and every transitory downturned lip at his failure to be acquainted with one or the other member of the local social register put up a little more of a barrier between Garven and Dr. Wilsonhulme's family. It was apparent after half a month that the blood in their separate veins was not the same color. It took all the stamina and inhibition Garven possessed not to respond to the slights he registered daily. Almost instinctively, he recognized them as a future resource, and one he could ill afford to squander for such a flimsy reason as gross incompatibility.

His old friends got him on at the Union Pacific Trucking Company again for the summer, and he toughened up over the rest of his vacation from school. Just before the fall medical school term started, Garven quit and went to Dallas to take Grantland Kurze up on his offer to go hunting, Texas style.

In his element, Grantland fit well and not only seemed to be able to persist, but to prevail. His element was Texas oil money. Everything about the young man was big: the money, the ranch, the house, and the sense of *joie de vivre* that accompanied even the most mundane activities of his life. Not that the recent Stanford graduate was a Pollyanna. He faced reality with wonderment and took what life had to offer—riches, power, intelligence, and comfort—with an ebullient and forward outlook, and without the slightest apology or shyness.

"Even my ranch fleas are rich enough to have their own dogs," he told Garven.

He reveled in the fun his money could buy.

"Glad to see y'all, Garven. I had about given up on ya. We got lots a drinkin' and huntin' and girlin' to do. Life is fleetin', and y'all been wastin' the best part of the year a workin'!" Grantland bugled when his garish white Cadillac convertible finally reached the Plano ranch outside north Dallas. "How was the ride out from Love Field, ole buddy?" he queried.

"Had a great ride, Grantland. Real style. I hate to admit it, but that was the first time I was ever in a Cadillac. That is truly the way to fly. And, as for workin', some us po' folks just hasta," Garven replied in a poor mimic of Grantland's classical drawl when he was given a small chance as his effusive friend took one of his infrequent breaths.

Garven noticed that Grantland's accent was much heavier than it had been when they were at Stanford. He seemed to have settled back into his old life and ways untainted by his foreign education.

"Okay, y'all must be tuckered out; so, I'll show ya to y'all's bunk room. Alejandro'll fetch in y'all's bags. Rest up; then we'll eat and plan our attack on the prey species of the world—four footed and two."

Alejandro had driven Garven from Love Field and now toted his bags into a spacious south facing room that was three-fourths the size of his mother's home in Cipher, Arizona. Alejandro was one of the workers on the place who did not file income tax forms and for whom social security taxes were not deducted. He was also one of those guest workers who was altogether glad to have a job and worked hard for his pay.

At a small supper of roast beef, baked potato with all the trimmings, four vegetables, pie ala mode, and coffee Grantland outlined his plans for Garven's next two weeks.

"Tomorra we'll take off to the back forty and hunt us up a little black tail buck or two and then I'll take you to where we keep the exotics. My daddy is takin' some senator out after an eland. We'll tag along. You ever seen an eland, bud?"

"I don't even know what one is," answered Garven feeling even more ignorant than he had earlier in the day when Grantland had patiently taken the time to elaborate the differences between Santa Gertrudis and Charbray, poled and horned, clover and jimsonweed.

"Those critters are big sorta deer or more like an ox with real long pointy horns. Daddy brought 'em over from Africa. My mother says they're just another big boy's toy, but that's not right. Daddy is savin' the species here on the ranch. They're a thrivin', and for twenty thou or so, he lets some New Yorker come out and have a hunt. Or he gives a thrill to some politician he needs. We are good to them, and they are good to us."

"Will my 30-30 be okay? I heard that the black tails aren't any too big," Garven asked, hoping that at least one thing he could produce would be up to snuff.

"Would be if you could get close enough to one of them. The fun of huntin' black tails is that they are so smart and fast. They can hear a skeeter walkin' tiptoe and can see belly button lint six miles off while they're on a full-out gallop. Y'all'll never get close enough to pick one off with that pea shooter. I got just the right weapon, if you wouldn't mind the suggestion," Grantland said.

He paused to give Garven the courtesy of an objection. A man took real pride in his gun.

Garven had no protest.

"I have a family heirloom for ya. Y'all take my old .257 Roberts with the Redman scope. Nothin' but the best for my old hall mate. This sweet piece has a Titus barrel and a genuine Mauser action, best money can buy. Try it out and see if y'all don't like it, ya hear?"

"That's real generous of you, Grantland. What time do we start?" Garven asked, indicating his easy capitulation.

"Crack of dawn. In fact, we got to be sittin' up there before first light when they come out to feed. Might as well sit around and whittle if you get out there after sunup."

"I'm pooped. Think I'll turn in, then, if we have to get up with the chickens," Garven said.

"Okay, for this one day until y'all get used to the country, then none of that wimpy 'early to bed, early to rise, make's Jack stuff after today. Have a glass of bourbon and branch water, whatever that is. See y'all in the mornin'. Alejandro and Pepe'll be goin' with us, tend the horses and all. Sleep tight, now."

They left before light and were sitting on a low rise overlooking a sagebrush and mesquite dotted open area as the Texas landscape began to take shape with the approaching dawn. The horses were on the opposite side of the hill, far enough away to prevent spooking the skittish little deer. Alejandro and Pepe patiently held the reins and talked with low voices while the two young Norteamericanos shivered in the cool morning air on the hill above them.

There was a very slight rustling noise in the clearing.

"One of 'em brushed a sagebrush," Grantland whispered directly into Garven's ear.

It was still too dark to make out any shapes, let alone to distinguish a rack of antlers from the bald head of a doe. Garven strained his eyes into the darkness and held his hunting rifle tightly.

The light of pre-dawn finally allowed for a view of the open plane. Huge clumps of prickly pears were almost as tall as the deer that wound in among them. There were eight deer distinguishable in the lightening gloom slowly moving through the dark forms of the sagebrush. As it became progressively lighter, the deer became more vigilant and nervous. A small, but beautifully proportioned, buck, carrying a handsome rack of five points on each side, pranced around his does, circling them and herding them along. He looked up frequently, made small false starts, and generally displayed the sense of tension that was the natural accompaniment of his responsibility to his harem.

Garven sighted at him through his Redman scope. Grantland was also sighting through the Zeiss variable power, high light retrieving scope mounted on his Winchester .270 with the lustrous hand-turned curly maple stock. Neither dared speak at this point. They had a 250 yard shot. Garven looked over at Grantland. Grantland nodded in his direction indicating that Garven should take the shot.

It was light enough. A light breeze blew cold air across the hill crest. The buck moved about with short fits and starts making it difficult to put the cross hairs on the kill zone of the animal. Finally, after a few seconds, but what seemed to Garven like hours, he drew in a deep breath; and as he exhaled, he squeezed of his shot. The buck leaped gracefully to the side and began to run in great distance covering bounds. His does followed behind in a dutiful single file line. Garven had missed. He fired a second shot at the fleeing deer, now a rapid moving smaller target, and missed again; this time his bullet kicked a small puff of dust to the left of the swiftly running buck.

Garven cursed himself. It was too far to waste another shot. Then, he was startled by the muzzle report of Grantland's .270 going off less than three feet from his ear. To his chagrin Grantland's shot dropped the deer that was now running at top speed and was upwards of 350 yards away. Garven cursed out loud.

"Just luck, amigo," said Grantland matter-of-factly as he stood up and began to stretch his legs to get the feeling back into them.

In fact it was the kind of shot Texas boys made almost every day.

Garven was angry and every thing about his demeanor conveyed that emotion. To Grantland it was all out of proportion.

"Hey, bud, take it easy. This is just a couple of us good ole boys havin' a little hunt—nothin' serious."

"I could have got him. You didn't have to shoot like I was some kid who couldn't hit the broad side of a barn. I had to get used to your gun. I'm not sure the sights are right on," Garven groused.

"The sights are just fine, amigo. It doesn't matter anyhow. Let's get the boys and clean that little buck," Grantland said, but Garven was out of earshot.

He had stomped away down the hill towards Pepe, Alejandro, and the horses.

Grantland shook his head and muttered to himself, "that boy is afflicted with the curse of competitiveness—got to win no matter what. Mighty tense. I hope I never get in his way."

He ambled down the hill to catch up with the other men.

The University of Arizona Faculty of Medicine 1952-53 calendar year started on September 21 with freshman class orientation. The medical school was only five years old, and its faculty was sensitive to the contrast with the venerable old Harvard, Yale, University of Pennsylvania type schools that could boast generations of department chiefs all over the country. The members of the Arizona faculty had been imported to Arizona at an exorbitant cost, and were working to deserve their enviable salaries and stipends. To their credit they insisted on a very strict policy of quality over quantity that limited their first class, the one that graduated in 1951, to eleven students. Garven's class numbered fifty-two on that first hot September day.

The demographic makeup of the class was unusual, if not unique, among schools in the United States during that era. Because of money available from the GI bill, the average age of the students was older—many were in their mid-thirties, and less obviously Caucasian; the pressure to accept students whose merit was in question just because of the old-boy route arrangements that characterized the eastern schools was slight. Arizona had a mixed ethnic background and did not particularly subscribe to the notion that woman's place was not in the medical school or that Negroes were constitutionally inferior. The faculty came largely from Yale and Princeton, and therefore was far more Jewish in complexion than the population of Phoenix would suggest.

As a result, Garven's class consisted of fifty-two diverse individuals—thirty-one white males and nine Caucasian women (all former nurses), six Negro males and two females, four Latinos (three Mexican-Americans and one

Venezuelan, all males). In a Christian nation, and a national medical system that was predominately Christian, Garven's class further showed its diversity or contrariness by being made up of twelve WASPS (male and female), one Mormon, four Roman Catholics, seven nonaffiliated and nonbelievers (of which, by his own entry on the admissions form, Garven was one), and twenty-eight Jews. All but one of the Jews came from out of state (i.e. eastern seaboard states) and that prompted a yearly acrimonious debate in the Arizona legislature about limiting enrollment to in-state residents. Each year that argument had been quashed by threats of an en masse resignation of the medical school faculty.

The Dean of the Medical Faculty, Dr. Bledsoe, described the diversity of the class on opening day. His orientation lecture included an enumeration of the qualifications of the students and how favorably they compared to the elitist eastern institutions.

Dean Bledsoe concluded the formal speeches with his observation and statement of purpose: "You have come here from different walks of life, different preparations, varied ethnic and social backgrounds, and with a host of different expectations and aspirations. However, there are certain elements about you that are the same. You can be confident that no person in your class is here for any other reason than that he or she merited the right to be here. The admissions committee was scrupulously color blind, deaf to the blandishments of important contributors or citizens for their children; and we rejected pre-conceived notions about gender, country of origin, or social background, even money. The great state of Arizona has been very generous with grants and stipends to provide seats in your class even for those who could not afford to be here. There is no stigma to any of the conditions of race, gender, religion, or origin here. There will be a stigma for poor performance.

"You were accepted here on a strict basis of merit, and we expect you to perform. We expect high effort and results from each of you. This is not college where you might slide by. This is professional school; and you will fulfill the requirements of the work here; or you will not graduate. Mark my words, my young colleagues, The Faculty of Medicine at the University of Arizona will produce only the best clinicians, academicians, and researchers, if we produce only one recipient of the Doctor of Medicine degree a year.

"Four years from now, when your class comes to graduate, fifty percent of you will not be there to receive a diploma. Twenty-five percent of your class will have come down from the classes above you because we think they need more work to reach the level of quality we will accept. Your class will be twenty-five percent smaller at graduation than it is this morning. Those of you who weather all of the vicissitudes and do all of the work will be among the best prepared fledgling doctors in the world and will embark on the most demanding and fulfilling career there is. And you will spend the rest of your lives learning. Remember this: five years after you graduate, all but the very rudiments of what you learn here will be obsolete. If you are not ready to make a life's mission of medicine, including a lifelong habit of scholarship, quit now and save yourself and all of us a great deal of grief.

"Medicine is a jealous mistress. She will require that you choose her over wife, children, church, community, or personal pursuits. If you cannot give her what she needs, this is the day to recognize that in yourself and to quit. Go on to something easier and more fun. Be a Renaissance man or woman, be an artist, a Thoreau, a business tycoon. You will not be a doctor. Save yourself misery and the profession shame.

"Welcome to the class of 1956. Now let's get to work!"

A nervous and intense young woman was sitting next to Garven during Dean Bledsoe's speech. She looked very somber when he finished.

"I'm Maria Stricker," she said and extended her hand.

Garven shook it. It was unusual to shake hands with a woman in his experience, but the woman offered the gesture as an indication of their equality, and Garven rather liked the idea.

"I suppose we all ought to go out and cut our wrists or become hermits after his talk," she said and smiled in mild amusement.

"It sounds like that would be the easiest way out. Maybe none of us knows what we are getting into," Garven answered Maria.

"I'm pretty sure those are true words; and we are about to lose our illusions very rapidly, I suspect," she said.

Garven smiled and nodded his agreement. He was feeling very insecure at that point.

The remaining four and a half days of orientation week involved tours of the classrooms and facilities, introductory talks from faculty members grouped by departments, and time to spend a fortune on the list of books, lab coats and equipment, and supplies handed out by the members of the faculty. The new students were convinced that there would be no time to do anything for themselves after the first class convened on Monday. Garven quickly dispensed with his plans to work part time to offset his expenses. The money from Dr. Wilsonhulme was dissipating rapidly, and his savings from the summer jobs were going to provide a thin existence. Money concerns had to be relegated to the back bench, the place in Garven's mind where chronic apprehensions were kept.

The first class on the first day of his medical school career started at eight o'clock on the dot. It was held in the oldest building in the complex of the medical school campus. The building was a hand-me-down from the university, as were two of the three remaining buildings. What had been spent on faculty salaries had come at the expense of grounds and classrooms. The basic sciences building needed paint, repairs to fire escapes and lavatories, and was woefully short of storage space which resulted in a plethora of teaching aids, specimen jars, blackboards, projectors, and lab equipment being left out to clutter the already narrow dark hallways. Gross Anatomy class was held in the largest and dingiest of the old building's rooms.

Garven took a seat near the front of the room fifteen minutes early. It was obvious that he would have to get there even earlier in the future if he were going to beat his fellow students to the front row. He took that as a small sign of the competitive nature of the men and women with whom he was going to live for the next four years, if he survived. It was a small sobering observation.

On the hour, the professor of anatomy entered a side door and walked briskly to the dais and stood behind the lectern. Behind him were two impeccable chalk boards and a small table on which stood an array of colored chalk.

"I am Edward I. Yosobuchi," he said.

He was a small, old, Japanese man with bright active eyes and face.

"I am your professor of gross anatomy. There will be laboratory assistants and the occasional guest instructor, but I am the one you need to fear."

He let that sink in.

"You don't have to fear me like those of my race who bombed Pearl Harbor. I am second generation Japanese American, and I didn't do it."

The students laughed dutifully.

"I did pay for the mistakes of my Japanese brethren. I spent the war years in Utah, a place called Keetley, where I learned to grow vegetables and to mend furniture. At least I can be considered useful instead of just ornamental," Yosobuchi said, then made a sharp about face and turned his back on them.

For the remainder of the lecture he faced the chalk board. Yosobuchi selected two pieces of flesh colored chalk then began to draw with both hands simultaneously because his subject concerned matching anatomical structures. He drew as he lectured.

"The breast," he began, "is a marvelous structure."

There were a few titters.

"And for more reasons than that," he continued. "These graceful organs are skin appendages served by arteries, veins, lymphatics, and these ligaments."

He drew swiftly and accurately, one breast diagram displaying the arteries and veins, the other the lymphatics and Cooper's ligaments.

"There are variations in size, shape, and texture, as you are well aware. For the purposes of this class in order to appreciate the anatomy better, we divide the types of mammaries into four classes."

He paused. The new medical students poised their pens over their notebooks.

"The classes are: Supers, droopers, super droopers, and pear shape."

He swiftly chalked in an example of each.

"Viva the pear shape!" he said as he finished that piece of art work. "Not every woman can have a pear shape, but with the proper effort anyone can end up with super droopers. The little Cooper's ligaments hold up the breast, give it that upturned lilt of youth. They are easily broken and when they are gone, and there are a finite number of them; they are gone. When enough of them disappear, the breast sags. Fortunately for mankind, the advanced nations, unlike our benighted Ubangi cousins, have the good sense to protect these treasures with that most marvelous of all inventions, the brassiere. Despite the relatively diminutive size of the device, it is remarkably strong—able to hold up two milk factories and a playground, as it were."

The class laughed appreciatively now. The professor's monologue was completely dry witted, and he did not pause for any of their responses.

"The breast of the male and of the infantile girl is a tiny disc, any definition it has comes from fat. I repeat, the breast is a skin appendage like hair or polyps. The postmenopausal breast, though often much larger, is once again largely fat. After a certain age, and I would not venture to give you that magic number, the sole function of the breast is to house cancer."

Garven was enjoying the lecture. He had been waiting a long time to sit in this chair, and he soaked up the serious information and the banter with equal appreciation. He was sitting next to Maria, who remained serious throughout the lecture, taking down everything the fast talking professor said in near court recorder verbatim.

"The breast is divided into four quadrants. The upper outer, or quadrant three is served by the perforating branch of the internal thoracic or internal mammary artery, and clinically is important because of the nodes that can be palpated in the axilla which tell the tale of cancer spread. If they are there in any number, the prognosis is dismal."

Professor Yosobuchi described the other three quadrants in similar detail.

"Now, the last quadrant—the aureole and nipple. The lymphatics drain to the anterior axillary nodes via the upper collecting trunk. The subaureolar plexus of Sappey drains the aureole and nipple and flows into the lower collecting trunk. It joins the upper and drains into the same anterior axillary nodes. Never neglect to examine the axilla, no matter what your specialty."

He described the nerve supply: the anterior branches of the lateral cutaneous branches of the anterior primary rami of the intercostal nerves. Here, he made a necessary digression and did another two hand symmetrical drawing, this time of the typical thoracic vertebra and a schematic thoracic nerve with all the branches and rami.

At nine o'clock exactly, Professor Yosobuchi finished his sentence regarding the skin, having to do with the difference between the epidermis and the dermis and the relationship of that concept to the breast.

He turned once again to face the freshmen students, put down his chalks, and said, "That is the end of the lecture for today. You will have a one hour lecture five days a week for two years on gross anatomy. It is very simple. You do not need to differentiate the important from the unimportant in these lectures. You will be responsible for every word uttered here. This is just like the scriptures—for every word that proceedeth out of the mouth of Yosobuchi; I think that is what it says."

Garven leaned his chair back on the two hind legs and took a deep breath.

"Boy," he said to Maria, "I'm glad we only have twenty-five quarter hours this session so we can work into this medical school stuff gradually."

She laughed in agreement.

"You will now receive your laboratory manual," Dr. Yosobuchi announced after the three minute rest interval. "Today's lab session is entitled 'Preparation of the Specimen', and the directions are contained on pages one through fifteen inclusive. Follow those instructions with all the care that you would with your grandma's secret recipe. If you do more, you may foul up your ability to study some part in the future. If you do less, you will not see or learn the necessary anatomy. If you do not see it or learn it in the lab, rest assured you will yet see in on a lab examination and will be rueful. I don't want you to have to be rueful."

When each student had a manual in hand, Yosobuchi tapped his fingers on his lectern like a gavel and got their attention again.

He said, "I think you might like to put on your lab coats now."

The fifty-two new students unwrapped their brilliantly clean long white lab coats and donned them. Every one of them worked to suppress a little smile of pride at their undeniable appearance of being medical students. Garven surreptitiously looked himself over more than once, his face mirroring his inward satisfaction with himself and the world for that moment.

"Nifty," Maria said, smiling at him.

"You look pretty sharp, yourself, doc," he said to her.

It was her turn to betray a streak of pride. She blushed.

"Follow me," said the little Japanese professor.

He was moving rapidly towards the far right rear of the room where four laboratory assistants in begrimed and tattered lab coats were assembled. The students gathered with the professor and the lab assistants around four large covered rectangular lead vats.

"I will now read off sets of four names. You will be lab partners throughout the course unless you make other mutually acceptable arrangements. By the close of the lab today, you will need to list your partnership group; so, we can assign your group to a lab assistant. The grouping will be used to schedule tests and all sorts of fun things like that."

The assistants passed out sheets of lined paper, one to each group of four, as the professor read off their names. Garven was partnered with Maria Stricker, RN, Elijah David Shapiro, an orthodox Jew from Crown Heights, Brooklyn, and Brent Battendorf from Apache Junction, Arizona. By no coincidence, none of the groups had more than two women or two persons of color.

"Now, if I may have your attention, ladies and gentlemen," called Professor Yosobuchi, having to raise his voice over the hubbub. "We have a great deal to do, and very little time to do it in today. You will now receive your cadaver, one for each group. You will be responsible for taking proper care of the body both for your own edification and because we will treat these people with the dignity they deserve. If I learn that any of you desecrate a body or treat it with disrespect, you will no longer be a student in this institution. Is there anyone here who has the slightest question about that?"

No one raised a hand.

"I will call out the number of your group. When I do, you will come and get your cadaver and carry him or her to the dissection table that corresponds to your number. We need to do this with all due dispatch. Number One!" announced the professor.

CHAPTER
Seven

The students were now a sober group as they watched the first four students advance and accept the long metal shepherd's crook handed them by the gnome-like pathology department deiner. The lab assistants had removed themselves to stand by the dissection tables until the specimens were brought to them. There was an embarrassed hush as the heavy lead cover was lifted off the first vat. The powerful sick-sweet aromatic, eye-drying vapors of formalin flowed out into the room. The smell was sickening and pungent. The students dutifully crowded up to the vat to peer in. For many it was the first time they had seen a dead person.

Garven inhaled a deep breath and pinched himself hard enough to raise a visible contused welt to make sure he would not faint. All around him there were pale green faces. Group One reached in with their shepherd's crook and snagged a submerged gray body and brought it to the surface. It slipped off the hook and sank again. One of the men in the group turned ghastly white, took two steps backward and fainted into Dr. Yosobuchi's arms. The professor had quietly walked up behind the group and anticipated the first casualty. He signaled to a couple of the larger men students who slid the unconscious classmate away from the activity.

Group One tried again. This time they were successful in bringing the cadaver to the edge of the vat. The three remaining students muckled the body of the thin old man over the edge and as delicately as possible laid him on the lab cart. His limbs were stiff and folded in unusual positions from the long crowded submersion in the preservative. Their lab coats were wet, stained and smelly. Group One had been blooded.

"Kind of looks like roast beef, doesn't he?" Garven said to Maria.

Elijah David whispered, "Kinda does, all right. Doesn't look kosher," he grinned.

Brent said, "Hey, lay off. Nothing about this reminds me of food. I don't know what restaurant you've been getting your roast beef at, but let me know; so, I can keep clear of it, Garven."

He was pale green in color and kept shaking his head to keep from losing consciousness. Brent was a UA football player all four years at the University, and he knew he would never live it down if he fainted.

Garven's group was number Two. Garven was given the privilege of snagging the cadaver. He had a hard time getting one loose from the pile of bodies on the bottom of the vat. Finally, he was able to bring up a leg. Elijah David reached out and grabbed the foot and pulled the body to the side. There was an identification tag attached to the great toe. 'Sydney Hollister' it read. The birth date revealed that Sydney was sixty-five years old at the time of his passing.

Brent waited to faint until after they went through the struggle of getting their specimen onto the deiner's cart. To be technical about it, he did not faint dead away; he just sat on the floor with his head between his legs.

It was ten o'clock before all of the cadavers were set out supine on the lead topped tables, and the once spiffy looking medical students were standing by their specimens with anticipatory excitement.

Dr. Yosobuchi called for attention and announced, "We will demonstrate the anatomical position, the external characteristics and lines; then you may begin your dissection from page one. You will open the integument of the back and left arm to begin. I do not want you to move ahead. When we are done, you can wrap your specimen in cheese cloth soaked in formalin until our next session."

He nodded to one of the male lab assistants.

"Yes, Doctor," the obedient anatomy grad student said.

"This is Mr. Grant, ladies and gentlemen. Since he is the best specimen among us, he has been volunteered to bare his chest so we can demonstrate the lines."

Mr. Grant removed his lab coat, shirt, and undershirt. Dr. Yosobuchi asked him to stand in the anatomical position.

"This is the standard anatomical position—a world wide convention so that all of us can understand each other. First, note that he stands with his arms dependent, slightly away from the body, palms forward. In that stance we have the front of his body defined as anterior, the back as posterior or dorsal; that towards the midline is medial; and that towards the sides is lateral. Towards the head is cephalad, and towards the feet is caudad. Face up is supine, and face down is prone. So you can see that the old phrase, 'prone to argue' is anatomical nonsense."

Dr. Yosobuchi swiftly made a series of lines on Mr. Grant's skin with a marker.

"We have several obvious divisions: the clavicular line, nipple line, costal line, umbilical line, pubic line."

Dr. Yosobuchi pointed these out.

"Above the line is supra, and below is infra or sub; so, we have supraclavicular or subumbilical; here and here," he pointed. "For purposes of anatomical description, we have vertical lines: this is the midline, this, the mid clavicular line, this, the anterior axillary line; and these are the mid and posterior axillary lines. It is crucial that you incorporate this language today so that you can learn the reference points used for the rest of the course."

"Latin," thought Garven. *"So, all that work on the dead language is paying off."*

Mr. Grant put on his clothing.

"Now inspect your cadaver as if you were doing a clinical examination. In effect, this is your first patient, the first person upon whom you will do a scientific examination. Take five minutes, then we will get on with today's dissection."

Garven, Maria, Elijah David, and Brent began to go over their Sydney in minute detail, noting tattoos, scars, skin blemishes, his below-the-knee amputation of the left leg, and his cauliflower ears.

"Had a rough life," Garven commented thinking about his own nose and ears.

No one could disagree. They recorded careful notations in their lab notebooks. Using their lab manual, the four memorized the locations of the supraclavicular and antecubital fossae, the external location of the femoral triangle, and the boundaries of the popliteal fossa behind the knee. Each of them resolved to memorize the contents of the fossae and triangles.

"Your attention, please," called Dr. Yosobuchi in five minutes. "Turn your cadaver prone."

He gave the young students a minute or two.

"Start with the lab directions and do only the first two pages—the opening of the integument on the left side of the back. Ask for one of the lab instructors or me if you need help."

"Who gets the knife?" Garven asked the others.

He was holding the scalpel in his right hand. His face had a look suggesting that one or more of his partners would have to fight him for the privilege.

"Go ahead," said Brent. "I hate to admit it, but I'm not up to that today."

"I'm going to be a pediatrician," said Maria. "I'll skip the cutting, thanks."

"I'm going to be a diagnostician, an internist; at least that's what my father tells me. So, I can pass on the cutting for the time being, too. Go ahead, Garven; something tells me that you are a cutter and sewer type," said Elijah David, feeling prescient.

Garven grinned. He was a little embarrassed at being so transparent, but not enough even to make a polite demurrer. The scalpel was an outsized one; it seemed clumsy, but appropriate for doing gross anatomy. His lab partners pressed in close. Maria held the manual open to the first page and pointed at the incision line outlined in the manual. Garven drew the knife from medial to lateral across the supraspinatus line. The skin was like moist waxed leather. The epidermis was scratched but not opened, even down to the dermis. It was like cutting rubber. Formalin oozed out of the tentative incision. Brent blanched and put his hand on Maria's shoulder. She looked at him with sympathy, but was careful not to make a big deal out of it since Brent was trying his best not to appear to be a weenie.

"Man, this is tougher than I expected. I always thought skin would slice like butter when I saw operations or when I cut my finger, or something," said Garven.

Brent emitted a little groan.

"I'll get it this time."

He pressed considerably harder and the dermal fat rolled into the incision in satisfying evidence that he was fully through the integument. The fat was glistening gray and wet with the pungent preservative. The skin was glistening from formaldehyde.

Brent squeezed Maria's shoulder hard enough to evince a short, "Ouch!" and then he crumpled to the floor.

The lab partners turned to lay him out in a reasonably comfortable supine position. He was completely out.

"Think we should put pennies on his eyes?" asked Elijah David with a perfectly innocent look on his face.

"E.D.!" squawked Maria.

Elijah David threw back his head and laughed, having elicited the response he wanted. Garven laughed with him, and Maria shook her head at the ascetic appearing Jewish boy and laughed, too.

Mr. Grant left a prostrate victim at one of the other lab tables and walked over to where Brent was lying. He broke an ammonia capsule and held it under Brent's nose. The big athlete woke up with a confused and pained start. The color returned to his face quickly; and, as soon as he realized where he was, he developed a very sheepish expression.

"Stay there for a little while. You will feel a lot better if you do," said the lab instructor.

His attention was already diverted to still a third fainter at a nearby table. He shook his head and fumbled in his pocket for another ammonia capsule. By now, there was general laughter in the lab room.

Garven finished the vertical incision from the dorsal spinous process of the seventh cervical vertebra down to the costovertebral angle junction along the midline, then as quickly as he could, undermined the adherent skin so that it hung in a flap, like a book cover. Brent recovered, and although pale and shaky, was able to join in the examination of the underlying fascia and muscles.

"Okay," said Mr. Grant, who had come up to their table. "Take the incision all the way to the intergluteal line then laterally across the level of the sacroiliac joint to the anterior superior iliac spine. What's your name, cutter?" he looked at Garven.

"Wilsonhulme," Garven answered.

"We are pretty informal here. Okay if we use first names? Mine's Nathan," Mr. Grant said.

"Garven."

Each of the others told the lab instructor his or her name.

"Now, when you get done with the back do the same thing on the front—left side only and only down to the costal line. Has to be a new cutter. Everybody takes a turn. Everybody here is going to be a fully trained doctor, and that doesn't let you skate out of messy stuff."

Maria finished the back, making a couple of button holes in the lower back skin, a 'no-no', as Nathan Grant was quick to point out, and Elijah David did the chest. He was quick and deft, more facile with the knife than Garven for all his protestations about wanting to be 'only a diagnostician'.

"Okay, everybody," called out Dr. Yosobuchi—no one called him Ed. "Gather around tables four, six, nine, and thirteen. You all need to see a female, and we only have four of them."

Anita Pressley, another of the lab instructors, then expertly dissected one of the woman's breasts; and with a little imagination, Garven and his lab team could begin to see some of the features Dr. Yosobuchi had drawn with his colored chalk earlier that morning. By the time she finished with that dissection, it was approaching noon.

"Use the remaining time to review your specimens, and get some lunch before you go over to histology," Dr. Yosobuchi suggested. "You have a full afternoon."

Garven was starved. He opened his brief case and brought out a sandwich and started to munch as the four lab partners poked and probed and recited the names of the muscles and principle fascial layers to each other.

"What kind of sandwich is that?" Brent asked Garven in a less than completely friendly voice.

His face was once again pale.

"Roast beef," Garven said and opened up the sandwich to show his lab partner the thick slices of gray-brown meat on a tomato.

"Why did you do that?" asked Brent plaintively, his voice trailing off.

He was no longer pale. He was green. He fainted again.

The four lab partners made an agreement not to eat while dissecting Sydney thereafter.

Garven was excited and enthusiastic for medical school by the time his first gross anatomy class came to an end. This was, to him, nothing of the drudgery of numbers, and symbols, and irrelevancies that pre-med had required—the inapplicable conglomerate of intellectual stuff that he had had to learn for no other discernible reason that to gain access to the medical fraternity. This morning had been full of the real thing—so real that he, like all of his classmates, was permeated with a penetrating stink of formaldehyde.

The afternoon was a return to prosaic educational reality. Following a thirty minute lunch break and time for the recent faintees to recuperate, the class of 1956 trooped over to the medical building and settled into four one hour didactic and soporific lectures, the real stuff, at least the kind of material that constituted the majority of pre-clinical medical education—Histology, microbiology, physiology, and biochemistry. Garven knew he was not supposed to be bored, but by the end of the day, he had made up his mind to be a surgeon; so, he would not have to put in one more day of his life than necessary at material that would make the telephone book seem entertaining.

The science of histology was taught by Japheth Bloom, PhD—the study of tissues and organology. The class heard about the classes of tissues: contractile, bone, connective, blood, conducting, and cardiovascular. Dr. Bloom described the morphology of the typical cell, and the idealized membrane, then embarked on a fifty-five minute machine gun speed lecture on the epithelium.

"Epi (upon), thelos (layer)."

At least, for Garven his little bit of prep school Greek was finally worth something practical.

Dr. Bloom included, the "integument, the glands, and the gut."

He classified the types of epithelium, "Simple columnar, simple squamous, simple columnar in glands, stratified columnar, stratified squamous, and transitional squamous epithelium which permits stretching as is found in the urinary bladder."

The professor described the techniques of tissue preservation, microtomes, and staining. Before he dropped off completely, Garven heard something about "differential staining with dyes of selective affinity—cytoplasm likes acidic and nuclei like basic—about H and E—hematoxylin and eosin—frozen sections, and florescein, and Prussian Blue, and the stains for bacterial cells—Gram's, methylene blue, Albert's, and Leifson's."

Dr. Bloom finished with his classical lecture on the history of the microscope, "Al Hasan magnified insects in 1000 AD," and gave a succinct but detailed history of the pioneer.

He went on to enlighten the class about the giants of histology—Kepler, Snell, Huygens, Hooke, and von Leewenhoek—and touched on light, polarization, and electron microscopy. Garven considered history a kind of hobby pursuit, and found that part of Dr. Bloom's lecture barely stimulating enough to stay awake. He only came to full alertness when the professor described what would be on tests, "Everything about cells, membranes, organization of cells into tissues, and tissues into organs."

Garven heard all of that and had notes to protect himself.

The professor continued with his list: "Laws of refraction from Snell, reflection from Newton, light interference from Lister, phase principle of microscopy and the phase contrast microscope, principles of cell division," which must have been presented while Garven was resting his eyes—a period that turned out to be a nearly fifteen minute gap in his note taking.

Dr. Bloom told the class that they would have "the opportunity in the near future to regurgitate the extensive list of structures under each of the types of epithelium."

He politely told the class "good day" and made his exit.

Microbiology—the study of pathogenic living organisms—was the crucial and clinically relevant course taught by Emil Gunther Gebhardt, PhD.

"The scourges off mankindt dating from pre-history are only now beingk understood und many of the attacks on these organisms vill have to come from future work. The treatment of viruses is a failure to date, und bacterial species resistant to antibiotics are becomingk a present day vexing problem.

"Let me tell you of dis exciting field," the bushy browed German said with his thick Bavarian accent. "Poliomyelitis vas found in Egyptian mummies.

Some off the people vere found to haf shortened legs. Tb vas discovered in ancient bones. Verro in 460 BC hypothesized that lifingk agents known as 'svamp creatures' caused disease, und, off course, ve know that malaria—'bad air' from the Italian—vas exactly zuch a disease. But it vas not undil 1909 that the virst pathological lifingk organism vas seen."

Dr. Gebhardt described the work of Plenciz, Jenner, Pasteur, and Koch, including the four Koch postulates that amount to the laws of microbiology as pertinent to the discipline in 1952 as they were in the nineteenth century. The professor told the class about the search for cures—the age of immunology, the age of chemotherapy initiated by Erlich, the discovery of sulfonamides, and Fleming's earth changing discovery of penicillin in 1929 by accident.

"You vill spend the year learningk about the classes of pathogens, the morphological types like cocci, bacilli, spirilli, spirochetes, vibrios, the qualities off the bacterial cells, especially their cell valls, und the principles off treatment. Today, since I haf the floor, I am goingk to tell you about the most excitingk field in microbiology, namely, virology."

Garven was glad to get the subject of viruses over with the first day. What did he care about bugs that couldn't be treated? About all he wanted to know was how to tell the difference between viral diseases and those caused by bacteria. He wondered if these ivory tower types would ever get around to the practical stuff he needed to know.

"Viruses cause flu, cat scratch fever, hepatitis, und encephalitis, but that iss not my field of interest," Dr. Gebhardt said. "They may cause cancer, but there iss no real proof, und that is Dr. Keating's field. Maybe measles causes multiple sclerosis, maybe mental retardation iss an in-utero viral infection. I don't know. My field of interest is a fery narrow one. I study the 'slow viruses'. There are brain diseases in sheep called Vishnu and the Blue Disease, that are clearly viral in origin. There iss a particularly terrible disease called 'kuru' that occurs in zome islanders who practice ritual cannibalism. They eat the brains of dead relatives in order to perpetuate the spirits of these departed lofed ones. It is not yet proved, but there iss mounting efidence that this human disease iss caused by a so-called 'slow virus'. Today, howefer, I vould like to concentrate on a fascinating disease only seen in Africa, called "autoimmune deficiency" which we think is alzo caused by a slow virus.

"So far in this country, the disease has only been seen in green monkeys imported from Africa, but there are some human examples that haf been very strongly suspected on the African continent. They probably caught the disease from the monkeys. At any rate, the animal, the host, seems to do just fine for a long period of time, just like the victims of kuru or Vishnu, then they fall apart. The disease causes a breakdown of all immune mechanisms undil the host has absolutely no resistance. He gets opportunistic infections like Tb, recurrent mumps, throat infections from what are usually considered to be benign bacteria, recurrent upper respiratory conditions, Yaba tumor virus, und efen an obscure tumor known as Kaposi's sarcoma. You vill learn more about that next year in Pathology, but for now, it is enough to know that the tumor only flourishes in the immunologically compromised host. There iss no efidence that the virus is air borne; there are some that haf suggested sexual transmission, but the efidence iss scanty, und I doubt it. Ve are quarantining anyone suspected off hafing the disease, und are trying to keep out all green monkeys. It does not look ass if ve vill efer haf a problem mit this virus, but viruses change, und ve could haf a real problem in the future. You should keep an eye open for news about this one."

Garven promised himself he would remember the lecture on slow viruses long enough to answer the expected exam question, then would get on with real disease. He had to laugh at the idea of standing around on one leg while some super obscure monkey condition called 'autoimmune deficiency' became a real disease some century down the line. This was what kept men like Gebhardt in medical schools, and real doctors out in the real world cutting out disease.

After physiology and biochem, possibly reasonable subjects but ones rendered unbearable by grad student instructors who read their lectures directly out of the textbooks for an hour, Garven went back to the apartment he shared with the truckers, Ray and Lyle, and took a nap. There was something about academics that made him very sleepy. He then showered twice in a vain attempt to get the formalin smell off his body. He hung his clothes out the window to air out the pungent chemical odor. He ate beans and hamburger with his roommates, studied until eleven, then gave his mother and Dr. Wilsonhulme their once-a-quarter telephone calls. He could see a pattern developing.

CHAPTER
Eight

There was no class work or labs Thursday and Friday of the second week. Both days were filled with examinations. In Gross Anatomy, Garven had the chance to regurgitate the contents of his notes and to demonstrate that he had memorized two hundred fifty pages of *Gray's Anatomy*. He used almost every little fact and memory crutch he had learned. When he was asked to name the small bones of the wrist, palm up,—Navicular, Lunate, Triquetrium, Pisiform, Greater Multangular, Multangular (lesser), Cuneate, and Hamate—he thanked some long ago student who created the mnemonic ditty that saved generations of medical students after him. "Never Lower Tillie's Pants, Grandmother Might Come Home." Because the navicular was also known as the Scaphoid, it was necessary to remember: "Some Lovers Try Positions That They Can't Handle."

Garven hurriedly wrote out the names of the structures passing between the calcaneus—heel bone—and the medial malleolus—bony protrusion on the inside of the ankle—the Tibialus anterior and flexor Digitorum longus. The other contents of the space were: vein, artery, vein, tibial nerve, and flexor hallucis longus which were memorized by "Timothy Doth Vex a Very Nervous Horse." The general and simple favorite of the male medical students was "I Love Sex", the mnemonic for the position and separate muscles of the erector spinae back muscles—the Iliocostalis, Longissimus, Splenius— from lateral to medial.

In the lab, he got to arrange the bones in order, recognizing them by shape. He was also given the opportunity to name every structure perforated by a long pin that passed obliquely through a shoulder, one that had had its skin redraped over it to obscure any hints from the dissection.

The histology lecture course test required identification of every kind of epithelium plus a few trick slides of muscle tissue and liver. He identified seventy-five percent of the cell parts required of him—plasmalemma, mitochondria, ergastoplasm, lysosomes, fibrils, Golgi bodies, centrioles, nuclei, nucleoli, and inclusion bodies. He was pretty sure that the instructors made up the names for debris in the cell just to have something to hold over the students, but he kept that opinion within his lab group. He tried to differentiate mast cells, lymphocytes, eosinophilic granulocytes, plasma cells, and pigment cells in the blood smears, mixing up the eosinophils with leukocytes and the mast and pigment cells with debris and missed macrophages altogether.

The essay question required him to describe collagen—physical properties: it consists of triple covalent alpha-helically coiled chains with tensile strength of 100,000 lbs/in. function: dense and loose fibrous tissue in tendons and ligaments and fascia. chemical characteristics: differential solubility: some in water, others in neutral salt, some in citric acid, and some insoluble. The lab test required preparation of the perfect blood smear using his own blood, leaving his fingers pricked and sore, written descriptions of most of the existent cell and tissue stains, a schematic drawing of the adult tooth with all the tubules, lines of Owen, Tomes' granular layer, lines of Schreger and Retzius, and then to identify the items under the pointer on a divided molar.

In the microbiology test, Garven wrote furiously. It was a test more of prodigious memory than insight or understanding. Garven had formed the opinion early on that the medical school education did not require a great and facile mind, but only a phenomenal memory. He had to rely on hours and hours of work to fill his test paper with the classifications of molds and fungi, the attributes of all forms of sterilization, the chemical formulae of natural and semi-synthetic penicillins, and the methodology of antibody measurement. With few exceptions, according to Garven, the information required of him in his freshman year was eminently forgettable and useless. His real test came in fighting off distracting boredom.

Physiology for the first quarter was renal physiology. Nights before the exam Garven dreamed of sodiums and potassiums sliding through semi-permeable membranes, and told his test paper about transport processes, numerical properties of osmotic filtration actions, enzymatic processes and useless equations he had memorized for the sole purpose of getting through that day. He got fifty percent on his exam and ranked third highest in the class.

Chapter Eight

The reason for the dismal performance from the class was that the instructor managed to create mental havoc out of even the intrinsically understandable segments of the course. A few brave souls had complained to the department chairman, who ignored them. Garven's only salvation in the course was that he did well on the lab where he was required to dissect out a living frog sciatic nerve, immerse it in oil, to stimulate it and to record the oscilloscopic results.

Biochemistry lectures and labs were as bad in medical school as all forms of chemistry had been in high school and undergraduate college. The test was worse. For Garven, it was rote learning; and the test as valuable a feat as memorizing the Book of Matthew or the Hong Kong phone book. The first two weeks had been spent learning, or more accurately, hearing lectures about fats. The test was an exercise of telling about and/or guessing the formulaic structure of saturated versus unsaturated molecules, stereoisomerization, conjugation, esterification, saponification, hydrogenation, oxidation, and classification. The only two words in the test that Garven cared about were 'atherosclerosis' and 'diabetes' because of the clinical significance of those disorders of fat metabolism. Otherwise, he relegated all of the biochemical information to the reserve shelf of his mind along with renal physiology and Latin conjugation from his prep school. His greatest desire was to get away from the rat doctors and onto the real thing.

Garven did not have time for dating, extracurricular employment, participation in sports, visits to his mother or his benefactor, or parties with his old friends from Cipher.

But he did become involved in what the papers called 'the Cold War against international communism' and specifically in the growing grass roots movement to make the hero of the anti-communist conservatives, Senator Joe McCarthy, the president of the United States. He read the newspapers and became incensed about the fall of Chiang Kai-shek in China and the discovery of communists in every niche in the U.S. government. Truman was a red or at least soft on communism; the secretary of state was probably a card carrier; the North Korean communists invaded the south; and Garven C. Wilsonhulme became converted to the need to get Joe McCarthy into the Oval Office; so, he could get rid of the communist nest in the state department, build up the army, and get on with the war against the Marxists in the country and around the world.

Garven's rare nonmedical reading became Mickey Spillane's *I, the Jury* because Mike Hammer, the protagonist, chased communist operatives. In his very limited spare time, he attended meetings and canvassed door to door to collect money for the Joe McCarthy-for-President committee. Phoenix, Arizona was ready to give to the cause, and became all the more generous as the American 24th Division lost more and more battles and ground in their heroic stand against the yellow communist hordes invading the peace loving capitalist south of Korea. Garven was successful and well liked in the campaign and was beginning to be looked upon as a comer in the organization. His work started to nibble at his medical school time, and Garven began to feel pulled in the two directions. He knew he would have to make a decision—give in to the heady ambrosia of political involvement and perhaps even ambition, or doggedly stay the course in medical school struggling to keep up his high grade point average.

CHAPTER
Nine

Brent Battendorf made an announcement to his lab mates in Gross Anatomy at the start of the morning on the last day of the third week of medical school. Garven had his hands deep in Sydney's left armpit.

Maria was describing the contents of the posterior wall of the axilla, "Latissimus dorsi, subscapularis, and teres major," when Brent suddenly stood up from the lab table, looked at his lab coat, and sniffed his hands, not liking the mortuarian smell of the formalin.

"I quit," he said.

The announcement was made with all the intensity as if he had finished a meal.

"What?" asked Elijah David.

Apparently, he was the only one who heard Brent speak; or, at least, upon whom the two words had registered at all.

"I can not stand this any more. I stink. I am exhausted. My body is turning to mush. I don't have any friends. This will go on for eight or ten more years. It's not worth it," Brent said with quiet emphasis.

"Take it easy, Brent. You're just tired. You're doing okay so far; don't let it get to you," said E. D.

"You're not serious, are you Brent? You ought to get some rest and think about it," said Maria.

Garven looked at the bone weary young athlete and said nothing. He could see how someone could feel the way Brent was feeling right then. There did not seem to be an end to it. Still, he thought Brent would get over it.

Maria went on, "Why don't you go home for the rest of the day? We can take notes for you, and you won't get too far behind. You look like you could do with a rest and a drink."

'Nope, I've had it. You guys keep on. I admire you, I really do; but I guess I just wasn't cut out for this. The thought of doing nothing but medical school and medical career and never having any fun or having time to myself is too much. I want to have some kind of a life while I'm still young enough to enjoy it."

"Can we talk you out of it?" Garven asked him.

Brent was taking off his lab coat.

"See you around. Have an extra lab coat; I won't be needing it."

With that, he turned heel and walked out of the laboratory. Just before he got to the door, he made a little jump and clicked his heels together.

The three remaining lab partners were in a deep blue funk over Brent's precipitous departure. Garven felt like it was his duty to re-invigorate himself and his friends, and he fished about in his mind for a method. It was a matter of serendipity that he came to a solution. A visiting volunteer anatomist Emil Hendrickson, served as a lab instructor on Wednesdays. He was a nervous eccentric pathologist from Tempe who wore a hand tied bow tie from his alma mater and taught anatomy as a hobby. His great love was cancer, and he fancied himself to be a virtual encyclopedia on data about unusual tumors. The second great advantage Dr. Hendrickson presented, so far as Garven's plan was concerned, was that he was severely myopic and wore coke bottle lens glasses. His gross visual acuity was hardly even marginal, but his ability to see under the microscope remained intact.

In anticipation of Dr. Hendrickson's arrival, Garven came to class early and sneaked over to a cadaver in the far corner of the room. He removed one testicle, then made a small incision in the side of his own cadaver's knee and forced the testicle into the knee joint. That particular Wednesday was set aside as 'knee day', and Dr. Hendrickson was to lecture on the joint then move around the room helping the students with their dissections.

When he finally got to Garven, Maria, and E.D.'s table, they were waiting with ill-suppressed laughter which the near-sighted doctor misinterpreted as enthusiasm. Garven became the spokesman.

"Dr. Hendrickson, we are not really sure what the text means regarding the description of the dissection. Would you mind getting us started?"

"Not at all, young man. I have to move right along; so, on the first knee, I'll take the knife, if you don't mind."

Chapter Nine

"Not at all," Garven said.

He and his lab partners pressed in close to watch the master anatomist begin his work. They were almost strangling in their effort to hold back their laughter.

Dr. Hendrickson felt around the knee then made a swift, accurate, and large incision that carried the exposure into the cavity of the joint.

"Now, we need a bit of brute force, if you don't mind," the teacher said.

He got Garven and E.D. to force the joint in hyperextension to open it up to full view. For the dissection, Sydney, the cadaver, was prone, so the testicle did not fall out.

"Gadzooks!" exclaimed Dr. Hendrickson like some cartoon character.

He had never learned to swear. Garven had to turn away lest his face betray him.

"I think we have a synovial cancer here! Very rare! This is worth a write-up! Let's gather 'round the rest of the students!"

He could not help speaking in exclamations. It was a red-letter day for him.

Garven, Maria, and E.D. swept around the room to 'gather the students round' which gave the three of them a few moments to compose themselves before they had to return and face the gullible instructor. Dr. Hendrickson was so effulgent over his finding that he nearly became poetic. He was aglow with happiness when he left for the day with the testicle floating in a jar of formalin. He had no intention of telling his associates about his finding until he had a paper ready for submission to *The Journal of Pathology*.

The prank was, of course, easily uncovered; and a terse note was conveyed from Dr. Hendrickson to Dr. Yosobuchi before the end of the week. Try as he might, Dr. Yosobuchi could not make the class recognize the gravity of this breach of scientific and medical decorum. They laughed themselves into a state of general silliness as their professor strove to chastise them and to restore order. One problem for the professor was that Dr. Hendrickson could not remember exactly which cadaver had contained the knee-testicle inclusion body; so, Dr. Yosobuchi was frustrated in his attempts to lay proper blame. Garven's reputation was established by the incident.

The following Monday two more members of the class announced to their lab partners that they, too, were leaving. After the fourth week tests, more of the same Herculean feats of memory, one more left the school, one of the Negro men. The class numbered forty-eight with one month elapsed in the first year of medical school. By the end of the quarter there were forty-six; two members of the class did too poorly on the final exams to be able to continue.

One good thing came out of Brent's leaving. Garven got to do considerably more dissection on Sydney and felt a little more like a surgeon every day.

During the winter quarter he stayed late to make a showpiece dissection of the brachial plexus of the right arm and made up a schematic diagram of the roots, trunks, divisions, cords, and nerves of the great nerve complex of the upper extremity that he placed by his work. He was buoyed up by the number of his classmates who came by to see the drawing and to compare Garven's picture and the illustration in *Gray's Anatomy* to Sydney's arm.

He was barely getting 'C's in physiology and biochemistry. He drove himself to learn the neurophysiology as taught by Maximillian Perle, PhD. The subject could have been interesting what with the concepts of neuronal transmission with neurochemical forces causing electrical impulses to course down nerves, leap-frogging across the Nodes of Ranvier and exciting sharp action potentials. Instead, Dr. Perle deadened his topic by demanding attention day after day to the mathematical intricacies of axonal transmission.

Biochemistry was biochemistry—several logrithmical degrees of interest below reading the *Kama Sutra*, but more necessary for Garven; and he would have to continue to persist.

CHAPTER
Ten

J ack Lefebra called Garven into his office at the Cadillac dealership one Saturday, near the end of the winter quarter. Jack was the head of the local "Elect McCarthy - Stop Communism" committee.

"Garven," he said, "The Senator is making great strides in his fight to ferret out the entrenched cadres and pinkos in the mid-west, but his efforts in D.C. are bogging down due to resistance. This is a turning point, a time for the people of the U.S. of A. to put up or shut up about their commitments to American ideals. He needs people, paid people, incidentally, to go to Washington as researchers to help find the Claus Fuchs and Alger Hisses hiding in the bureaus. He needs help from people with pure American backgrounds, good white folks, and people who have stood up against the perverts and the commies. I'm proud to say that we nominated you, and the Senator sent me a letter confirming your job. Here it is, boy! This is your big opening in politics!"

Garven read the letter with its impressive 'Senate Office Building' letterhead. This was the chance of a lifetime. He could feel it in his bones. He envisioned himself on McCarthy's coattails as the great man moved swiftly into the presidency. A guy like him, ambitious and smart, could do great things for himself, and for the country, of course, by being a part of the official anti-commie team. He thought about Brent and the unassailable logic of his lab partner's final speech to his fellow medical students. Getting a job with McCarthy would make the snobbish Wilsonhulmes of Providence sit up and take a notice of him.

"I'll give it a lot of thought. I'm pretty tired right now, Mr. Lefebra. I need to get my head clear before I make such an important decision."

"Call me Jack, Garven. I expect great things from you. Anybody can be a doctor. I put in two years of med school myself when I got out of the army after the big war. I look for bigger things from you. Why don't you come over to the house for dinner tonight? We can talk about it."

Garven intended to wring his hands and to sweat out his decision through the day, and to give his answer to Jack Lefebra that night over barbecued steak; but he got too busy trying to memorize the qualities and activities of Ribonucleic Acid. He had looked at the lecture notes telling him that "the sugar group linkage is diesterified by phosphate at 3′ to 5′" and "mild alkaline hydrolysis yields 2′ and 3′ phosphates" for the hundredth time when he realized the passage of time. He also realized that he had just been putting off his decision. When he did put aside his copy of White's *Principles of Biochemistry* and began to consider seriously what direction his life was to take, he could see so many negating advantages, disadvantages, and unknowns for each of the options that his deliberations came to a blank end. The last thing he did was to read the newspaper before he set off for Jack Lefebra's party.

The *Arizona Republic* headlines blared, "THERE IS NO SUBSTITUTE FOR VICTORY", and the lead article extolled General MacArthur's triumphant march to the Yalu despite the objections of President Truman. Garven could see the path opening up for American conservatives as never before. He knew almost instinctively that this was his opportunity to be in on the ground floor, and that his chance would never come again. Medical school had been more a drudgery than the unparalleled excitement he had envisioned as an undergraduate, and he could only anticipate more of the same for as far as he could look ahead. He was a sorely tempted young man as he knocked on Jack's front door.

"Ah, Garven, come on in! Everybody, here's our soldier of the American Way. Give him a hand!" Jack Lefebra bellowed dragging the young man to the center of attention.

Garven's face was scarlet.

"Hi, everyone," he responded tentatively.

"Congratulations, young man!" exclaimed the Methodist preacher clapping him soundly on the back.

The rest of the American Conservative League, Phoenix branch, flocked over to Garven and pummeled him with good will. Garven basked in his brief moment of limited celebrity and enjoyed the evening immensely. The food was good and hot—chipotle chili and Jack cheese sopes, salsa made with a mixture of chilies—yellow banana, long red cayenne, Jalapeño, and green serranos. The company was convivial and like-minded with him; and he was pursued by Geraldine Lefebra, Jack's seventeen year old daughter and heiress to his Cadillac distributorship and considerable estate. Jack smiled down on the beginnings of puppy love and made it abundantly apparent that he approved.

When Garven left the party around ten o'clock, nothing had been said about his decision. Jack Lefebra, his guests, and his daughter all presumed that there was no decision, simply a chance to pursue a great opportunity and that the up-and-coming young man was one to watch. Garven did nothing to dissuade them of their presumptions.

"Come by on Monday. I have the particulars in my office, Garven. You can start in Washington next week. No more business tonight. Why don't you take Gerrie for a ride?" Lefebra called after him as he was leaving.

"See you Monday," said Garven. "Want to come, Gerrie? My car's a wreck, but if you promise to push when it breaks down, maybe we can make it."

Gerrie looked askance at Garven's 'wreck' then called out to her father, "Daddy, can we take the yellow '52?"

"Sure," have a good time. "Not too late, hear?"

He beamed as he tossed his daughter the keys to last year's big V-8 caddie.

Gerrie insisted that Garven drive.

"Aren't you just too, too excited?! You'll be one of the top men in Senator McCarthy's office. I just know it. I would just die to be able to go to Washington. Will you think about me while you're up there, Garven?" she twittered as she snuggled against him.

"Hey, Gerrie, this job is only to be a researcher or investigator of some sort, and there are probably an army of other ones like me," Garven answered her. "But, yeah, I'll think about you, a lot."

It was not hard to think about the nubile girl warming his arm with her curves. It was hard to think of anything else at the moment.

"Wanna take in a movie?" Geraldine asked.

"Sure, there's a Gene Autry at Liedman's, that okay?"

"Yes, but you have to get me a Coke at the new place, the MacDonald's, after."

Garven was embarrassed that he had not even heard of the new place. He was aware of how much he was missing by being stuck away in medical school.

The date was a great success. The two youths hit it off well. Gerrie all but asked him to take her out again Monday night. She wanted to hear what her daddy had to say to him. It was all so exciting to the girl. Garven had never before had anyone take such an overt interest in him, and he was flattered. He left her and the Cadillac at home, and drove his wreck back to his room. The evening with Gerrie had gone by so fast that Garven had not had a moment to think about his decision, and it was put off once again as he collapsed into bed.

He spent Sunday immersed in neuroanatomy pouring over the systemic plan of *Gray's Anatomy* and the regional arrangement of *Grant's Atlas*. He memorized the schema of the lumbosacral plexus, anterior and posterior divisions, and the contributions of the several nerve roots making up the separate nerves—a major feat of separation of details. At the top end of the body, he memorized the cranial foraminae and structures traversing them and started on the twelve cranial nerves. By the end of the day he could remember the old mnemonics: "On Old Olympus' Towering Top, A Finn And German Viewed A Hop" (Olfactory, Optic, Oculomotor, Trochlear, Trigeminal, Abducens, Facial, Auditory, Glossopharyngeal, Vagus, Accessory, Hypoglossal) for naming the cranial nerves in order from front to back. Garven and the other men preferred an updated mnemonic for the cranial nerves, however: "Oh! Oh! Oh! To Touch And Feel A Girl's Vagina - Ah Heaven!" The order of the nerves passing through the superior orbital fissure of the skull: Lacrimal, Frontal, Trochlear, Lateral, Nasociliary, Internal, Abducens, he memorized by learning the mnemonic: "Lazy French Tarts Lie Naked In Anticipation." When he was too tired to keep at it any longer, he set aside his books and notes for the following day's classes.

Then he remembered. He had an appointment with Jack Lefebra at the Cadillac dealership in the morning. He could not exactly be in class and at that meeting. It was time to choose. While he watched *I Love Lucy* and then Edward R. Murrow on the news, more about the yanks chasing the yellow hordes back across the Yalu River into China, he came to grips with who he was, who he still was. He finished arranging his books and papers into his brief case. He would be in his place in medical school as usual the following morning. Although he had not really put in much worry time over the decision, it was a relief to have made it. Garven had really known all along what his direction would be; he had known it all his life. He picked up the phone and asked Central to give him the Lefebras.

Jack had been understanding as well as disappointed which surprised Garven. He had told the young man that he had always half regretted dropping out of medical school because he thought doctors were the most important people in America. He had succumbed to the lure of quick money.

Garven was more surprised at Geraldine's response when he asked her father if he could speak to her. She had been outright frosty; no date on Monday; and, no, don't call for another date. She was not about to get entangled with anyone who was going to be a student for the next ten or twelve years like doctors had to do. No thanks.

Having lost his bid for timeless great romance, Garven Wilsonhulme showed up early to work on Sydney on Monday morning. He had the right section of the pelvis dissected so that all of the lumbosacral plexus was displayed. His two lab partners were impressed.

"You seem more like your old self, Garven," Maria told him.

"I've been involved in some stuff that was taking too much of my time. That's over, and it's a weight off my mind, that's all," Garven said, indicating no great desire to pursue the subject further.

At the end of the sixth week, there was something of a stir in Gross Anatomy. Johannes Müller, a German-American farmer's son from Minnesota, rode the city bus home to his apartment every day. From time to time students took laboratory specimens home to complete dissections or to cram for lab tests, and Johannes, who was an obsessive-compulsive in his Germanic study habits, made it a habit. The lab instructors had dissected one head and neck, separate from the cadaver's body, for the students to study and kept it in one of the formalin vats. Johannes took it home—against policy—to use it to cram for the anatomy final.

Johannes was very tired. The following day he returned to class without the head, and no one, including him, even realized that it was not in the lab. Everyone in the class knew it the morning after that, however. An excitable Mexican woman, who worked as a domestic for one of the senior medical school professors, happened to sit next to an abandoned package on the same bus Johannes had used two days before. Being by nature a good citizen and helpful, Mrs. Garcia, had opened the package to see if it was something that should be placed in the trash or if it were something that should be brought to the attention of the bus line officials. She decided it was the latter.

When Mrs. Garcia discovered the dissected cadaver head in the sack beside her, she created an upset on the crowded bus by letting out a sustained keening wail, a sort of stygian noise that created a general panic. She fainted and had to be hospitalized. Thinking that the package belonged to her, the sack with the head was placed on the gurney with her when she was delivered by ambulance to the Salt River University Hospital causing her and the attendants in the ER to experience another episode of noisy panic. The uproar died down only after it was established that Mrs. Garcia was all right, just scared white headed, and that no ghoulish crime had been committed. The head was returned to its vat, and the class received a vituperative scolding.

There were those on the faculty who were in favor of expelling Johannes for his crime, and they very nearly prevailed. He was saved by Dr. Staphanakis, the head and neck surgeon and anatomist. Dr. Staphanakis reminded the faculty of his own close brush with disaster, and bade his fellows to show the student the same compassion and understanding for his mistake as had been shown to himself two years previously. That argument carried the day.

Dr. Staphanakis was famous for his incident. He was a somewhat eccentric person, not far different from a number of odd university types. First of all, he was a blond, blue-eyed Greek, a rarity itself. Secondly, he had a PhD in ichthyology as well as his M.D. He had wanted to study fish for the rest of his life, but his father would have none of it; so, he had had to become a medical doctor. He pursued the study of fish as a serious hobby. He was the world's foremost expert on the lateral line sensory organ.

In his capacity as a head and neck surgeon and anatomist, he was regularly asked to give lectures at outlying hospitals and at other universities. It was his habit to place a dozen heads in various states of dissection into a heavy gauge plastic sack and to load them into the passenger seat of his Volkswagen bug and to drive to his lecture.

On one of his travels to a lecture appointment, he was pulled over for speeding.

The Arizona Highway Patrolman who pulled him over started to recite the tired, "Where's the fire, buddy?" routine when he saw the curious bag on the passenger seat.

"What's in the bag?" he queried the somewhat absentminded professor.

"Oh," said Dr. Staphanakis now paying attention. "Heads."

The patrolman was nauseated. He fought back an urge to turn away and to stick his finger down his throat, but he remained pale and professional. He had the bewildered Dr. Staphanakis get out of car and to assume the position. He cuffed the unworldly professor and took him into Phoenix where he was jailed. The patrolman gingerly carried the evidence at arm's length. It took nearly a day to straighten out the mess, convince the local gendarmerie that they were not dealing with a mass murderer with a weird head fetish, to reschedule the lecture since Dr. Staphanakis was hopelessly late, and to convene an extraordinary meeting of the medical school faculty.

There would have been peace, quiet, and easy forgiveness had the second episode of the class of 1956 not occurred that very same week. Once a year, prospective medical students from the university were given an in-depth exposure to the medical school with a tour of the facilities and the chance to be in the labs and with the medical students. A crowd of eager pre-med students flocked into the Gross Anatomy lab and milled about oohing, aahing, and ugging at the partially dissected corpses. Dr. Yosobuchi gave a short talk, and the lab coated students were given the chance to talk to real live med students about their experience and about whether or not they should go into medicine. It was all very nice.

But one particularly effusive co-ed, a Phoenix debutante from one of The Families, checked in the pockets of her lab coat before returning it to the lab instructors. Thereupon she fainted. The instructors rushed to her side with their ammonia capsules. When they moved her into the supine position, a formalinized penis dropped from one of her clenched hands. Once she came around, she was altogether forgiving, thinking it was one of the great kinds of pranks that medical students were known for, and that she would have to stop being such a prudish sissy if she were ever going to be a med student.

The professor and lab instructors were considerably less understanding and forgiving, however. Once the pre-medders were ushered out, snickering or expressing indignation, depending on the intensity of their moral or religious convictions, the faculty members ordered the Gross Anatomy students to line up for a grilling and a severe censure. The questioning produced no culprit, and the chastisement did not seem to have caused a superabundance of sorrow for sin because, even during the most angry remonstrances by Dr. Yosobuchi, occasional snickers could be heard in the ranks.

Partly because he had been seen to saw through his cadaver's pelvis with a borrowed chainsaw on the day when it was time to display a hemipelvis and was regarded with suspicion by his lab instructors, Garven was questioned very closely as one having a penchant for practical jokes; but he kept an expression on his face like the inscrutable sphinx, and denied every suggestion of wrong doing. Garven's alleged involvement in the penile prank was overshadowed by the official review of Dr. Stephanakis' bag-of-heads incident. Two incidents that could besmirch the medical school's reputation became two too many, and the professor had to accept a letter of reprimand. From the point of view of most of the rest of the faculty and every student, the official rebuke only enhanced the affectionate attitude held by his defenders for the surgeon's eccentricity and quirkiness.

When Winter Quarter finals were done and the results recorded for all to see in the Basic Sciences building lobby, Garven found that he had done well—'A's in everything but Biochem, and even in that nightmare class, he had achieved a 'B' instead of the gentlemanly 'C' he was expecting. Two members of the class were informed that they would have to repeat the year in order to have proper credit in Biochemistry. One more student quit, a nurse who had gotten pregnant, and her long-suffering husband and declared that "enough was enough."

CHAPTER
Eleven

S pring Quarter was notable for a near mutiny among the medical students, and was the nearest thing to genuine public excitement that ever happened at the University of Arizona Faculty of Medicine. Senior students finished their academic courses three weeks before graduation and two weeks before the rest of the classes came to a close. The class of 1952 had a total of twenty-eight survivors who were preparing for graduation as of one month before the ceremonies. The ceremonies were always impressive with the candidates for Doctor of Medicine marching at the head of the line just behind the faculty. Each year it was the tradition of the school for the audience and the other students and candidates to cheer the newly minted doctors as they finished receiving their diplomas, the only true parchment documents given by the university. The celebration was, by now, an integral part of graduation, so much so that the local press and state and local government and religious leaders joined in the noisy welcome to the fledgling physicians.

Three weeks before graduation in June, 1952, on the last day of classes for the seniors, two of them received notice that they would not be allowed to graduate. The "faculty had determined that their work was unsatisfactory" overall. When the rejections became public among the rest of the medical students, and even some sympathetic faculty, they were aghast and became progressively angry and vocal. There was a mood of tremendous threat hanging over the other students, but for the seniors there was a funereal pall.

The president of the senior class called an extraordinary meeting of the class. He presented the results of the investigation the class officers had made into the unprecedented action by the faculty. The officers had learned that it had not been a faculty decision; and in fact, several of the faculty members had dissented strongly. The rejection and the denial of graduation had come from one man, the preeminent chairman of the department of medicine, Maxwell Cartral, M.D., Ph.D. who had almost single-handedly made the school what it was. It was his opinion, devoid of specifics, that the two who were selected out were simply not of the quality his medical school should produce. He would make no apology for the lateness of his decision, and made it clear that it was him or them. The class voted to mutiny.

The mutiny came in the form of a declaration sent to Dr. Bledsoe, the dean: The class of 1952 would not participate in graduation ceremonies unless their two classmates were reinstated. When Dr. Cartral was shown the ultimatum, he issued one of his own: none of the class would receive their M.D. degrees. The situation remained at a noisy impasse, an ugly Mexican standoff, until two days before the actual baccalaureate and commencement. The officials of the university were frantic; the medical school faculty members were implacable; and the potential graduating class members were uniformly distraught, bordering on frantic over the public relations nightmare.

Finally, the president of the university called a meeting with Dean Bledsoe. Dr. Cartral refused to attend stating imperiously that medical school was not a democracy and that he knew far better what constituted a properly prepared physician than did some student class president or the president of the university, for that matter. Following the closed door meeting between the university president and Dean Bledsoe, the senior class presidency was told where the bear slept.

Bledsoe convened a special faculty meeting to which the senior students were given an invitation they could not refuse, and the dean told an assembled majority of the faculty that there would be a graduation, and that diplomas for doctor of medicine would be handed out amidst the traditional hoopla. He told them all that there would be a compromise.

"Gentlemen, we will not leave this office until there is no longer a problem with medical school graduation for 1952."

The men debated for two hours with the university president prevailing in matters of civility. Finally, there was a compromise. The class would graduate but without the two that had been summarily dismissed by Dr. Cartral, acting well within his rights as dictator, rights spelled out in his contract. From the faculty's side, it was agreed that the two students would be allowed to repeat the senior year and would not have to be on Dr. Cartral's service. Dean Bledsoe was assigned to inform the eminent professor of medicine.

Garven needed money. He really needed money. Dr. Wilsonhulme could no longer contribute enough to cover the expenses of graduate school, and his mother could not give Garven anything. Garven talked to his adopted father at length and was finally convinced not to take his truck company job again. Instead, he should find a medically related position. He needed to be committed to medicine thereafter. Garven agreed with the logic, obtained a loan at a usurious interest rate, and found a job as a lab assistant in the biochemistry department for half what he could have made from the Union Pacific Motor Freight Company, despite the growing money fears.

The job was a nightmare from the beginning. It consisted of washing laboratory glassware under the supervision of an imperious senior laboratory technician. The process had to be scrupulous. Every beaker and pipette had to be absolutely free of all contaminates, not just clean. Each glass container was soaked in a series of solvents to remove as much of the adherent chemicals as possible—blood solvents and soaps, alcohol, acetone, and water. Garven had to rinse each piece multiple times in each solvent. No matter how much he washed and rinsed, they still seemed to end up with a streak of soap or salt, or the glass was etched and rough. He could not please the senior lab technician, Henrietta Slicebaum, no matter what he did. She had a friend, a German woman who worked in the next door lab who joined in the general denigration of Garven's work which contributed to his sense of frustration and anger.

Henrietta took perverse pleasure in pointing out the flaws in Garven's work to the biochemistry professor, Dr. Sievers, who ran the lab, taking pains to point out that Garven was 'just a medical student' as if that were prima facie evidence of ineptitude. Garven's recent experience in the biochemistry course had set his teeth on edge before he ever got to the summer job in the department, and this treatment was rapidly becoming intolerable. The blowup occurred at the end of the second week of the summer. Garven caught Henrietta intentionally dirtying an Erlenmeyer flask.

"Planning a little experiment of your own, Miss Senior Laboratory Technician?" Garven snarled at the obese spinster.

She stood there holding an open tube of silicon gel in one hand and an Erlenmeyer flask, in which reposed a smear of gel, in the other.

"This is none of your business, Mr. Wilsonhulme," came the defensive response.

"We'll see. We'll see. Dr. Sievers might be real interested in seeing this flask, Henry."

He deliberately mispronounced her name, suggesting a possible dyke status. Before she could react, Garven had snatched it from her hand. Her face registered a continuum of responses from surprise to indignation to perplexity to chagrin.

"Perhaps we can talk about this between us, just between co-workers. Please, Mr. Wilsonhulme. *Please.*"

She had not wanted to include the plaintive tone, the 'please' especially the two 'pleases'; but she knew she was in a bad position; maybe this even threatened her job.

"Perhaps," said Garven coldly.

His face was set in angry lines.

"I know you have had some difficulty getting started here. I think now you will find it better. I would be happy to be of help to you. Together, we can see to it that the glassware meets Dr. Siever's standards, and that you get proper credit."

"And you don't get humiliated or even canned for this adolescent stunt, not the first one either, I think he will suspect."

She shook her head in resignation. What did this over privileged medical student know about the reality where a woman had to struggle in a man's world to get to where she could make a decent living, maybe even start to get ahead? She had no choice but to eat humble pie one more time.

"I'll need a raise. That shouldn't be a problem with your help, should it, Henrietta?"

"No more problems, okay, Mr. Wilsonhulme?"

"It's Garven. And you've got a deal. Don't cross me, Henrietta. I am not a nice guy," he said with narrowed coyote's eyes that convinced her he was telling the truth.

Garven finished the summer as a supervisor of the lab maintenance crew in Dr. Eugene Jelesnad's Cortical Steroid structure lab—a promotion with an increase in pay—for which Henrietta provided the key recommendation, one that took him to a different building to work. He was even given a credit mention in Dr. Jelesnad's article in *Analytical Chemistry, Silica Gel Microcolumn for Chromatographic Resolution of Cortical Steroids and Separation from Closely Related Entities.*

CHAPTER
Twelve

The second year of medical school—the pathology pre-clinical year—started on Monday morning, September 24, 1953 in the Salt River Valley Hospital morgue. The old county hospital was built in 1910 and haphazardly accumulated new and uncoordinated wings and additions at intervals. The morgue was in the basement of the oldest part of the hospital that was now under the direction of the medical school. The autopsy room was a dungeon with cement walls that sweat in the summer and fall heat, polished linoleum floors permanently stained with blood and other brown markings, and a clutter of steel tables, utilitarian steel frame glassed-in cabinets, lead lined sinks, and laminated wood specimen cutting boards. Here and there was a human organ, each in a different state of dissection and preparation, and everywhere was the characteristic mucous membrane and eye dehydrating odor of formaldehyde.

One fourth of the class of 1956 was present in the stuffy, smelly, undersized room. The diener rolled in a sheet covered corpse on a steel frame gurney through the parting crowd of nervous medical students, and unceremoniously slid it onto the autopsy table with its four inch deep floor, hoses, and drains. He slid the cover sheet off the body without looking at it, and stepped to the back of the room. Dr. Anderson, the professor, pathologist, and county medical examiner, walked briskly into the room from a side entrance and made his way up to the body.

The dead person was a red-haired female, no more than thirty, and looked as if she might have been reasonably attractive in life. The most conspicuous thing about her was a single hole the size of a penny in the left side of her chest between the fourth and fifth ribs near the sternum. Dr. Anderson picked through several instruments on the tray beside the autopsy table and selected a scalpel with an outsized detachable blade. Without introduction, not even a "Good morning, students," he made two large diagonal cuts across the woman's chest from the lateral ends of the clavicles to meet at the midline just below the xyphisternum, taking less than two seconds total. The incisions opened skin, fat, fascia, and muscle and bared the ribs. In another second, the pathologist extended the tail of the 'Y' from the sternum to the pubis passing expertly through all layers of the abdominal wall but leaving the internal viscera intact.

Three students had to be helped from the room temporarily by the grinning diener. This was his favorite day of the whole year.

Dr. Anderson then picked up a pair of large shears and chomped through the rib cage opening a triangular shaped window into the chest cavity. The chest was full of blood, and the heart looked to be two or three times normal size. Two more students backed away from the table's edge.

"Cause of death is obvious," commented the pathologist as he evacuated blood from the sac surrounding the heart with a huge needle attached to a syringe.

"Specimen," he said, and handed the full syringe to the diener.

Dr. Anderson began to talk as he snipped little pieces of organs and ran his fingers along stripping the bowel. He described the findings, demonstrated the pathology and the otherwise normal anatomy of the young woman, and asked questions of the students. Garven identified the pancreas and was pleased with himself. The pathologist gave a short dissertation on the great value of pathologists to the world of medicine and the contribution of autopsies to the advancement of medical science. Garven did not quite buy into what Dr. Anderson was selling, but he conceded that there might be something to the specialty. It just was not for him.

The rest of the first day of the second year was spent in lectures—infectious diseases and liver tumors in the morning, bowel pathology and arteriosclerosis in the afternoon—and laboratory diagnosis. The lab course was run by the hematology division of the Department of Medicine. Maxwell Cartral was chairman of both. That afternoon was Garven's first encounter with the august majesty.

The grad student lab instructors cringed and seemed to shrink a little when the Old Testament prophet faced professor strode into the lab at the head of a retinue of white coated followers.

"That's the medicine rounds group for today. I can hardly wait to go with him. He's the most important member of the faculty. A recommendation from Cartral is a guarantee of getting the internship you want," Elijah David whispered to Garven.

Garven wanted to say that a bad word from him was the death knell of your medical career, and that he was going to take the prudent course of keeping himself out of the man's main focus if it was at all possible. He did not get to reply, however, because the chief resident, fourth in the line of internists walking in order of rank, threw E.D. a look that turned him to a pillar of salt.

"Good afternoon, students, I am Maxwell Cartral," the best known member of the faculty announced unnecessarily. "This is your introduction to patho-logical diagnosis in the lab, and the first time you will see and participate in medicine. Your performance here will be scrutinized very carefully."

Garven could just bet.

"You will make a perfect blood smear today by pricking each other's fin-gers. You will not go home tonight until you are passed on by one of the lab instructors. There will be a short lecture by our senior hematology resident, Dr. Holbrooke, at four thirty. He will cover the normal blood cells, their morphology and function. Pathological hematology will be the subject of the lectures for the rest of the quarter. I suggest that you pay very close attention."

There was something at once threatening and chilling about the man's pro-nouncements. His main message, the unspoken one, had been received by the students: "Look on my works, ye mighty, and despair."

The retinue followed the Great Leader in a serpentine file out of the lab and back towards the medicine wards, and the sophomore class got down to the day's business of making their fingers miserable by pricking them and squeezing out drops of blood and placing them with infinite care on slides. They placed H&E stain on the smeared blood drops and covered the smears with slide covers. Then they lined up to have the lab instructors tell them why the slides were not perfect. Every student had at least one small wound in every finger before he or she left the lab that night. Garven was convinced that it was all a sadistic game because around six o'clock, the lab instructors began passing the students' smears in wholesale lots. Garven played it foxy and brought up one of his early slides at quarter to the hour, and it was certi-fied as 'perfect', the same slide that had not been up to snuff an hour ago. He had just gotten another one of those holes that needed to be punched in the medical training card for admission to the hallowed halls of the fully initi-ated—the M.D.s—he decided.

That quarter Garven learned how to do a complete blood count and that required that he learn to do a venipuncture. That art was learned, as usual, by practicing on each other. Garven drew his first blood sample from Elijah David. It only took him three punctures to get into the vein, a near record for the class. The problem occurred when Garven was ready to take out the blood. He had forgotten to push the plunger of the syringe all of the way in before he had the needle in the vein. The problem now was how to get the air out of the syringe. He did not want to stick E.D. again; so, he quickly pushed 20 cc's of air into E.D.'s blood stream without thinking. E.D. was a hypochondriac on the best of days. When he saw the air enter his vein, he almost toppled off the chair. He looked at Garven with a pleading look, and Garven looked back with undisguised horror and fear. He was sure he had killed his friend and lab partner. E.D. looked as if he would faint. As it turned out, nothing happened.

Other useful skills were learned in the laboratory diagnosis class like how to smear pus and to stain it and to differentiate on slides between TB red snappers, strep, staph, and meningococci, and how to do a urinalysis in under three minutes complete with a differential cell count unless it was something exotic.

By Christmas, from his path course, he could tell a breast cancer from normal or pregnant breast tissue most times, a primary malignant brain tumor, glioblastoma, from a cancer of the lung metastatic to the brain, whether or not a melanoma on a surgical specimen had a sufficient tumor free margin and if there was malignancy in lymph node sections. He personally did twelve autopsies, all on Mexican victims of knife wounds, and all for the coroner's office. He became good enough that they gave him a job as an assistant during the Christmas autopsy over-load season.

That job saved him for a few more weeks. He had applied for and been turned down for financial assistance; he was not in a status that would allow him to be a staff or lab assistant, and he could not bring himself to be enslaved by more student loan debt with the bank that he thought of as loan sharks in suits. He was behind in his rent, and he was living on two meals a day with meat only once a month. He had begun to get desperate.

For his new work he was given a title that placed him just above the morgue diener and well below the pathologists; he was paid less than either and even less than the janitor; they could always get another medical student. His job description said that he was a general helper and cleaner-upper, but what he actually did was exactly what the medical examiners did on the obvious traumatic death cases. He performed the autopsy from stem to stern, describing in detail and for the forensic record the cause of death and any other obvious findings that the pathologist might have to mention if, by some remote chance, his testimony in court were ever needed. Sometimes if he had a question Garven would seek out one of the coroners; but mostly they were too busy; and he had to look it up in a book. If they were too busy, and if he were too tired, which was often, he just dry-labbed it. Garven did everything except sign the final report which nowhere indicated his contribution.

The job made him nearly solvent again for a while. He got straight 'A's that quarter because now he was interested. It was not quite clinical medicine, but a lot closer than the basic science drivel he and his classmates had had to put up the first year. Only one student failed to show up for Winter Quarter, 1954. The class size increased by three at the start of the quarter and two more at the start of Spring, students who dropped down from the class above. Garven was too busy to get to know the new students; and he noticed that the competitiveness required of them, or perhaps just the natural inclination of medical students and doctors to act independently and in competition with their colleagues made the class less close and cohesive. He could not say that he had a single friend in the medical school—only acquaintances and enemies, given the arena in which they had all been thrown.

Spring quarter gastroenterology lab was the worst experience of medical school. It was infamous for the suffering it caused. The students divided up into pairs and obtained and examined fecal samples (their own) for the presence of ova, parasites, and pathogens. The instructors made it an important part of the class' education to be able to recognize the streaking of BRB— bright red blood—on stools from actual patients with hemorrhoids, the black stools of old blood, the yellow floating fatty stools, and the hard droppings of dehydration. The standing joke among the students was that outstanding feature of gastroenterologists was their obsessive scrutiny of their own bowel evacuations every morning. The enthusiastic students evaluated stomach contents to understand principles of forensics and to diagnose g-i tract disease. That was just unpleasant. What constituted real suffering was the first true clinical procedure the students performed—the placement of an NG (nasogastric)—tube.

Each of the students had to push the red rubber tube down the nose and throat of his partner and into the stomach several times for different purposes of education. Garven could scarcely stop retching as the tube dangled uncomfortably down his gullet and was vomited on when he passed the tube into Elijah

David. The worst assignment of all was the experiment designed to teach the students how to recognize the differential amounts of blood in the stomach via NG tube measurements and in the large bowel via stool measurements.

Each partner of a set was given a dose of steam heat sterilized then chilled blood to drink, the exact amounts were unknowns in the experiment. Garven's luck of the draw was a quart of whole blood. The blood appeared gray and frothy and tasted like rusty burnt toast mixed with old bouillon and was the consistency of chunky nasal mucous. Other sets of student partners had placebos—iron salts mixed with milk to produce the correct gray purulent look, feel, and taste. The students measured and calculated, and all produced wrong answers. They were privileged to try again until they got it right.

Hematology lab taught Garven the rudiments of iron deficiency anemia, sickle cell (sick as hell) anemia, falciparum malaria, polycythemia rubra vera, and the different kinds of leukemia. In that class, Garven learned his first lesson in psychiatry. During the fourth week of the quarter, the off week for tests, the class was pouring over example slides of lymphocyte disease on a hot sleepy spring day. There was quiet conversation and a few jokes and a sense of general well being, one of those temporary respites from the chronic attack mode method of education employed by the medical school.

"Attention!" shouted one of the lab instructors.

Every head alerted to the sound of his voice and turned in his direction. The door of the lab opened and a troupe of four similarly lab coated staff people marched resolutely into the room.

"Put down your work. Remove all books and papers from your desk. We are going to have a surprise quiz. You will separate yourselves now."

The students assumed a uniform look of shock and obeyed like robots. Each of them could see his GPA going into the trash basket because none of them were prepared for any kind of test on the blood. The newcomer lab assistants rapidly moved through the class passing out blue books and test pencils.

"I will read the instructions first, then the questions. You will have three minutes to answer each of ten essay questions. Ready."

There was an ugly hush in the room. The only noise was ragged breathing. Despair was the mood of the day.

"The first instruction...," he paused momentarily. "Take off your lab coats and roll up your sleeves."

There was general consternation.

The new lab assistants then moved very swiftly through the shocked looking students drawing a sample of blood from each. A label with the student's last name was affixed to the tube.

"Now, relax," called out the lab instructor, jovially, his face aglow with merriment, an emotion unshared by the students. "There is no test, as you might have surmised. Instead, you are going to learn something about lymphocytes. Pick up the vial with your name on it, make a smear, and examine it for the number and condition of the lymphocytes."

The students moved quickly to comply and soon were pouring over the slides made from samples of their own blood.

"Tell me what you see," the instructor said as he bent over Garven.

"I'm not sure," Garven said. "I don't see any lymphocytes that I can be sure about. There are a lot of cells the same purplish color, but these look twice the regular size, like they're swollen. Are they immature lymphocytes?"

Very immature lymphocytes could be a sign of lymphocytic leukemia, and Garven was confident that he had not suddenly contracted that uniformly fatal disease.

"Good description. Yes, they're the lymphocytes. They're best described as 'stress lymphocytes'. They are produced during periods of sudden severe stress—a sort of fight or flight mechanism of uncertain teleological significance. You have a passel of them, Wilsonhulme. Better lighten up. Your stomach lining will never last the rest of med school if you don't."

And that was the first introduction to psychiatry.

At the end of the sophomore year, two students were found to have a more or less chronic swollen lymphocyte problem and left medical school for a more reasonable life. Three members of the class of 1956 flunked and were asked not to return and two were told that they would have to repeat the year. Only one of them did. Garven maintained a chronically high stress lymphocyte count, but he was officially going to be one of the students starting the 1954-55 first clinical year.

CHAPTER
Thirteen

Garven now supported himself, barely making enough to pay rent at the humble dwelling he shared with his old friends from Cipher and to make up his past due rent, by working at two jobs. He seemed to be eating cardboard and drinking ditch water most of the time and was losing weight he could ill afford to lose. He was chronically hungry and grouchy. The first of his jobs was as an autopsy technician for the county as he had done during the Christmas vacation, and the second was to prove to be a pivotal experience in his life. He got the job through the help of one of his classmates, Lynn Stion, a Mormon from Provo, Utah, who had been rejected at the University of Utah med school before being accepted in Arizona. He had family in Phoenix and seemed to have a handle on every new happening at the medical school for some inexplicable reason.

"Want a great job for the summer?" Lynn had asked Garven towards the end of the sophomore academic year.

"I'll say. The thought of washing dishes by day and being a ghoul by night is repulsive, especially the washing dishes," Garven replied with enthusiasm.

"I heard from the surgery secretary that Dr. Larry Shephard has two openings in his lab. I don't know exactly what he's working on; and I don't even care. He does surgery on big dogs and cats and cows, I hear. I just want to get my hands into surgery, even if it's not on humans. I sort of thought you felt the same way."

"You bet," Garven told him.

"I knew you did; so, I made us both an appointment for Friday to see Dr. Shephard in his office about the jobs. Ten o'clock."

"I'll be there with bells on," said Garven.

And he was—ten minutes early, arriving after Lynn. Lynn went in to see the general surgery staff man first. When he came out, his face was noncommittal.

"So'd you get the job or what?" Garven asked him.

"Yeah, I did," Lynn answered. "Your turn," he said and moved away from the door to the professor's office, obviously not anxious to prolong their conversation.

"Hello, Dr. Shephard, I'm Garven Wilsonhulme," Garven said as soon as he was shown to a seat in Larry Shephard's office.

"I understand you have come about the lab assistant job," Dr. Shephard launched right in without preliminary, not even a hand shake.

"Yes, Sir," Garven said.

"I'm sorry, Garven. Okay if I call you Garven?"

"Yes, Sir," Garven told him masking his disappointment at the 'sorry' he had heard.

"There was only enough grant money for one position, and I gave it to your friend. First come, first served."

Garven's face fell. He had been counting on the job. He would probably have done it for free.

"Do you know of anything else going on, Dr. Shephard? Anyone else need a labby?" he asked as he started to rise to leave.

"As a matter of fact, I do. Let's see, what was that I read?"

The professor thumbed through several scattered piles of papers on his messy desk.

"Ah, here it is."

He produced a list of new faculty appointments and their lab assignments. He ran a finger down the list.

"There's a new surgeon coming the first of June. In fact, he's going to open up a new division of the Department of Surgery. Name's Oliver Wendall Harralsen, of all things. You might go over and sign up with his secretary. He's not even around yet; so, I don't think anyone else is even aware yet that he is going to exist here. I'll write down his name and office number for you."

"Thanks a lot," Garven said. "I really appreciate your help."

"Have a good summer, Garven," Dr. Shephard said and turned back to the drudgery enshrined in the piles of paper on his desk.

He often wondered what would happen if he simply, as a matter of routine, took all of the contents of his in-basket and transferred them to the out-basket each day without even looking at them.

Garven found the office and met Dr. Harralsen's secretary, Maggie Penrod. She was young and inexperienced, low on the pecking order, just like her new boss was going to be. Garven was hired for the summer. He was glad of the job, and she was glad to have one more administrative detail out of the way; so, she would look good to her boss when he arrived the next week.

Garven started to walk out; but, as and afterthought, inquired, "What kind of doctor is Dr. Harralsen?"

"Neurosurgeon, first one we've ever had," Maggie answered.

She was not altogether sure what a 'neurosurgeon' was.

"Okay, thanks, again," Garven said in parting.

He arrived at Dr. Harralsen's lab at eight o'clock in the morning on July first, two days after the school year ended. He was the only one there; so, he took a seat. He waited until nearly ten when the doctor and a woman in a lab coat sauntered in. He looked young and eastern, tall, blond, and Scandinavian, in a hand tied bow tie and tweed suit, much too heavy for the region and the season. She looked stern and in charge.

"Hi," Dr. Harralsen said as soon as he saw Garven. "You must be the lab assistant."

He extended his hand in a surprisingly friendly show of warmth.

"Yes, Sir," Garven said and smiled.

He was glad to be there. His only concern was the woman. Was he going to be the fetch and carry boy for another ball breaker spinster senior lab tech?

"Where are my manners?" the doctor asked rhetorically. "You two haven't met, have you? This is Rose Cochran. She is the honcho of the lab. You and I will have to do what she tells us. We'll do the surgeries, and she'll do run the lab."

Garven interpreted her job as taking care of the scut work, and he began to like the woman even before he shook her hand.

"Hi, I'm Garven."

"Rose," she said and smiled warmly.

She was middle-aged, but he decided not to hold that against her since she seemed genuinely pleasant.

"Okay, Rose, we'll leave you to take care of the lab, and Garven and I will take a while to go over the experiments."

Garven followed the neurosurgeon into the lab's tiny office. Dr. Harralsen swept the clutter off the small table and the two men pulled up chairs.

"Let me show you what I'm working on. It's an anatomical problem for the time being: then later, I may work on the chemistry and physiology of the structure I'm interested in."

Dr. Harralsen opened his brief case and brought out some preliminary sketches and laid them on the table before Garven.

"This is the subject. It's called the 'suprapineal arachnoid body', for lack of a better name. I abbreviate it to 'SPAB'. Pardon the crude drawings; art was never my forte. I expect you to do better. Anyway, this little gadget is found in the very midpoint of the brain, right down in tiger country. It is situated dorsal and posterior to the pineal body and just above the superior cerebellar vermis."

Garven strained his memory of neuroanatomy to its limits.

"A great anatomist named LeGros Clark first described it; but nobody paid any attention because nobody has the faintest notion what its function is. I, personally think, Descartes was wrong about the pineal being the seat of the soul. I think this thing is the soul. But, that's just my own opinion. A little work has been done in humans, only on adults and largely old people, and very little has been done in lower animals. That's where you come in. I'd like you to spend the summer dissecting out the structure in a number of species, get us some human cadaver specimens for photography; so, the art department can get some decent drawings; then, if you have time, you can get some infant brains and look at them. I suspect that this gadget is more prominent and important in neonates, and maybe we can get the basics done this summer. Then I hope we can devise some experiments to find out something about the function come next year. What do you think?"

"Sounds great to me," said Garven.

"One thing that you might find interesting about our friend, the 'SPAB', is that it has ganglion cells in it—maybe it's some kind of gland—and also, curiously enough, it contains erectile tissue."

Garven smiled, "Sounds sexy. Where do we start?"

"Well, first we have to have a lab. What we have right now is a mess. If you wouldn't consider it demeaning, we could clean up today and tomorrow while Rose gets us some equipment and animal cages, and you can start on your first animals the day after," said Dr. Harralsen.

"I like scut work," said Garven, dryly. "But it is a means to the end of getting at the fun stuff; so, I am ready to start right now."

He went out into the lab and found a push broom and began to get the floor in order. No one called about him doing an autopsy that night; so, he, Dr. Harralsen, and Rose worked until bedtime. They got the lab scrubbed and in order in only the one day. Rose was surprised and pleased at the help. Young Dr. Wilsonhulme shot up a couple of notches in her estimation.

The following day Dr. Harralsen tended to the necessary administrative details of moving into the surgery department while Garven and Rose shopped. They went to the main university storehouse and bought rat and guinea pig cages and enclosures for larger experimental animals that would be kept later. They bought dissecting instruments, a set of drills and saws to take off skulls, an operating light, and a variety of sizes of animal tracheostomy tubes.

"Having fun, Garven?" Rose asked him as they loaded up her station wagon with all the new equipment.

"Yeah," he answered. "It's great having an expense account. It's like the university is one big sugar daddy."

"You can get to like spending OPM," Rose said.

"I give up, what's OPM?" Garven asked.

"Other People's Money—it's the great government and university pastime. It gets to be addicting."

"I can see how," said Garven. "Want to get some lunch—on me?"

He was feeling good.

"Sure, never pass up a good meal. I equate 'good' with 'free'," she said.

They laughed.

In a week Garven learned that it was impossible to dissect a fresh brain and find out anything useful because the brain was too soft and fell apart. He learned how to cut the brains out without damaging them; then he learned how to preserve them. By the end of the second week, he started the dissections only to learn that he was inept; at least he lacked the necessary skills. Dr. Harralsen watched him struggle for a day or two then stepped in and showed Garven some techniques that permitted exposure of the SPAB without mangling it. Garven was impressed with the skill and delicacy with which the neurosurgeon worked around the fragile structures. He was patient and efficient of movement. Garven began to develop a progressive low grade case of hero worship.

Except for lunch and the occasional necessity to run off to the morgue to do a post trauma autopsy, Garven worked from dawn to bedtime five days a week on the project. He was fascinated, and his skills improved very rapidly. So did his diet, since he could eat free in the employee's mess. Soon he had a series of specimens out, diagrammed and photographed. Dr. Harralsen was effusive with his praise, and Garven was the happiest he could remember being. Dr. Harralsen was a real gentleman who was masterful at dealing with people. He was nothing like the products of the SOB school of neurosurgery Garven had heard so much about whenever brain surgery came up in conversation around the medical school.

"I think it's time to look at this little gadget in a living animal; what do you think, Garven?" asked Dr. Harralsen near the end of July.

"Absolutely," Garven said.

It would be a chance to watch Dr. Harralsen operate, and that had to be good.

"I am going to bring in five or six goats tomorrow. Why don't you do the first one since I'm going to be in the OR all day? I'll help you with the next ones on Thursday. Okay with you?"

He had a faint wry smile. Garven took it as a challenge.

Garven arranged with Rose to assist him. It was a comfortable arrangement since neither of them had ever seen a neurosurgical operation; so, neither could put the other down. Before sun-up Thursday, the two of them brought the goat in from the little enclosure located in back of the lab building where it was being kept. It was a scraggly brute, as uncooperative as a mule. They had to drag and push it all the way into their lab. Swearing seemed to work best.

Garven knew they had to put it to sleep, and also knew from general acquaintanceship that the bottle of pentobarbital was probably for the anesthesia. He had no idea how much to give; he had forgotten to ask. They shaved a place on the balky animal's leg and found a vein. Garven managed to insert a needle for an intravenous line after half a dozen tries. The skin was a great deal tougher than he would have imagined. He drew up some pentobarbital in a syringe—half full seemed like an example of the Grecian golden mean—and slowly infused it into the unruly goat. In a matter of seconds, the animal slumped to the floor. Miraculously, it was not dead. Garven considered that a very good beginning.

He and Rose lifted the goat onto the lab operating table and laid it in what appeared to be a comfortable position. They cleaned and shaved the scalp then put clean towels all around and under the head. Garven took the scalpel and made a midline vertical cut between the horns. Rose knew enough to press on the skin edges to control the bleeding. Garven scraped the skin aside, and Rose found a self-retaining retractor to hold the skin edges open.

"That was pretty smart," Garven told her.

She did a little self-conscious theatrical bow.

"How do we get the skull open?" Garven asked Rose.

"Haven't the foggiest, doctor. That's your department. You're the big surgeon." She smiled.

It was perplexing. It was something else Garven had not given adequate thought to. He took off his gloves and rummaged around in the equipment drawers until he found a hand drill and two chisels. There was no hammer. He picked up a piece of pipe as a substitute.

Garven drilled and drilled and drilled. The skull was as hard as granite and unbelievably thick. Every now and again, he would stop and gauge his angle, wondering if he had somehow missed the brain altogether. Rose wondered out loud if the animal had a brain. Garven's arms were weary.

Suddenly, the drill plunged through the opening and penetrated three inches into the open cavity.

"That can't be good," Garven said, thoroughly chagrined.

His miracles held. The animal did not die.

"Maybe we will have to be real careful from here on out," Rose suggested tactfully.

"Thanks for sharing your phenomenal grasp of the obvious, Miss Rose," Garven said.

His forehead was sweating and his hands were trembling a little, but he managed a wan smile.

"Okay master brain surgeon, how do you propose to take off that skull?" Rose asked.

"I'd like to make another couple of holes," Garven said. "But I'm not sure I'm up to it. I also doubt that I could finish in my lifetime."

Rose laughed.

"I guess I'll give the chisels a try," he ventured.

Garven tapped on the skull with the chisel using the length of pipe as substitute hammer. That did not even chip the surface. He banged harder. Nothing. Then he whacked with all his might. He was able to chink a small chip of bone away from the dense skull. Rose had to sit down for a minute; she was laughing too hard to keep on.

"Hey," Garven said, a little miffed. "I'm open to suggestions, if you have something to offer."

Rose held up her hands in defeat.

Garven knew he did not have the luxury of surrender. He had to do something. He took off his gloves again. This time he found a large pair of slip handle pliers. He spent an hour gnawing at the bone edges, finally beginning to make a little progress when he ran out of miracles.

Brain started to well up into the drill hole opening. Soon it seeped over the surface of the skull, a yellow-gray ooze. This really looked bad. Garven began to chip off the bone as fast as he could. He looked like a beaver on amphetamines. Rose could only work intermittently because she was laughing so hard. Blood began to well up around the oozing brain. Garven scraped it off and the viscous fluids kept on coming. He could not believe that the animal could have that much brain in its cranium.

The goat died.

"Well, I'm glad that's over," Rose said.

Garven looked very unhappy. Where she saw humor in the sheer hopelessness of the attempted operation, he saw a personal defeat. It was not that he felt great sympathy for his patient; he saw the whole fiasco as a personal failure; and Garven Wilsonhulme was not very accepting of failure—his or others.

"Not for me," he said. "At least I'm going to have a look." He finished the removal of the cranium. It was infinitely easier now. He slit open the animal's dura mater and found brain that had been turned to the consistency of heavy whipping cream. He could not make out a single piece of brain topography or recognizable structure. It was the aftermath of Armageddon in microcosm. He certainly could not make out the suprapineal arachnoid body of Clark in the devastation. Garven was a much chastened budding scientist when he finally finished the first craniotomy of his career.

CHAPTER
Fourteen

Garven sheepishly told Dr. Harralsen every gory pathetic detail of his experience, taking care not to spare himself in the least, the next day after the professor announced that he was ready to do the second goat.

"Perhaps I can show you a thing or two to make it go a bit more smoothly," the unflappable brain surgeon said.

"Perhaps you can," Garven said knowing that was real mastery of understatement. "I will just bet that you can."

He was overjoyed that his boss was not angry with the mess he had made of things.

He and Rose brought in the goat. Dr. Harralsen put in an IV and attached a normal saline drip to it. He made the process all seem so simple. Then the doctor checked the goat's weight and calculated a dose of sodium pentathol that corresponded to a dosage chart. Garven had already learned three principles of surgery, and they had not had the goat in the room for five minutes.

When the animal was asleep, Dr. Harralsen had the two assistants hold the goat supine with its neck straight while he deftly performed a tracheostomy. He inserted a tube with a balloon around its tip and inflated the balloon to keep it in place. Garven was fascinated. It was all so smooth and efficient.

"Why the tracheostomy?" he asked the senior man.

"So we can control the respirations, give him some O twos, and most importantly, so we can bag him to keep his CO_2 down. That keeps the brain swelling down to a minimum."

"Boy, could I have used that tidbit yesterday," Garven said shaking his head in wonderment.

Then Dr. Harralsen gave the goat an injection of urea solution through the IV.

"Dehydrates the brain to keep down the swelling during the procedure. Can't have brain pooching up into our faces while we're trying to operate, now can we?"

"Nosireebob," Garven thought, as he contemplated lessons four and five in brain surgery 201. *"Shoot, with that stuff, anybody could do brain surgery,"* he joked to himself.

"Mind shaving the scalp, Garven? I'm having a niki-fit," Dr. Harralsen said.

He was very casual and completely calm. He stepped to the side of the room and smoked a Camel while Garven removed the hair. Garven would have given anything, right then, to have that kind of coolness.

"So, when I make this incision in the scalp, how are we going to control the bleeding, Garven?"

"Have Rose mash on the skin, that's the way we handled it," Garven responded.

Dr. Harralsen and Rose laughed, glad to see that the earnest young man still retained some of his sense of humor.

"And how did that work?"

"Not great," Garven admitted. "And I'll bet you have a better way that you are just dying to show me," he laughed.

"You are a smart kid. So I'll show you. Put your fingers along the incision line."

He had drawn a line on the scalp with an indelible pen.

"Press hard; dig your fingers in; right, like that."

The surgeon drew the knife through the tough skin without the slightest hint that it was an effort. His fingers were controlling the bleeding on his side of the incision. Garven felt like the little boy with his finger in the hole in the dike. Blood sneaked out from all sorts of places on his side.

"Curl your fingers. That's better."

The bleeding stopped altogether, even on Garven's side. Lesson number six. Garven had a sneaking suspicion that there might still be more to this than he knew. For one thing he could see no way out of the dilemma of having to let go of the pressure on the skin edges eventually.

"So, now what," he asked. "It'll just start to bleed again as soon as I let go, right?"

Dr. Harralsen reached around with his free hand and picked up a fine surgical clamp with bent tips. He clamped the layer of connective tissue adjacent to the skull bone and laid the clamp down. He swiftly repeated the process multiple times until the entire incision was everted with the lower layer lying above the skin surface. There was not a drop of bleeding. Lesson number seven. That was slick and clean.

"This guy is great," thought Garven.

"In the OR we usually use little metal clips on the skin edge to accomplish the same thing. They're called Michele clips. They take up much less room, but this is still a pretty good method even if it is a little old fashioned. Furthermore, it's cheaper."

Dr. Harralsen joined the clamps with rubber bands and covered them with another towel to keep them out of the way. Then Rose handed him a self-retraining retractor. He spread the jaws of the instrument in the scalp opening, and it gave a three inch diameter of bone dry exposure.

"Compared to my performance, this was presto chango and shibam," said Garven enviously.

"Give yourself ten more years, young man. Be a bit patient. For one thing you are going to have to learn not to be so hard on yourself. I didn't exactly fall out of the tree knowing how to do a craniotomy. It took a week or two," Dr. Harralsen said looking directly at Garven and grinning.

By the time the miraculously efficient and clean operation was over, and the SPAB had been seen in the living animal, Garven felt like he could hardly wait to be able to do what his hero had just done. Garven Wilsonhulme said quietly to himself that he would become a brain surgeon if it took him the rest of his life.

In August Garven was efficient enough in the lab to have completed the literature search and to have written the review section of the paper. He could do a craniotomy on most animals in less than two hours and was able to describe the appearances of the SPAB in vivo in the various species and removed the specimen en bloc with a section of brain for preservation and comparative study.

Dr. Harralsen complimented Garven on his work, then asked, "Looks like you don't have enough to do—you've worked yourself out of a job. Want to get some human specimens?"

Garven looked incredulous.

"Rose?" he joked.

Dr. Harralsen laughed.

"I wasn't suggesting that you start doing major brain surgery in the hospital until you at least graduate from med school. And I wasn't thinking of kidnapping or grave robbing. What did occur to me was that no one has seen this structure in a newborn or a stillborn. In addition to our work on comparative anatomy of the SPAB, we can make a contribution by getting hold of some babies and harvesting their brains."

"Do you have a source of mothers and fathers that are willing to make a small sacrifice for the interests of science or something?" Garven asked.

"Not quite. I am going to dispatch you to all of the hospitals in the state as well as here in Maricopa County. You will need to get on the horn and arrange with the pathologists in each hospital to put you on call for when they get a baby's brain. You probably should go and meet them and their staffs and dieners; so, they will be favorably disposed to think of you. I would hope you could get close to a dozen brains before you have to go back to the salt mines this fall."

"Okay, but I have a sneaking suspicion that I am going to get a reputation as the village vampire or ghoul."

"Just tell them you are Dr. Frankenstein when you call; should work magic. The name still holds a great deal of meaningfulness out here in the wasteland, I am told," Dr. Harralsen said with his best dead pan expression and Transylvanian accent.

"Thanks for all the helpful suggestions," Garven said.

He could not keep a straight face.

The pathology departments did give Garven a hard time about his intentions—on a jocular level. They did require a letter from his sponsoring research physician on a serious level, but they were entirely facilitating. He received his first call to come to the autopsy of a neonate two days after his first call. He took the requisite letter with him.

The mood in the morgue was grim. It was difficult enough to deal with the family of a deceased adult; it was a matter of personal gravity to everyone concerned to deal with their own feelings about an infant, let alone coping with the baby's family. Garven was immediately aware of the complete absence of any banter as he entered the autopsy room. He carried a plastic bucket half full of formaldehyde in which to store the brain.

"Hello, Sir, I'm Garven Wilsonhulme," he told the pathologist of Phoenix Presbyterian Hospital as soon as he entered the room. "I'm the medical student, here about the infant's brain. I really appreciate your help."

"Glad to be able to push back the frontiers of science, Garven," the doctor said and gave him an indulgent smile. "You ever been to an autopsy?"

"Yes, Sir."

"Ever done one?"

"I work for Dr. Conrad at the Salt River Valley Hospital University Medical Center. I've had a bit of experience."

"Are you any good?"

"I think so."

"Ever do a baby?"

"One."

"Great. You can do this one in keeping with the oldest medical school dictum of them all—see one, do one, teach one'."

"Okay, where's the scalpel?" Garven asked without a hint of hesitation.

"That's the spirit. Give him the knife, Ralph."

The diener handed over the scalpel, and Garven went to work.

When he opened the chest, he found a very peculiar looking arrangement of the heart and great vessels, like nothing he had ever seen before.

"Know what you're looking at, Garven?" asked Dr. Strickland, the pathologist.

"Not really. Something congenital. Was this the cause of death?"

"Yeah. Looks like Taussig-Bing's, maybe. I think we're looking at transposition of the great vessels—they all seem to be wrong. I think that's the pulmonary artery although it looks bigger than the aorta. As I recall, this is a rare congenital disorder with an atrial septal defect... or was it ventricular? I'll have to look it up. Kid may have died of pulmonary hypertension. We won't know until we get it out and go over it and the great vessels. Take 'em all, Garven. We will likely have to send the specimen over to the Ivory Tower, or maybe even the AFIP or NIH."

Garven felt like one of the insiders because he knew the initials indicated the Armed Forces Institute of Pathology and National Institutes of Health.

This was the first congenital anomaly Garven had seen, and he found it fascinating. But he had come for the brain. He moved quickly through the rest of the autopsy with Dr. Strickland guiding his hand.

"Good job. You just a second year?" the pathologist asked when Garven finished.

"Starting my third."

"Remember pathology—best career field in medicine. Don't judge too hastily about the big money—big prestige specialties. Come on over and see me when you get done. Maybe I can convince you to be a real student of medicine."

"Maybe."

"Need help in getting the brain out?"

"I think the diener and I can do it," Garven told him.

As it turned out, Garven was in for a fiasco—another learning experience. He had no trouble getting the scalp open or in getting the cranial cavity open.

The main difference with the baby's skull and the adults with which he was familiar was the extreme thinness of the baby's cranium. It was as flexible as heavy paper. Instead of using the Strykker saw as he did on the mature skull, Garven was able to snip the skull open with scissors. As soon as he opened the tough covering of the brain, the dura, he began to run into trouble.

The brain was so soft—the consistency of corn-meal mush—that it could not be handled. It began to fracture as he tried to keep it in place as he snipped of the tethering cranial nerves, vessels, and brainstem. It was in a dozen pieces by the time he got it into the bucket of formalin.

"Nice work," chided the diener.

Garven was already frustrated and embarrassed. It was all he needed now— to have his medical efforts criticized by a guy with a third grade education who had to take off his shoes to get to higher math.

He was pretty sure the guy knew how it really should be done; so, he swallowed his pride and asked, "Okay, doc, what should I do on the next one?"

The diener was not used to having anyone think his opinion was worth anything, and he looked at Garven suspiciously.

"Really," Garven said, "I need all the help I can get."

"A humble doctor. First one I ever saw," said the diener. "My name's Ezekial."

He extended his hand.

"Garven," the frustrated young man said. "And I'm just a medical student, a peon like you."

Ezekial smiled broadly, and the two shook hands.

"Now I'm agoin' tah show you how it's done," the muscular black man said.

Ezekial then demonstrated how to hold the tiny porridge consistency brain with cheese cloth as it was gently teased out of the cranium and to lay it in a cotton mesh sack; so, it never suffered pressure or distortion.

Garven thanked the man.

"You're a good brain surgeon, Ezekial," he said.

"One of the best," the old man said with a toothless grin. "'Ceptin' I don' get the big bucks like them fellas."

"You're underpaid," Garven said as he took his bucket and left. Among his successes that day, he counted the fact that he had made a friend.

The enduring lesson of the day for his future career was never to discount the contribution of the people on the lower rungs of the ladder; they could make his life easier.

The second best surgeon that Garven had occasion to observe at work that summer was Daniel Melton Giocci, employee of the Steele Brothers Slaughter and Meat Packing Company. Garven was privileged to watch the master at work on several occasions. These occasions presented themselves as a result of a favor Garven did for one of the endocrinologist researchers at the behest of Dr. Harralsen. The researcher needed immediately fresh bovine adrenal glands to obtain active enzymes for endocrinological reactions. He was short staffed, and Garven, who was considered to be in need of activity by his boss, was dispatched to obtain the adrenals.

Daniel Giocci was the foreman at Steele Brothers and met Garven on the dock that ran along side the slaughter shoot.

"How many does the great scientist need today?" Daniel asked as soon as the introduced themselves.

"Four; two pairs," Garven said.

"You ever harvest adrenals, son?" the powerfully built middle-aged Italian asked.

"Nope."

"Well, we ain't got much time, as you'll see down below. So this time, I'll do it, and you watch. Next time you do it, okay?"

"That's fine with me. Lead on."

"You got to catch on quick and move right along in my business, Garven. We got a sayin': 'See one, do one, teach one' so you pay real close attention because I ain't got no time to be teachin' you every time you come out here from the university. Don't think too much about college boys; they don't seem to catch on real quick. I hope you show me to be wrong."

"Do, my best," Garven responded.

Daniel led Garven into a change room where they put on rain suits and rubber knee boots. He looked scornfully at Garven's box of small knives and dissecting forceps.

"Won't need none of that piddly stuff, boy. Just put it back in your pocket."

They descended a utilitarian steel stair case and onto the slaughterhouse main floor. It was a maelstrom of activity. Heavily muscled men dressed in rubber bib overhauls and boots labored and swore at a frenetic pace on the blood soaked and riverine floor. The process started with an unsuspecting steer sliding head first down a narrow tunnel—the chute—and into the room. As soon as its head poked through, the first man in the line swung a long-handled twelve pound hammer and struck the brute square in the middle of its forehead. The beast toppled to the floor having never experienced the least fear or pain. The first man never missed, eight hours and hundreds of steers a day. The second man put large hooks in the tissue in front of the large tendons in the animal's lower thighs and a hoist swung the inert brute into the air. Two more men opened the thoracic and abdominal cavities and swept out the internal viscera with a few deft strokes of their razor sharp knives. The heart, liver, and kidneys were saved from the mess of offal by a third man—this one a teenager—and another pair skinned the animal and cut it in half vertically with a large narrow chain saw. About a minute and a half elapsed between animals.

Water ran from strategically placed hoses moving the viscera into a large sump causeway and out of the room. Hoses continuously washed down the accumulation of blood. The assembly line ordinarily swept the hemi-carcassas onto washing, wrapping, and storage areas away from the main slaughter room. On this occasion, however, Daniel Giocci commandeered four half steers and had his men move them to a side track.

Garven was spattered with bovine blood and nervous about dodging the knives, huge saws, hard working men, and the steer carcasses. He slipped and slid on the blood slick floor trying to keep up with Daniel. Garven could scarcely make out any structures inside the gutted animal.

Daniel shouted over the din in the work room, "I had them leave the kidneys on these. See, here."

He pointed out the kidneys flush with the back wall of the half beef.

In a matter of a few seconds, the slaughterhouse foreman removed the kidneys without so much as nicking a muscle. He cut, rather than tearing, each blood vessel and never touched the top of the kidneys.

"These here are the adrenals. They also call 'em the suprarenal glands; you can see why."

Garven took note of the position of the glands sitting on top of the kidneys. He had not been able to pick them out from the other fatty and gristly tissue before Daniel showed him. The foreman completed the removal of the glands in about two minutes work. Garven put the glands into warm saline and sealed the containers.

"That was slick, Daniel," he said to the foreman who was about to leave and get back to his job.

"Nothin' to it once you know how. You'll do the next ones, now that you know how," he said to Garven with a hint of a smile lurking behind his stern toughness.

Garven collected forty pairs of suprarenal gland that summer. He got his time down to ten minutes per gland, but could never match the surgical skill and assurance of Daniel Giocci. It had been a pleasure to watch a master at work.

Garven cajoled Maria Stricklin into helping him with the baby brain collections. She was interested in the project at first, being enthusiastic about the scientific endeavor; and besides, she liked Garven and did not mind helping him.

It was a shock to her the first time they collected the small soft specimen; and she complained to Garven that, "I'm going to be a pediatrician. This is tough on me, seeing all these dead children. You are going to owe me big."

After the eighth brain, she refused to go on. It was causing her nightmares. Garven had gotten on to the technique by that time and was beginning to enjoy the technical challenge of it. He figured it was just the difference between the real doctors (surgeons) and the rest. Dr. Harralsen told him he had enough specimens; so, he did not press Maria into service any longer. He had just enough time to preserve the brains and to get them dissected out to show the very prominent character of the SPAB in infants before it was time to start the fall quarter of his junior year in medical school, the first clinical year.

CHAPTER
Fifteen

The first foretaste of being a real doctor took place on the first day of the 1954-55 medical school year in the first class of the day. Physical diagnosis—examination of patients; it was the first time Garven and his classmates could say that they had done something that was fun in medical school. One of the chief of internal medicine, Dr. Cartral's, retinue taught the class. He gave a week of lectures on what to get out of examining the general appearance—the presence of jaundice, wasting, splinting, limping, enlarged chest, bowed legs, and twitches. The resident told the students how to examine the eyes, ears, nose, and throat for squint, cross eyes, diminished vision, deafness, ear drum infections, inflamed and scabby nostrils, plugged nasal passages, bad teeth, furrowed and furry tongue, and halitosis. Garven and his classmates learned how to evaluate the chest—strange shapes, pathological noises like stridor and rales, and pathological diaphragm motion. Another resident presented the heart—irregular rhythms, and murmurs which Garven could not hear and pretended that he did, like the rest of his classmates.

At the end of the week they were able to use a sphygmomanometer, stethoscope, reflex hammer, oto and opthalmoscopes, and their gloved fingers. It was then time to do their first physical examination on a patient. The students in the class before them had told Garven and his friends to be ready for a surprise but steadfastly refused to let them in on the secret.

"Don't want to spoil it for you," the upperclassmen had said.

Saturday was the day for the first patient. Class was held in the general clinic at the Salt River Valley Hospital, a sprawling warehouse sectioned off into dozens of curtained cubicles. At the beginning of the class, each student received several packages. Garven opened his in front of the cubicle to which he had been assigned and found a black leather doctor's bag embossed with his name and the logo of the drug company that donated it. Different companies had donated hammers, scopes, the best stethoscope available at the time, and all of the paraphernalia of physical diagnosis.

"Attention, ladies and gentlemen!" sang out the instructor's voice, and the room grew quiet. "You have been waiting for your first patient. He or she is standing next to you, on your right."

Garven looked to his right and saw no one except his classmate, Tina Vasquez, an attractive and feisty girl from Colombia, the youngest member of the class, and probably the smartest.

There were murmurs.

"We have a great deal to do today; so, please keep with me. You will take turns examining each other. The student on the right will examine the one on the left, then vice versa. This is to be a complete, with the emphasis on the word 'complete', examination. One of the instructors will be by frequently to check you out and to give you pointers; and, I might add, to prevent any hanky-panky."

Nervous laughter rippled around the room.

"Get all your clothes off, put on the open-in-the-back gown, and sit in your exam room. Let your partner know when you are ready."

Tina looked pale. She had not expected anything remotely like this. Garven had practiced keeping a sober expression for when he examined a female; so, he would appear professional, but he was unprepared for being examined by a woman. This was going to be a thoroughly leveling experience.

"There are not enough females in the class; so, the women will have to be examined more than once. We will limit the second exams to the pertinent parts where differences can be expected," continued the instructor.

The women in the class groaned.

By the time Garven had experienced the methodical medical student examination by Tina including a rectal exam and checking his scrotum for masses or tender epididymis, it was more than a leveling experience. Garven and Tina had learned the great medical art of objectivity or at least the facial expression of caring and detachment at the same time. Tina was inexperienced—he was virtually free of false modesty. Tina had been careful of his feelings of self-consciousness as she had examined him. She was thorough, as only a nervous medical student can be, but she took care to keep him covered and looked at one part at a time.

"Thanks," Garven said after he had redressed. "That was only half as bad as I thought it would be."

"You mean for me," Tina said with a shy smile. "Now be nice to me."

Tina was a devout Roman Catholic, the cherished daughter of a wealthy South American planter. She had been protected and sheltered her entire life and had not so much as kissed a boy. As Ogden Nash said, "her breast no randy hand had pressed." She was truly frightened. Her father would have had a stroke.

Garven did the same examination on her as she had done on him except that he rigidly followed the guidelines for the breast examination and had to have help doing the pelvic. He was surprised to realize that he had not felt the slightest sexual urge during the examination of Tina's breasts which were full and attractive. He was nervous and fumbled as he tried to put the small speculum into her vagina and finally had to give up.

"Sorry," he kept saying as she jumped when he made another attempt.

Finally, he covered her and waited until the instructor came in.

"What's the trouble?" the internist asked.

"I'm not doing too well on the pelvic. I can't do the speculum right," Garven admitted sheepishly.

"Let me see," said the instructor and opened the cover without the slightest hesitation.

He examined the girl for a minute or two then said, "I've found your problem. I can't get a speculum in either. She's a virgin."

He said it as if it were a disease. Tina blushed scarlet.

"I should get the rest of the students in here," he said. "They aren't likely to see this on an adult woman in this hospital again in medical school."

He turned to leave.

Tina clapped her thighs together and looked genuinely afraid.

Garven said, "Hey, doc, she's shy. She's a good girl. That wouldn't be right to show her off like a freak. How about just forgetting it?"

"This is the day for you all to lose your inhibitions, the day to learn how to cope with your feelings about medical examinations. She's a grown-up, and she's going to be a doctor. Even women have to get over being so finicky. I, personally, don't think they ought to be here. They just take up a medical school seat then go out and get married and have babies and never practice. If she can't take this, she won't be able to take medicine as a career," the young doctor said.

"Still not right," declared Garven. "Nobody ought to be forced to be examined. She can get tough by doing the exams on patients; she doesn't have to be humiliated to be a doctor."

"Now, there's a novel idea. Every new generation of doctors gets crapped on by the generations in head of them. It's a hallowed tradition," the instructor said cynically.

"Well, it's a bad one," Garven said. "Let her alone. She's doing her best. She doesn't need this grief."

"Oh, all right, Sir Galahad, get her over to one of the other women so she can practice doing a pelvic. Most of the women in the class are married, and it's no big deal for them."

Tina was pale. She had dressed during the time the two men were discussing her body and its use.

"Thanks, Garven. I was really embarrassed. In Colombia we are virgins when we get married. Some men never even see their wives naked. It'll take me a while to get used to this, I guess," she said.

Garven gently smiled at her.

The experience was a good one for the majority of the class. The members developed a bond of friendship that came from the mutual cooperation and respect they had been obliged to display to one another. At the end of the day, Garven's class was one small but discernible step closer to being clinically detached and had developed a portion of the polish and dignity they were going to need to pursue their lives in medicine.

One man, a born-again Christian, quit the class after the first physical examination experience. He had found the probing and touching of another person than his wife so repulsive to him that he decided that he could not endure a lifetime of doing examinations. His departure came as a great surprise to the members of the class, but the main instructor commented that it was expected. Some people were not cut out for medicine, and this was a good time to find out before the investment in time, effort, and money was so heavy that they could not afford to quit. They would just go on to be unhappy doctors, or worse, bad ones.

Garven's first examination on a real patient came two days later. The third year class was divided into Medicine, Surgery, and Pediatric sections. Garven was fortunate to be in the third of the students who started on the internal medicine service and had the opportunity to take advantage of the large number of patients that entered the clinics and the hospital through that major department.

His first patient was an elderly woman who had entered the hospital complaining of nausea and vomiting. Her symptoms had ceased after a day on the ward with an IV. To Garven's untutored mind, she might have only been suffering with a touch of the stomach flu initially. He saw her at the end of her second week. The old lady was happy to see him, glad to have someone with whom she could talk. Garven took a three hour medical student's medical history from her, the bulk of the time being spent on the 'review of systems', following the outline for the history from Danberger's *Physical Diagnosis* textbook.

The pleasant old woman had a positive review of systems; she was old enough and garrulous enough to answer yes to every symptom on the extensive list. Garven guessed that she had over three hundred symptoms without including her allergies. She was allergic to every known drug, to all members of the plant kingdom, and to the hair, skin, and scales of every member of the animal kingdom with which she had had contact.

Garven performed an extensive physical examination, duly recording every wart and mole, her vital signs in the standing, sitting, and recumbent position on both arms, and the estimated size of her liver and spleen. Then, as required, he asked if it would be all right if he got some blood, urine, and some stool for the lab.

"Why, yes, dear," she acquiesced without hesitation. "Everyone else does."

Garven laughed and patted her arm.

He drew her blood. He was quite facile at venipunctures now after his lab diagnosis course. He collected all of the specimens required, and then headed for the lab to run the tests. When he was done, he had a page of lab results to add to the sixteen pages of history and physical examination. Next, he did a chart review, graphing the temperature, pulse, blood pressure, and two score lab values. She had a truly impressive set of lab data available.

He typed up his report, including his impression and conclusions. He had half an inch of paper to confirm his thesis as to what was wrong with the nice old lady. She was anemic. All of the evidence pointed to blood loss—iron deficiency anemia. She had denied any evidence of bleeding. She had not menstruated in thirty years; and since she was one of those who assiduously checked her bowel movements every morning like the gastroenterology specialists, she could say with certainty that there was no blood issuing from there. Garven was very careful to document every opinion. He included a two page long differential diagnosis taken directly out of Dr. Cartral's *Textbook of the Diseases of Blood* in anticipation of having to make the dreaded presentation to the autocratic chief of internal medicine.

For the purposes of educating medical students, ob-gyn was divided into arbitrary segments. Nonsurgical gynecology was assigned as a medical function. Garven's second patient was in the gyn screening clinic (known more commonly as "dirty bottom" clinic). His patient was a ponderous jolly black woman in for her yearly pap smear who did not at all mind having the new medical students practice on her year after year. She was a nice, clean, patient woman, unlike many of her sisters in the clinic.

Garven had great difficulty finding the right entrances, and once he did, to palpate anything he was supposed to recognize. She was so large and his fingers so short that he had to push and to feel about to try and get some perception of her uterus and ovaries. He concentrated mightily, excluding all else as he probed and pushed. It required multiple attempts, twists, and reinsertions.

Finally, the woman, who had been quiet and tolerant up to that point said, "Hey, doctah?"

"Yes, Ma'am?" Garven answered, looking over the drapes covering her protuberant abdomen.

"Efan you all keep that up, y'all auh agoin' ta rang ma bell, ya heah?"

Garven blushed, and that would have been a minor amusing anecdote for a cocktail party someday and no more, had not the students in the cubicles on either side of him not heard the conversation. For the rest of the month, he had to endure remarks about 'bell ringing' and would he 'please explain his technique; so, I can run a successful gyn practice someday'. Garven had a fairly thick skin and liked the minor notoriety as much as his fellow students enjoyed giving him the raspberry.

CHAPTER
Sixteen

E very Friday morning the department of medicine held Grand Rounds presided over by Maxwell Cartral—the fourth member of the Godhead—himself. Nominally, one of the junior staff men (there were no women) chaired the conference; but there was never any question about who was in charge, whose opinion mattered, and who got in the last say. Practicing physicians from the tri-state region attended faithfully, contributing patients and case reports with fawning and trepidation. Every member of the medicine staff was to maintain a perfect attendance record; the only exceptions to that rule were formally excused absences. The staff men produced excuse chits like school boys when their duties required them to be elsewhere. Dr. Cartral personally perused the excuse chits and rejected some of them out of hand no matter how senior the requester.

Grand Rounds was a great game. The rules were for a brilliant faculty member or guest lecturer to present an arcane topic then for the captive audience to attempt to come up with pertinent articles from the literature to refute the lecturer's thesis. One-upmanship was the order of the day, and the professor who could successfully find an unanswerable challenge carried the day. It was rumored that some of the references to the medical literature were out-and-out faked, but no one had ever publicly challenged anyone. It was also rumored, with more credence, that Dr. Cartral was always given advance copies of the lecturer's talk, including his references. The most irreverent of the students and house staff suggested that the Chief of Medicine was so venal as to look up the bibliographies of the articles cited and from them gain insights that allowed him to score veritable intellectual coups and to perpetuate his reputation as a scholar with omniscience or at least an encyclopedic memory. It was at least remarkable that he could, week after week, come up with such apt citations of the most up to date work on the issue at hand, no matter how far afield the subject might have been from Dr. Cartral's own work.

The second phase of the conference was the medical student presentation of a selected patient currently on the service. The house staff men responsible for the patient and therefore for the medical student's work were in as much jeopardy as the student, and they all cringed inwardly when the fledgling scholar faced the man they all referred to as 'Ozymandius' behind his back.

The junior staff man, Dr. Stephen Weinstein, last year's chief resident, allowed the discussion of the presenter's subject 'Enzyme Mechanics in Challenged Polymorphonuclear Leukocytes' to run its course then he introduced Garven, "Our student presenter today is Garven Wilsonhulme, a junior student on the service. He will present a case of anemia of uncertain etiology."

Garven was pale and felt shaky. He knew that a wrong nod of Dr. Cartral's head could spell career doom for him. His only desire was to get through the presentation and the gauntlet of questions to follow without stepping on his tongue or worse, on some other pendulous part.

"The patient is E.W., a sixty-nine year old Caucasian woman from Apache Junction who presented in the emergency room with a chief complaint of nausea and vomiting present for two days. She developed mild diarrhea while in the hospital, but by the morning of the second day, she was asymptomatic and requesting to go home."

Garven then rapidly recited the remainder of the history in excruciating detail, having memorized his presentation so as to prevent the possibility of missing even the most insignificant point.

He continued with the physical examination.

"I examined her after she had been in the hospital for two weeks. Her general appearance was that of an elderly white woman..."

Dr. Cartral interrupted, "Caucasian, not 'white', young man. Remember the formalities; we are discussing a patient and will accord her all due respect. You wouldn't call a Negro a 'black' person, would you?"

"No, Sir. Sorry."

Garven was flustered and lost momentary track of where he was in the recital of the history. He started over again, careful to use the proper race designator. He described her pallor, general easy fatigability, and her habitus in great detail. As benumbing as the detail was, no one complained or risked looking bored.

Chapter Sixteen

Garven's details would serve as the point of departure for the discussion to come, and could provide clues whose judicious use might yield brownie points.

Then he launched into the lab giving every single value to the enraptured audience. He made the data orderly by showing the studies in graph form. Although dozens of BUNs, creatinines, electrolytes, biliribins, cryoprecipitates, whole blood differentials, and individual cell line counts had been done, the only abnormality was the decrescendo course of the red cell hemoglobin and hematocrit values which measured the thickness of the blood—the relative amount of blood elements to the transporting plasma.

After Garven finished his presentation, Dr. Cartral, as he did with every student, asked, "What is your differential diagnosis, Mr. Wilsonhulme?"

Garven rattled off an impressive list of the causes of anemia taken from Dr. Cartral's book. He included iron deficiency, disorders of the marrow and the spleen, blood cancers like leukemia, and red cell abnormalities. Dr. Cartral then gave a short discourse on anemias and suggested further lab studies that could be drawn, and Garven would have been able to sit down with credit for having done a workmanlike job on an uncontroversial patient and would have gotten a 'C' or even maybe a 'B' for his efforts.

However, there was in the audience a young Harvard trained internist who had not been associated with the Medical Faculty of the University of Arizona, and therefore had no stock in the maintenance of the myth of Dr. Cartral's infallibility. He chose to pick on Garven to make his point.

"I have a couple of questions for the student, if I may, Dr. Cartral," the LMD—Local Medical Doctor, a term usually spoken with a tone of patronizing disdain by the faculty—said with care to preserve comity.

"Of course, Doctor...?" Dr. Cartral said.

"Dr. Wingate, Jeremy Wingate, from Phoenix Presbyterian," the LMD responded.

That explained everything. Phoenix Presbyterian was the only hospital that deemed itself to be on a par with the university, and took every opportunity to demonstrate the caliber of its staff. All heads turned toward Dr. Wingate.

"My first question is, why did you collect all those BUNs, creatinines, bilirubins, and electrolytes when her first set was normal and even a follow-up set was unchanged?"

Garven loved that. It was like it was his fault all of those irrelevant blood studies were done.

"To establish a pattern, Sir," he finally answered, although he had a more testy retort in mind.

"To serve what purpose?" the LMD asked.

Garven could not think of a good answer; so, he fell back on the most dangerous reply possible in a Grand Rounds presentation, the truth.

"Because someone like you might ask what the value was," he answered.

There was a moment of mild shock and silence, then a ripple of laughter flowed over the audience. This interchange was beginning to look interesting. Dr. Cartral gave the chief resident a threatening look. Garven was too low on the totem pole to warrant a glance.

"You gave us an impressive differential diagnosis, Mr. Wilsonhulme," the Phoenix Presbyterian internist said. "Do you think it's possible to narrow the diagnosis down some. I mean, practically speaking, what do *you* think is wrong with this woman?"

Garven had been afraid someone would ask that question.

"Iron deficiency anemia," he replied, hoping against hope that the LMD would let it go.

"And what...," he paused for effect and a wry smile, "do you think caused her iron deficiency anemia?"

"Well, most likely...uh...blood loss." Garven's voice trailed off.

The acoustics were good in the old student amphitheater, and the doctors and students heard him despite his soft reply.

"From what? You didn't find a source of bleeding, right? Nothing in the stools, no evidence of trauma, or a hematoma, no fractured hip, right?"

"That's right," Garven said, unhelpfully.

"So where did she lose the blood?"

Garven really did not want to say. But he could not just stand there mute.

"Well, the only place I could think of; I mean, the only thing I could measure... was that she had so much blood drained out of her every day that we made her sick."

There was a great deal of poorly suppressed laughter. Dr. Cartral and his house staff did not laugh. It was a serious matter to them, the need to take blood for a myriad of studies—this was a university, after all—and this laughter was an implicit criticism of the methods they held sacred. Dr. Cartral was glowering at Garven. Garven looked fixedly at his shoes.

There followed a truly spirited discussion, unlike the nature of most Grand Rounds, and the clashes of the titans left Garven out of it. He was able to take his seat by E.D. without anyone noticing that he had left the limelight.

"Jeez, Garven, whyn't you just cut your wrists? You are now on Cartral's list. If you ever graduate, you will probably do your internship in Apache General Hospital!"

There was no such hospital, course; it was the figurative Arizona equivalent of being banished to Novosibirsk. Garven just groaned.

CHAPTER
Seventeen

Three days a week, the junior medical students returned to didactics for lectures in Preventive Medicine, Pharmacology, the medical subspecialties, the surgical subspecialties, and psychiatry. Far and away the worst class in the medical school year in and year out was Preventive Medicine. No student from the University of Arizona had ever taken a residency in the subject; it was that bad. To compound the poverty of useful information imparted by the teachers, Preventive Medicine was its own freestanding department, unassailable by any other discipline. The professor was a quirky nonclinicial whose passion was statistics, and he insisted on giving a very extensive lecture series on the subject that held absolutely no interest for the students.

To make his points, Dr. Feingold kept huge jars of colored beads with only himself and a few trusted assistants knowing the exact counts of the various colors. He illustrated his lectures by passing out unknowns—jars of yellow or white beads in which were contained a few black beads. The student was expected to stay awake during a lecture on Gaussian distribution, the chi square test, point estimation, method of maximum likelihood, or the Bayesian approach and then to do an experiment of bead counting to test the theories of probability about the frequency with which a black bead would show up. The medical students were uniformly thinking about their current clinical workups, or about the opposite gender, or about money—more exactly, lack of money, and how to get a little more—and found it impossible to take bead counting seriously.

The class was held in a steeply inclined auditorium. Student protest at the absurdity of counting beads while life and death went on in the hospital came in the form of covert civil disobedience. There were two methods of action: the milder form consisted of removing beads from the bottles and hiding them, especially the dark ones, to throw off the count. The more severe form had to be well orchestrated. During the hush of intense interest as Regression Analysis was being elucidated or during a pop quiz on null hypothesis versus alternative hypotheses, students at the top of the hall, in several strategic locations, would let fall a marble; so, it could clatter stepwise all the way to the bottom. After seven or eight such random occurrences, neither the rest of the students nor the instructors could accept that the forces of chance were in operation, and there would be a stern lecture. The problem for the students was to act as if they thought it was a serious matter.

Pharmacology was the opposite. The students were fascinated by the class and by the eminent practicality of the discipline for their own situations. Here was information they would take to the wards and to their patients—real doctor material. The professor of pharmacology, Random Wilder, PhD was the only head of department who was not an M.D. There were M.D., PhDs, but only one nonM.D. degree holder. He was nothing to look at; he did not have a scintilla of charisma. He wore blue serge suits, heavily starched white shirts, and a plain blue tie. He had five of each and wore them in rotation. He drove a 1938 Studebaker, an automobile that had proved itself reliable enough to get the professor to and from work for nearly two decades; and he saw no reason to make any alteration in his conveyance. He had a Gerber baby round face set off incongruously with a toothbrush Hitlerian mustache. He wore old fashion round glasses as if in protest of the modern black plastic horn rim style.

But when Ransom Wilder, PhD talked, he commanded the attention of everyone in the room. He knew everything that was known about pharmacology. He knew everyone who had ever done anything worthwhile in the subject. He never condescended or scolded, or name dropped, but always demanded the best from his students and from the faculty he commanded. The Department of Pharmacology was the stellar unit of the entire medical school by national and international ratings and compared favorably with the best anywhere. The textbook, *Wilder and Goodhue, General Principles of Pharmacology*, was the bible in every medical school in the country.

Garven was a pragmatist of the first order. He wanted to know the name, dose, form, and toxicity of medicines. Very little emphasis was placed on those properties in the course. He still loved what he was learning. Day by day and week by week, Garven was accumulating an ever deepening sense of how drugs worked and how they could be understood and evaluated by classes. He recognized that he was becoming able to make judgments about chemicals used in medicine based on a firm foundation of basic principles and stopped agitating internally for the instructor to get on to the good and useful stuff.

Dr. Fingl, one of the pharmacology professors, taught him to distinguish action and effect of drugs; effect being the observable result, and the action being the locus of interface of chemicals resulting in the underlying result which caused the effect. He learned about drug-receptor interactions, the conflicts of effects and actions between mixtures of drugs, the temporal characteristics of drug effect including the factors of absorption, distribution, biotransformation, and excretion. From Dr. Fingl, Garven knew the interaction between potency and dose, reliable experimental information, and the difference between hypothesis and superstition.

Dr. Carlyle led the class through the host factors in pharmacology: age, gender, race, associated pathology, physiological reserves, and heredity. Dr. Moesser helped them with the problems of toxicity, side effects, selective effects, and the use of drug combinations to counteract the deleterious effects of primary acting drugs. They worked their way through homergics, hetergics, addition, potentiation, synergism, and summation. Before the year was over, Garven had a grasp of how to select a principle drug out of the jungle of therapeutics available, how to avoid the pitfalls of under and overdosage and addiction, and how to make sense of the plethora of new drugs coming onto the market every week. For the first time in his educational career, a lab seemed pertinent to the real world.

The first lab involved observing the effects of intravenous morphine on dogs and cats. Garven was paired up with Johnathon Holbein and Samantha Jordan. They wrote down the characteristic behavior of their dog: tail wagging: alert, friendly, active. His pupillary diameter was ten millimeters. Samantha drew up ten milligrams of morphine per kilogram, and Garven slowly injected it in the vein that had been cannulated by Johnathon. Shortly the dog became listless, weak, inactive, and finally very nearly stuporous. His pupils now measured three and four millimeters in diameter. One of the other dogs developed a peculiar reaction as if it had gone crazy or was very angry—a sham rage. On the same dose, one of the dogs had a convulsion and died. Garven was impressed and would ever afterwards remember the different reactions to the same dose of the same drug.

The second lab in Pharmacology involved human experimentation—the subjects were once again to be fellow students. The purpose of the lab was to have the students learn about the history of general anesthetics and why the modern ones were preferred. It was neither necessary nor possible to administer chloroform because of its risk of acute liver damage, and no one would accept a day or two of semistupor from barbiturates. The instructors prepared the class to learn about open drop ether—a form of anesthetic that was still in use in backwards areas of the United States and throughout the Third World because of its safety and ease for the administrator. The problem with ether was that it was so unpleasant.

Having been told that fact up front, the class provided no volunteers when the instructors requested. It finally fell to a drawing of lots. Two hapless men picked the short straws and became the guinea pigs; and Garven and Maria Stricklin drew the two long straws and the opportunity to administer the drugs.

One of the men, the first subject, lay on the examining bed. Maria held the small wire cage covered with gauze over her classmate's nose taking care to keep the apparatus away from his eyes. Garven slowly dropped ether into the gauze. At first, the 'patient' squirmed and complained of eye and nose irritation, then he developed profound eye and nose watering. He began to fall asleep, and as he did, he became very agitated and combative. Then he slumped into a profoundly deep sleep. The class unanimously agreed that open drop ether was best considered a relic of the past.

The second student subject went through the same process except that he was given atropine before being given ether. He went through the same stages of excitement followed by unconsciousness, but he did get to miss out on the eye and nose watering.

CHAPTER
Eighteen

G arven's second patient for presentation on the medical service was a morbidly obese man. The attending was a stickler for detail, but a man with a sense of humor and one who seemed genuinely to like the students, a distinct anomaly in the faculty ranks so far as Garven could tell. Garven prepared for two days. When it was time for him to present the case to the attending endocrinologist, he suffered his first humiliation in school.

"Wrong patient," said the attending.

He looked over his student-patient list again to be sure.

"It can't be!" Garven exclaimed.

He had done all of the work. It was impossible.

"But it is," the attending explained patiently. "You misread the patient list and took the man listed one below the one to which you were assigned."

Garven checked the list himself and was devastated. He tried to compose himself. While his guy was not a great case, there had to be some interest in a man who weighed five hundred pounds.

"Can I present him to you anyway," Garven asked in a controlled voice but with pleading eyes.

"You can present him for the experience, but I can't give you credit. You will have to take an incomplete on him. There will be plenty of others. In fact, the man you should have worked up, the thyroiditis, is still in the house. Why don't you work him up for next time?"

Garven felt thwarted and angry. It was unreasonable. He had just made a little clerical error. He hated being in such a weak position. He wanted to punch the professor.

Instead, he said, with ill controlled animus, "I didn't make a mistake. I took the patient assigned to me, and now I'm being penalized. It isn't fair!" His voice was rising. "I... you are... "

"Stop. Don't say anything more, Mr. Wilsonhulme. You are okay now, but you will get yourself into hot water if you go on. You have a long way to go in your medical education, and this is a lesson you must learn. Even you can make a mistake. You will get further ahead if you just admit it—to yourself and to the patient or your colleagues—accept the problem, and try to fix it. If you get angry and insulting every time you make an error, you won't last long in medicine."

He looked very pointedly into Garven's angry eyes.

It took an overwhelming effort to keep his tongue, but somehow Garven remained still. He shouted inwardly at himself to remove the expression of outrage and personal affront he knew that he must be wearing so blatantly. He learned an important lesson, and all it cost him was a little more stomach lining and some more work to get the thyroiditis patient's H&P—history and physical—and lab ready for the next endocrine rounds. He lost a bare few points on his overall medicine record, not enough to make a difference. He mulled over what had happened and decided that he had gotten a valuable insight for very little cost.

Garven experienced his first death the following week. He was working in the Maricopa Veterans Administration Hospital. There was an old, befuddled vet named Marvis Jacobs who, as near as Garven could tell, was a permanent inmate. He had a three volume thick chart; most of the contents were minor, not enough to require hospitalization in the first place, and certainly not enough to warrant the long hospitalizations. The old man wore a sign on his back that said, "I'm Marvis Jacobs. I belong to 7B. If I am lost, please bring me back to Mrs. Curtis on 7B. Thanks."

Mr. Jacobs was senile and had a perseverant speech fixation.

Every person who entered the ward was accosted with, "Take me to the terlet! I gotta go. Why don't no one take me to the terlet."

This happened twenty or thirty times a day and most of the help and the interns and residents ignored him. Garven found it very difficult, because the old man interrupted his conversations, broke in on him when he was doing an H&P on another patient, and embarrassed the farmer's wives who came to visit their husbands.

Garven had been at the VA for nearly a month and now worked fairly independently getting the general scut work done without having an intern on his back. He could start IV's, change Foley catheters, put Ace wraps on legs, and do a highly passable H&P without taking all day. One Saturday afternoon he was doing a history in the cubicle next to Marvis Jacobs. The old man had driven him to distraction with all of his interruptions, and it had doubled the time he had had to spend with the other rather confused old vet.

Finally, Garven got up and yelled at the old man, "Shut up! Go sit on your bed and just shut up!"

Marvis blinked in wonderment then started to cry. "I'm sorry! I'm sorry!" he wailed. "I jist wanted to git somebody to take me to the terlet. I gotta go to the terlet."

"Just do it in the bed!" snapped Garven and went back to his H&P despairing.

After a while it was quiet. Garven sneaked a peek between the curtains separating Marvis' cubicle from the man on whom he was presently working. The old man was lying on his back with his mouth open. Garven thought for a brief second that he perhaps should go in and check the old vet, but it was so wonderful to have him quiet that he decided to presume that the old man was asleep. Garven was tired, and the H&P was his last bit of scut for the day.

When he finished the write up, Garven checked on old Marvis one more time. He knew he should not have. Mr. Jacobs was dead. Garven felt a little guilty for not having had a higher index of suspicion earlier and for not really caring now. The old man was a burden to himself and to everyone else and would never have gotten better. He took his time and reported the finding of the dead man to the charge nurse, Miss Pittynap—the RN everyone called 'Miss Pittypat' because of her propensity for fussiness instead of substantive action. Miss Pittynap rushed out to tell the intern.

Dr. Sapire was an intense, harried, brilliant Jewish man of forty, well over the usual age for interns. His mother had finally nagged him into being a doctor; so, he could finally snare a wife; and ever the dutiful son, he had plunged in with messianic zeal. He ran at a full gallop to the old man's bedside, his stethoscope flapping about his chest.

He screamed, "Cardiac arrest! Call a code!"

Then he tore off Marvis' shirt and hoisted him up so the nurse could place a board under the old man's back. He started mouth to mouth resuscitation while Miss Pittypat began chest compressions according to the manual.

Dr. Sapire came up with some solid material from the old vet's mouth and spat it on the floor. Garven could hardly bear to look. Dr. Sapire tried to keep on, but had to go over into the corner and retch for a few minutes.

He gasped out an order to Garven, "Do the mouth to mouth. I'll be back in a minute."

While the intern retched, Garven came over to the dead man who was bouncing around the bedboard from the vigor of the nurse's chest massage. The old man's ribs were all broken now, and the chest wall gave like an infant's.

Garven brought his mouth down in the general direction of the old man's and held his breath. He moved his head around as if he were forcing air into the vet's dead lungs, but he never came closer than three inches from tissue. Dr. Sapire was busy ordering all of the helpers to fetch this drug and that and starting big IV lines, and watching the flat EKG tracing with overt despair. He did not notice Garven's lack of real effort. After forty-five minutes of futile effort in which practically every rubber glove, cutdown tray and trach set on the ward had been opened and the area looked like a MASH unit major frontline battle surgery center, the senior medical resident arrived on the scene.

Dr. Sapire was visibly relieved.

"Jeb, Jeb," he said puffing, nearly exhausted. "We've done everything I could think of: massage, intubated him, epi IV and intracardiac, shocked him all the way to 400. Nothing works!"

Jeb Stafford was as serious about the old vets as Dr. Sapire, but he did have a modicum of common sense. He puttered around with a few more drugs and had no better results than Dr. Sapire.

"Let's call it quits. You've done a great job, everything you could do."

"How about a trach? How about open chest massage?"

Dr. Sapire was pleading, distraught.

"Nah. David, let's call it quits. You can't win 'em all. It's over."

He patted David and Miss Pittypat on the back consoling them. Sapire, Stafford, and Garven left the room; and the nurse set about to clean up the colossal mess.

A rabbi appeared at Mr. Jacobs' bedside as unobtrusively as a shadow. Garven had not known that Mr. Jacobs was Jewish, had hardly thought of him as a person until the rabbi, in a strikingly beautiful baritone voice intoned, "*Yisgadal ve yiskadosh shmei robab.*" [Extolled and hallowed be the name of the Lord in the world which He created according to His will.]—the Hebrew Kaddish for the dead.

The following day in rounds Dr. Stafford came directly to the incident as soon as all of the attendings and house staff and students were gathered in the conference room.

"I have to tell you," he announced in general, "I have had some pretty disturbing information brought to my attention. Mr. Wilsonhulme, did you know that Mr. Jacobs had had an arrest?"

"Sure, that's why I got Miss Pittynap to call the code," Garven said.

He had a pretty good idea where this was heading, and he worked to keep calm and matter-of-fact.

"I mean earlier. One of the nurses saw you look in on him. Was he okay then?"

"I figured he was asleep at one point," Garven answered.

He did not appear defensive and was pleased with his control.

"Did you check him?"

"No, I didn't see any reason to."

"He could have been in trouble. He could have been dead. Did you think about that?"

"Not much," Garven said.

It was not the answer the chief resident wanted to hear.

"Maybe you thought of him as just an old vet, a senile worthless old man."

It was the ultimate populist challenge in the VA.

"Maybe. But that had nothing to do with my decision. Now that you bring it up; he was old and completely senile and life was not worth much. It seems almost cruel to me to do CPR on him."

"Are you God?"

Dr. Stafford was angry and indignant now.

"No more than you are."

Garven worked to control his temper.

"Maybe Dr. Sapire could have saved him if you had reported his trouble in time. Next time get yourself a higher index of suspicion. We are here to save these patients. Don't forget that!"

"When Dr. Sapire started to work on Mr. Jacobs, the man had been stone cold dead for quite a while. It was an exercise in futility. Some people just die, you know. We can't save them all. It isn't even right to try," Garven said evenly.

"As long as I am chief resident, we will resuscitate them all. We will do everything we can to help these old vets. *Everything*. Clear?"

"Clear."

Everyone calmed down, and the incident was forgotten as the rest of the rounds were completed. When all of the doctors, med students, and nurses and dispersed to take care of their individual ration of scut work, Harry Rample, the surgical intern doing a rotation on medicine because he thought it would round him out better, caught up with Garven.

"Hey, don't take it too hard. You sound like a surgeon type. We think different that the swamis."

Garven loved it when someone spoke disrespectfully about internists, especially right now.

"It seems like such a crock to break up an old man's chest, particularly a dead one's just for a drill or something," Garven groused to the intern.

"Look, come on over and meet Dr. Humphrey, the Chief of Surgery. Maybe you can get a different perspective," said Dr. Rample sympathetically.

Dr. Humphrey was unique. Not only was he a superb technical surgeon; but he was also a better than middling researcher; so, he was able to keep up his position in both spheres—the workaday world of cut-and-sew at the VA, and in the publish-or-perish arena of medical academia. So far as the house staff and students were concerned, Dr. Humphrey's unique quality was that he was accessible. Unless he was truly too busy, he would take time to answer the questions of underlings. More importantly, he had the uncommon quality of having common sense.

Rample knew where the surgery chief was. The portly bear of a man had been in a conference with NIH grant investigators and would be just going back to his office. The two younger men caught up with him before he could disappear in to his inner sanctum.

"Dr. Humphrey!" called Harry Rample.

"Oh, hello, Harry, what's up?"

"Could you please take a minute to answer this student's question? He's had a tough day of it over with the lice and fleas."

"Now, Harry, it isn't the best thing to call our internal medicine brethren 'lice and fleas'. I've told you that a dozen times."

It was obviously a standing joke because the surgery professor could hardly manage a look of even mock severity.

"Yes, Sir. You're right. I repent," the intern said.

He did not look remorseful.

"Anyway what's the problem?"

Now Dr. Humphrey was looking at Garven.

"By the way, what's your name?"

"Garven Wilsonhulme, Sir."

"Well, Garven, it's your nickel, shoot."

"Okay. Dr. Humphrey. If you were walking down the hall and came on one of the old vets on the floor unconscious, had a cardiac arrest, what would you do?"

Dr. Humphrey looked at the young man thoughtfully.

"Well, my boy, I would think about how many of these fine old patients of ours have TB. I would think about all those red snappers milling around in his orifices. I might call for an EKG, or some lab work, or a chest x-ray."

"How about mouth to mouth?" Garven interrupted.

"Don't rush me. I'm getting to that," Dr. Humphrey said.

He was smiling.

"Sorry," Garven said feeling gently chided.

"Then I would bend over the old gentleman and check his pulse and respirations, maybe even his blood pressure. Then I would look sadly on him and say, 'poor old fella'. That's basically my approach."

"Sounds right to me, too," Garven said, relieved.

"So, what's the problem? Don't they do it that way over in swami land?"

All three men laughed conspiratorially. Garven knew for sure that day that he was a surgeon type. The conversation with the Chief of Surgery only served to corroborate his decision of the summer with the neurosurgeon, Dr. Harralsen, that surgery was his thing.

It would be wrong to think that the internists were nothing but humorless medical automatons even though there was a growing body of evidence to that effect in Garven's experience. In the last week of his medical rotation, Garven was back at the university hospital on the endocrinology service. It had been a rather eventful day for the service because their major paper had just been completed. Every staff man and woman and all of the house staff had participated in a project to see if morbid obesity—greater than fifty pounds over normal weight—could be treated with a successful long term result. Three hundred patients had been put on diets, pills, exercises, and psychiatric counseling for two years. Social workers had gone to their homes when they failed to keep appointments. Everything possible had been done to make the massively obese people adhere to a diet.

The results were finally tabulated and the conclusion was presented at rounds although most of the people involved already knew the general outcome of their efforts. Massive amounts of fat had been lost as a result of the tremendous effort on the part of the endocrinology department. All of that was duly noted. The end result was that, on the average, there had been a net change of two pounds—two pounds gained per person.

At the time of ending the effort, the experiment, not one single person had lost a single pound. There had been five deaths, four directly related to the obesity, and one due to suicide.

Garven listened as the professor intoned the awful conclusion, "And now, the last word on obesity. We shall hereafter define it as a medical condition of excessive weight gain that is hopeless; deterioration and death are inexorable and inevitable; and no sustainable weight loss can be expected long term in this fatal disease."

There was a mood of profound gloom on rounds that day. There was also an incongruity in the picture. It took Garven a while to recognize what he was seeing. As the professor was finishing his paper, the five junior residents on the service were calmly sipping drinks. That would not have been particularly noticeable—discourteous perhaps, but not conspicuous—had it not been for the fact that they were calmly sipping from urinals. The male patient urine collection vessels were metal and had a broad tube for insertion of the appropriate organ to prevent splashing and spilling. There was something inherently indecent and nauseating about the actions of the residents. Apparently no one but Garven noticed at first.

As rounds began to break up, the residents made more of a display of drinking. Now it was evident that the urinals contained pale yellow liquid. Finally, one of the secretaries took notice of a resident as he chug-a-lugged a satisfying swallow. She let out a small shriek and threw her hand to her mouth. Professors, students, interns, and visitors turned their attention to the residents as they swilled the yellow liquid. There was general subdued consternation and looks of nausea and disapproval. Dr. Hendrickson, who had just presented the division's paper and was in charge of the day to day clinical service, strode over to one of the residents and locked him in earnest and serious discussion. They abruptly left the room together. Garven wished intensely that he could be a mouse in one of their pockets while the in camera conversation took place off stage.

In a very few minutes, Dr. Hendrickson and the resident reappeared in the room, now largely cleared of its audience. The professor was laughing uproariously. Garven sidled up to one of the residents involved and asked him what was going on.

"Oh, we knew it was going to be a bad day; so, we thought we would lighten things up a bit. We scrubbed out some of the chamber pots, and autoclaved them. I did mine twice. Then we filled them up with apple juice.

Think it had the desired effect?" the resident asked Garven, no longer able to keep any semblance of a straight face.

Dr. Hendrickson chanced to bump into Garven at the end of rounds. "My spies tell me you're interested in surgery, that you want to be a technician instead of a real doctor, too bad. I guess today gave you some idea of the deep level of reverence we have for science and the benefit of our patients. Maybe you will give thought to being a real doctor. You're smart enough. Think about it."

CHAPTER
Nineteen

Garven started on the Surgery Service after Christmas and discovered several small ways to help meet necessities. It was serendipity, the way the food problem was solved. Eating in the cafeteria was cheap by ordinary standards, but for Garven, who had next to nothing, it was too expensive. Besides the food was bad, all carbohydrates, cheap gristly meat and weaners, and none too clean. Maria Stricklin put it well when she described the fare as being "just offal."

On the other hand, the food provided the patients was several quanta better despite their poverty and the unlikelihood of them complaining. Garven discovered that he could eat regularly by snatching up unused patients' trays. This was a rather hit and miss and often hungry process until he learned the ropes from a surgical intern whose finances were on a par with Garven's. Interns were paid $30 a month, which was below the poverty level. The intern caught Garven wolfing down a patient's untouched food one day and made an invaluable suggestion. Instead of prowling around hoping against hope to find an unused or at least undirtied tray, he suggested that Garven take matters into his own hands. Garven had the privilege of writing orders in the chart, although they had to be countersigned by an M.D.

"Why not just order a full regular diet for the belly cases just out of surgery? No one keeps track; the county pays for the meal; the nurses don't pay attention; and you happen by and get the meal. Good idea, no?"

It was a good idea, yes; and Garven solved the problem of hunger for the rest of the time he was in medical school by that ingenious bit of dishonesty.

Lyle and Ray were good old boys and made a concession on the rent deal that amounted to a contribution to Garven's medical education expenses. Since he was in the hospital so much, it was an easy thing to find an empty room more often than not; and he essentially moved into the hospital to live. They kept his things in the apartment and rented out the room to another trucker. It was necessary only occasionally for Garven to sleep in his car.

It became nerve-wracking to have to find a new room every night and embarrassing when he had to be kicked out; so, the nurses could admit a patient to that room. He solved the problem once and for all, and never had to pay a dime of rent for the remainder of his year and a half in medical school by finding the ideal room for himself.

Perhaps 'ideal' is a descriptor that should have some qualification as to the situation. The room was dirty, musty, old, and grossly inconvenient—about as homey as a cell at San Quentin. It had originally been a quarters for Mexican nurses' aids for the psychiatric and male g-u services, both of which required male help exclusively. As the hospital expanded and modernized; and the pay scale improved for paramedics, they were no longer provided with room and board. Their room became a repository for old filing cabinets, typewriters, obsolete suction machines, broken IV standards, and irreparable hospital beds. The shower stalls moldered and became crusty with lime deposits, and the toilet became gray with disuse.

Garven had made friends with one of the old Mexican aides on the surgery service, and the old man remembered the old days in the loft room. He showed Garven the abandoned stairwell and the obscure door. It was up to Garven to test out the sink, the shower, and the toilet. When he discovered, to his delight, that they all worked after a fashion, despite their decrepit appearance, he set about to shove things aside and to pile things on top of other things until he had room to get in and out. He fixed up one of the beds and procured bed linens from one of the wards on a midnight raid. He now had the ideal room—rent free, and virtually unknown to those who might wish to take exception to his use of the facility.

While he was solving his rent and food problem and contemplating his problem of how to pay for his tuition and books, Garven went about his daily work as a subhuman on the surgery service. The residents on the surgical services were regarded and paid as poor white trash; the interns were even lesser citizens and were overworked, underfed, and poorly treated. All of them were entire biological classes above the lowly medical students, the subhumans. Even the nursing students, who were considered important and useful to the hospital and therefore were accorded common civility, were regarded as a class above the med students.

Garven and his contemporaries were assigned to one or another of the interns—six students per intern. It was a classical master-slave relationship. One might think that the abused interns would see in the students fellow sufferers and would make an effort to befriend them and to treat them with a measure of compassion. Not so. It was more like the relationship between rural poor white trash and poor Negroes in the South. The interns saw in the medical students, as the rednecks did in the Negroes, a class even lower in the social strata than themselves; they revelled in the distinction; and they were merciless.

Garven got up early and did H&Ps, urinalyses and blood work, collected and plated out stool specimens for ova and parasites, made up IV solutions, cleaned up pus and changed dressings, and tagged along behind the intern as he did his own scabrous daily scut work. Garven felt that he was becoming the world's foremost expert on starting IVs and doing cutdowns. If he could not find and put a needle or a cannula into a vein, it couldn't be done. He came to know all of the secret sites for cutting over veins and putting in a court of last resort IV line, a cutdown. He learned how to swab and culture pus; and there was a lot of it on the charity wards where the patients did not take care of themselves and were chronically rundown before they came to the operating rooms. He was allowed to open infected wounds as his share of the surgery on the wards. He lavaged the wounds, packed and repacked them, cleaned them with iodine; and at times when nice healthy pink granulation tissue formed in a wound on which he had worked, he was permitted to sew up the wound to achieve healing by second intention as another surgical sop thrown to him as a token payment for his labors.

The real, regular payoff for the hours of miserable labor on the wards was that the students were assigned, two to a patient, to every person who went to surgery on a scrupulously fair rotation system. The presence of the students was a tolerated encumbrance to the work of getting a patient through an operation in a big city-county-medical school system already rife with impediments. Two is company and welcome in an operation—a surgeon and an able assistant. Three and four are a crowd. The students were forbidden to touch anything, to lean over, to cough, to talk, or to ask stupid questions. Sometimes they were assigned to reach in at arm's length and to hold greasy bowel with a retractor. Sometimes they could see a little; and at those times, they learned a little more about surgery.

By the luck of the draw Garven assisted on a wide assortment of general surgical procedures: gall bladders, hernias, stomachs, bowel resections, colostomies, radical mastectomies, amputations, and a few aortic aneurysm resections. The University of Arizona and the Salt River Valley Hospital and University Medical Center did not do heart cases or thoracotomies except for the simplest abscess removals or emergency ligature of a posttraumatic bleeder inside the chest. There were not enough neuro cases being done that Garven ever drew one of those.

He saw surgical *tours de force* by the chief resident and staff men, clever maneuvers, slow and sloppy intern and resident efforts, and the world of nighttime surgical emergencies coming up from the emergency room. Gradually, Garven became able to tie a decent knot, to sew up simple lacerations, to find and clamp off a bleeder, and generally to be useful and to learn. Daily, he recognized a meager change in himself; he was becoming slightly more competent and confident with the passage of time and with experience. Although he still had a long way to go, Garven was now able to see himself as a doctor someday; and he was able to surround that self-vision with a growing reality. He ignored the abuses heaped on him by interns and residents, and scratched and clawed to get to do any procedure he could. He had the soul of a surgeon, Dr. Stevens, one of the staff men, had commented, once when Garven had inveigled his way to be first assistant when his intern had gotten the flu and could not stand up long enough to assist. It was nothing but the truth, Garven said to himself. He liked being recognized for that; nothing could be bigger or better than being a surgeon. Nothing.

Garven had a great deal to learn, especially about the halls of academia. He was assigned to write a paper on a general surgery subject with the solitary proviso that he actually participate in the procedure about which he wrote. He fished around for two or three weeks before finally settling on a subject. He observed that people in renal failure routinely had to come in to have a peritoneal lavage to leech off some of the accumulated nitrogenic toxins that built up as a result of their kidneys' inability to excrete the wastes. He could not find any decent review articles on the subject.

First, he made himself the school's technical expert on the procedure. The interns were only too happy to turn the onerous task to him. They wanted to spend their time operating, and considered peritoneal taps and lavages scut work that took up their time and energy. Garven, being fresh and enthusiastic to do procedures, almost any procedure, approached the assignment with gusto. He liked to prep the protuberant abdomens, put in the procaine, make the small incision (the only one he was allowed to make as a student) and to push the large blunt tri-edged trocar into the abdominal cavity. It was satisfying to see the proteinaceous yellow fluid gush out and the patients give a sigh of relief from the pressure. He learned to put in just the right amount of lavage solution to keep the patients' blood pressures and electrolyte values stable. He liked being an expert.

Garven wrote a well thought out and well accepted paper and submitted it to the surgery department's publications committee. They sent it back with a few suggestions, and Garven made the changes and re-submitted the paper. Dr. Stevens called him to tell him that the paper would be published in *Surgery, Obstetrics, and Gynecology* in the July volume. He sent Garven a copy of the manuscript.

Seeing that manuscript, especially the list of authors, was a startling lesson about medical academia for the naive young man. Where he had expected to see, Wilsonhulme, Garven C., *The Dynamics of Peritoneal Lavage,* he saw instead a list of four authors starting with the head of the surgery department, then Dr. Stevens, the resident who was on the ward before Garven came, and the intern presently on the service. His own name was last. When he brought the change to one of the attendings and almost voiced a complaint, he learned the lesson that in the publish or perish world of medical schools: every paper was going to have several authors, the most senior man was going to take the credit, and it made no difference whether or not some of the listed authors had made an actual contribution. As the Bible so pithily intoned, "the scales were falling from his eyes."

Garven was in the rapid process of shedding his illusions.

Not that he harbored that many illusions. Not after a few days on the service. It took no time at all to learn that, like admirals, surgeons had to put their pants on one leg at a time. He saw them tired and crotchety, pompous and self-seeking, flippant and condescending towards internists. Garven agreed that internists were deserving of a lot of condescension. And he saw the surgeons' unadmitted mistakes, and more than once, their disasters, and not rarely enough, their hypocrisy.

CHAPTER
Twenty

The first disaster Garven saw in the operating room occurred for an inexcusable reason. The surgeon was a young staff man and a show-off. The intern and the two students assigned to his case were a captive audience, and the operation was a simple one, beneath the expertise of the unrecognized star of the surgical theater. Garven had worked up the case, a large, nonthyroid neck cyst. It was so large that the woman's trachea was shifted, and she had trouble breathing. She had to hold her head at an unusual angle. All of the labs, including thyroid functions, had been normal; and the woman was young and healthy.

"Give me the differential diagnosis, son," ordered the surgeon as they fitted the last drape in place over the scrubbed and iodinized skin of the neck.

Garven hated being called 'son' by anyone, especially by a guy that did not look more than a couple of years older than himself.

"Thyroid cyst, branchial cleft cyst, inclusion cyst, tumor..."

"What kind of tumor?"

"Thyroid, maybe a lung carcinoma extending up into the neck, maybe a muscle tumor,"

"Rare as hen's teeth."

"Uh, something like a metastatic breast tumor?"

"Never saw one in the neck."

That settled that. If the staff man had not seen such a thing in his vast experience (two years out of residency) then it could not be.

"Expanded lobe of the lung. That's about all I can think of," Garven finished.

"Dr. Parton?" the staff man turned his attention to the intern.

"Most likely some kind of benign cyst. I guess it could be part of the lung like Wilsonhulme says, but I doubt it. At least, I've heard of that. Too soft to be a cancer."

"I agree," said the surgical attending.

He made a neat transverse incision across the base of the neck just above the sternal notch.

"Did you hear about the guy that went to his doctor for a checkup and the doc told him he had to have an operation immediately?"

"Nope," both Garven and the intern answered.

One of the things Garven liked best about the operating room was the jokes. They served to calm everyone down and to create a bit of a leveling influence in a highly stratified microsocial unit.

"Anyway, the guy says, 'But I feel just great. I have never been better.'"

The attending opened the fascia and was using a mosquito clamp to separate and open the underlying connective tissues. He was staying in the midline to keep out of the muscles because they tended to bleed easily.

"'Well, my man', says the doctor. 'I checked you over very thoroughly. Doctor knows best. You have to have this operation'."

"'Okay', says the patient, 'you're the doc. But how much is this operation going to cost me?'"

He clamped a small bleeder, and the intern tied a silk ligature around it.

"'About $5000', the surgeon told the guy.

"'Five thousand bucks!' the guy says. 'I don't have that kind of money!'"

The attending paused to have the circulating nurse mop his brow.

"The doc says, 'That's okay. You can pay me on the installment plan.'"

"'You mean like you was buyin' a car,' the guy says."

The attending clamped two more bleeders; the intern tied them off; and the attending picked up a number eleven blade stab knife scalpel.

"'Yeah, that's right,' the doc tells the man. 'How did you know?'"

Garven, the intern, and the two nurses laughed heartily. Nurses loved jokes which put doctors down. The attending had a quirky self-deprecating sense of humor for all his arrogance, and the nurses generally liked him.

"Look, I have to get back to my lab. It's been nice, but I have to get this thing done. I could dissect this cyst all day, but I'll show you a little trick. I'm going to deflate it, then the cyst wall will probably just fall out. We'll be out of here in fifteen minutes," the attending surgeon said and flourished his stab knife like Zorro wielding his rapier.

"I just had a thought," said young Dr. Parton. "What if it's an aneurysm?"

"Too firm. I don't see any pulsations, do you, Dr. Parton? Remember the old adage, 'When you hear hoof beats, you should think of horses first, not zebras'. This looks like a cyst, smells like a cyst, feels like a cyst. It must be a cyst."

He swept the knife down in a theatrical plunge, inserting it into the cyst a careful half an inch.

"*Voila!*" he cried in a mimic of D'Artagnon.

He withdrew the knife as swiftly as he had inserted it and looked down to watch the cyst fluid evacuate under pressure.

Instead, a horrendous column of blood a full inch in diameter shot out of the opening clear to the OR ceiling—a surgical Krakatoa. In the next instant the incision in the 'cyst' opened up like a slit open seam of a silk dress. Blood erupted from the opening splattering everyone and everything in the operating room. The attending's eyes were flooded with the viscous opaque blood; Garven's face and chest were soaked. He could not see a thing. Only the intern had the presence of mind to clap his hand over the bleeding site. It was a pitiful attempt, like the Dutch boy with his finger in the dike when the whole dam caved in. Blood flushed out around his hand in a torrent and poured out onto the floor making a pool all around the operating table.

"Her BP is diving!" shouted the anesthesiologist who had been taken completely unawares by the disastrous sudden hemorrhage.

He had been thinking about the toxic effects of pentobarbital in preparation for his anesthesiology boards when the bottom dropped out of everything.

"Blood!" he yelled at the circulating nurse. "Get O pos, uncrossed! Get plasma or albumin. Let's start another IV. Get me a fourteen gauge needle. Hurry it up!"

He hung a fresh bottle of Lactated Ringers solution and ran it wide open.

The attending surgeon had abandoned sterile technique and wiped off his face with his gloved hands. He scrambled the scrub table to find a large clamp. Any large clamp. There were none. It was to have been such a simple case. In and out. An innocuous little cyst.

"She's gone!" shouted the anesthesiologist. "Arrested!"

"I'll beat on her chest," shouted Dr. Parton over the din.

The OR was now filling up with helpers. By some miracle a unit of blood appeared from somewhere, then another.

"I can't get a vein!" the anesthesiologist said in desperation. "They've all collapsed!"

"I'll cut down!" shouted the attending.

For some reason, everyone was shouting. Garven felt completely useless. He shrank back and tried to keep out of the way.

"No use. She doesn't have any blood to pump around!"

"I'll crack her chest!" the attending yelled.

He tore off the drapes over the woman's chest and sliced through the entire chest wall between the fourth and fifth ribs in a single swipe. He pried open the ribs, causing a loud crack as one of them fractured. He reached his hand in and closed it over the woman's heart.

"It's empty!" he said.

It felt like a deflated thick walled balloon, and it was motionless. The attending surgeon's eyes looked stricken, like a cornered animal. He squeezed the limp vital organ, but it was futile. There was no blood to pump. The woman had exsanguinated. Virtually every drop of blood she had had in her body was external—caught in the drapes and surgical gowns, dripping from the ceiling, or puddling on the floor.

After an eminently frustrating and fruitless hour, they stopped their efforts at resuscitation. The surgeons and medical students left the room for the nurses to clean up. The patient's body was taken to the morgue. There would be an autopsy. The hospital and the university would insist on that. Garven did not have the stomach to go with Dr. Parton when he went to face the woman's family. The attending left for the lab.

In M&M—morbidity and mortality—meeting at the end of the week, the case was discussed in detail. The conversation among the operators was not mentioned nor was the Zorro method of swordsman incision method described. The autopsy revealed that the so-called cyst had been, in reality, an anomalously placed segment of the arch of the aorta which had pushed up into the root of the deceased woman's neck. It was not only a benign lesion; it was nothing more than an unusual, but not unheard of, variant of normal anatomy. And because of the surgery—the unnecessary surgery—the woman who had entered the hospital healthy, was dead.

The effect on Garven was profound. He grew up, in a sense, that day. No longer was medicine and surgery a far away dream. It was now a soul shaking reality. He was deeply affected, and it was an experience he would never be able to erase from his mind. He had been responsible, at least in part. He had examined and diagnosed. He had been as wrong as everyone else. He did learn a lesson, a deep one. The OR was a temple where nonsense could not be permitted. He would carry that lesson with him for the rest of his career.

There was no announcement and no explanation. The surgical attending quietly resigned and rumor had it that he had gotten a job working in a drug company lab with no patient care responsibility. The intern, Dr. Parton, found a new job to complete his internship in internal medicine in a private hospital in the mid-west somewhere. Garven thought that was unfair; it was not Dr. Parton's fault. Garven learned another lesson from the terrible fiasco. When a disaster occurs, there usually has to be a scapegoat, and it always rolls downhill. Dr. Parton was in the wrong place at the wrong time. And he had missed the diagnosis along with the rest of the team; so, he was not entirely guiltless; but he was a nobody and therefore fully vulnerable.

CHAPTER
Twenty-One

Garven was witness to a near medical disaster that would have eclipsed the importance of the operating room tragedy. It occurred while he was on the pediatrics rotation during spring quarter. Polio was a great and terrible scourge in America. Every day children were brought to the peds ward suffering with the viral illness. The wards were lined with iron lungs where children afflicted with respiratory or bulbar poliomyelitis lay unable to breathe without the assistance of the miracle cylinders. Nurses hurried from lung to lung making sure they continued to function and worrying whether there would be a disastrous power outage every time there was a thunder storm.

The orthopedic clinics saw long lines of children with misshapen legs, children in wheel chairs, children carried by their parents. Poliomyelitis, infantile paralysis, was an epidemic disease—33,344 cases in the U.S. in 1950, alone—so fearful that congregations prayed that God would forgive them their sins and would have the polio angel pass them by. Parents kept their children indoors and often, out of school. Summers were times of near panic because there seemed to be an unholy predilection of the disease to strike during the most pleasant and carefree time of the year.

Then Jonas Salk invented a vaccine for all types of polio I, II, III, which used killed virus and was injected under the skin. The vaccine was not yet on the market when Garven was on the pediatric service, and was still considered experimental. The university pediatric professors were part of a study of the safety and efficacy of the vaccine set up through the National

Institutes of Health. They received large quantities of the vaccine from Coutering Laboratories and began the carefully monitored administration of the vaccine to hundreds of screaming children. Parents begged to have their children on the study. The lines for the vaccine extended from the pediatric clinic well into the street. Garven worked ten and twelve hours a day administering the new vaccine and caring for his polio patients on the ward.

Then, in the midst of the euphoria, a specter of disaster presented itself. Dr. Hathaway, chief of pediatrics, made the announcement. The vaccine was faulty. Some batches, and it was unsure which batches or how many, had been inadequately sterilized; and live viruses were concentrated in the vials. Recipients around the country began to develop the disease.

"I greatly fear that, in our haste to save our children," Dr. Hathaway announced to the stunned students, house officers, and faculty assembled in the pediatrics amphitheater, "we have infected most of the children of Phoenix. We may well have destroyed a generation. God help and forgive us."

The venerable old man stood with his head bowed, tears glistening in his eyes.

"We can give gamma globulin, but no one knows if it will do any good. Roll up your sleeves and let's get to work. It's all we can do."

It was an enormous and unpopular effort. An emergency educational campaign had to be mounted to inform every parent of every child who had received the potentially live virus vaccine. They flocked into the medical school in a panic. Every child with a cold or the flu became a major emergency, and the pediatric beds were overfilled by the second day. The wards were stripped of nonessentials, and more beds were brought in. In a week, there were children in broom closets and on futons on the floor. The house staff and every available medical student worked around the clock to give gamma globulin to the children. The hospital became a bedlam of screaming children being injected with twenty cc's of the viscous gamma globulin through a huge needle—every child's worst nightmare. It was a wholly absorbing drama. On the eighth day, they ran out of gamma globulin and the people taking care of the children suffered the fear that they were about to see their worst nightmare.

When poor, exhausted Dr. Hathaway had to make the announcement to the parents lined up into the street for the lifesaving antidote that they would have to wait until more became available, there was a near riot. The parents vilified Dr. Hathaway and the university for using them as guinea pigs. They all but stormed the wards and clinics to get at the gamma globulin they were certain was being hoarded there for the rich. Garven was knocked to the ground by a huge Negro man who accused him of holding out for white children only. The Coutering Company rushed new supplies in as fast as they could be produced. The Red Cross mounted a massive campaign to obtain donors. Finally, after two weeks of hell on earth, every available child had been given the antidote. Not a single child got polio, but two children died of anaphylactic allergic reactions to the gamma globulin. Their parents filed the first two malpractice suits in the history of the university.

When the epidemic and the pandemonium quieted, Garven settled down to the routine of learning to care for children. He learned first that they were not just small people, sort of diminutive adults; but, in fact, they were special medical entities unto themselves. They got different diseases, required different drugs and doses of drugs, and most importantly, the fledgling doctor had to learn how to deal with the parents as much as with the children. Garven learned to cope with hand wringing, fault finding, clinging, threatening, neglectful, fearful, and in every way, excessive, parents. Every child's illness was serious; every one was an emergency. No matter what was the matter with the child, the parent wanted him or her to have a dose of antibiotics.

In the clinics Garven saw dozens upon dozens of children with upper respiratory illnesses (URIs). By decree, every child who presented with a fever or a URI had to have a complete blood count (CBC) to rule out a blood dyscrasia. Every once in a while a child would appear in hematology clinic with a case of leukemia that had been missed by his LMD because his or her symptoms and signs were of a URI but were caused by the underlying leukemia. In their busy practices, the pediatricians could not get a CBC on every patient, and the occasional one slipped through the cracks. Then the faculty and house staff would sneer at the LMD as if the very label was rightfully pejorative. LMDs were the lowest form, too dumb to make a medical school diagnosis. The message got through to the house staff and the students. They were not about to have to wear an LMD dunce cap by missing a leukemia.

Real leukemics were a tremendous amount of work. They had to have IVs; they swelled up; they caught every opportunistic infection. Their parents anguished and pleaded with the doctors and nurses for some sort of solace. There was really none to give. There were no medicines or surgeries available to treat the children. The kids had to undergo painful sternal bone marrow punctures, venipunctures, lumbar punctures, and changes of their IVs. Garven thought he had died and gone to hell when he did his rotation on the pediatric oncology service. His observation was that cancer in children was all but uniformly and miserably fatal. The counter from the faculty was that they could not afford to give up; they worked on finding causes and cures for the terrible diseases of childhood; and somehow, they would persist and finally prevail. Dr. Hathaway went so far as to predict that one day they would see children who lived fifteen years from the time they were diagnosed as having leukemia. Garven thought it would be more like 'when hell freezes over'.

CHAPTER
Twenty-Two

The family of one of Garven's classmates in medical school, Gordon Fitzpatrick, lived in Phoenix within walking distance of the center. Garven was issued a standing invitation to come to their house "anytime" for a chance to catch up on the newspapers, current events and gossip, and to see the occasional TV show.

It was there that he became a fan of the new cartoon by an illustrationist named Charles Schultz called "*Peanuts*." He identified with the main character, Charlie Brown, who was continually being taken advantage of, who was the eternal optimist despite his girl friend Lucy's fiendish habit of sweeping the football aside every time Charlie Brown came to make a place kick. On the radio, over a game of cards, Garven learned that American Airlines was announcing same-day service across the United States east to west and west to east on a Boeing 707. He and the family had marveled at the modern age, and his friend's father had described excruciating cross country trips of his day in contrast.

It was there that Garven learned that Truman relieved General MacArthur of his command of the troops in Korea in April of 1951 and rekindled Garven's anticommunist zeal. He remained unshakably convinced that Truman was either an outright pinko communist or was an unwitting tool in the communist empire's hands. He learned of the political conventions' selections of Eisenhower and Nixon on the Republican ticket and Adlai E. Stevenson, a socialist, and John J. Sparkman, an Alabaman, on the Democratic Party ticket. He watched the silly antics of Lucille Ball and Dezi Arnaz on the *I Love*

Lucy show and enjoyed with unabashed enthusiasm the heroic adventures of Roy Rogers and Dale Evans and the magnificent horse, Trigger.

There were 3.8 million TV sets in the United States; 9 percent of homes bragged of having a set. Garven enjoyed TV as a diversion, but knew that the silliness of Lucy, the 'Raslin' matches, and the limits of human creativity would keep the medium a novelty, and probably a short lived one at that. At any rate, Garven Wilsonhulme had more important things to think about.

During the second to the last week of the 1954-55 academic year, Garven scored his first single-handed triumph of medicine. It was a feat of diagnosis and perseverance, of fulfilling pleasure and self-satisfaction; and, perhaps most importantly for Garven's specific personality, an achievement of undiminished one-upmanship.

He was assigned to the pediatric rotation in the emergency room. The triage desk screened out the vast majority of minor colds, childhood exanthems, and clinic follow-ups; so, most of the cases were genuine emergencies; or, at least, genuinely sick kids. He saw all of the kids first, then the intern checked him off or referred the problem on to the resident when he was unsure or admitted the child to the ward. It was a week of flu epidemic and an overflow of patients with gastrointestinal upsets and URIs filtered through the ER to the annoyance of the intern who had to see every child whether they were 'really sick or not'. It was his next to the last week in his clerkship; he had no intention whatever of going into pediatrics; and he would never be happy until he was able to be back in the real world of internal medicine, surgery, and big people.

A little boy was brought into Garven's cubicle in the emergency room with an obvious cold. He was shaking and fussy. Garven examined him—four years old, listless, crying, nasal passages congested—typical URI. He was about to get him signed off when he became aware of a few purplish blotches on the child's skin. The little boy was the blackest child Garven had ever seen, and the blotches were obscured by lack of contrast. He picked the child up, and the boy tensed and let out a scream.

"He always been a screamer," the boy's mama said. "Don't you pays him no mind, doctah. Ah kin see that y'all ah verah busy. Ah'all take him home and put a plaster on his chest. Ifen he acts up, Ah'all just whup him one so's he be good."

"Have you noticed any stiff neck on little..." Garven looked down the admitting sheet for the boy's name. "Little Andrew?"

"No Ah ain't doctah. He jist have a little cold in his chest and nose. Ain't no big thang." she answered.

"Anyone else sick in your house?"

"Nope, nobody."

"Anyone with the pneumonia or black lung or meningitis?"

"Nevah had anyone with any of those thangs. Y'all doan thank Andrew could has the smilin' mighty Jesus, does ya?"

"To tell the truth, Mrs. Pinkston, I do have a suspicion of that," Garven said guardedly.

He did not want to panic her, and he did not want to appear to be a wet-behind-the-ears-medical-student-zealot who sees serious disease behind every sniffle.

"O-o-oh, Laudy, Laudy, massa, tell me it ain't so, doctah. It cain't be so. This little boah nevah done nothin' wrong in his whole life. We ah good Christian people. Doan deserve the smilin' mighty Jesus, no way."

"Don't get upset, Mrs. Pinkston, I'll check it with Dr. Specialist."

That was the standard name for the house staff by the medical students. The very sound of it was magic to the untrained ears of most of the uneducated clientele—the great unwashed—who streamed through the ER and the indigent clinics.

Garven brought the intern to see the patient. Dr. Patton did a three minute physical, found the URI signs, and thought Garven had an overactive imagination when it came to the purplish blotches. He signed off on the diagnosis of URI.

"C'mon, Garven, they're backing up on us. We'll be here all night."

That was true for Garven no matter how many patients he saw or how rapidly. Garven remained uneasy.

He said to Mrs. Pinkston, "Ma'am, your little one probably has nothing more than a bad cold or the flu, but I care about him, and I'm kinda worried. I'd like you to stay here with him for a while, maybe an hour or two; so, I can watch him. Okay?"

"Okay, you is the doctah," the tired woman said.

Her weary weather-beaten face was a topographical map of fear and sadness.

She patiently took her seat in the middle of the hoard of screaming children and exhausted mothers. Garven had the lab draw a CBC, and for good measure, had a chest x-ray done. He lost track of the child in the welter of confusion and pressure of the emergency room.

When he took a breather an hour later, he caught up on the lab tickets that had collected in his in-box. There was an x-ray report on Andrew Pinkston.

"Normal Chest." He rummaged down through the pile and found the CBC. The findings leaped out at him. "WBC: 20,000", four times normal! The differential cell count of the white blood cells read: "All PMNs, strong shift left." The little boy had his blood full of infection fighting pus cells, so many that there were a lot of immature cells. The bone marrow was working overtime, and it was fighting a bacterial disease, not a viral URI.

Garven sought out Andrew and his mother. She was sagging with exhaustion. Little Andrew was limp as a wet wash cloth. He tapped on the mother's shoulder.

"Mrs. Pinkston," he said softly.

The tired woman worked to focus her eyes on him.

"Oh, ain't you the doctah what waited on us. Ain't you nice to come back."

"I think Andrew may have a serious infection, Mrs. Pinkston. I think we need to do a lumbar puncture."

"What's that?"

"A spinal tap."

"Whafo?"

"I'm afraid he might have an infection in his spinal fluid."

He did not dare to say meningitis because of the horrendous portent the word held.

She was surprisingly calm.

"Y'all mean the smilin' mighty Jesus doan ya?"

"I don't know for sure," he said. "But I think we better find out."

She was crying softly. It was one more misery in a life full of disappointments, inconveniences, and deprivations. Garven looked into the face of despair.

"It's very hahd, doctah. Ah doan know what all his fathah would say; he cain't git here. He works for the city, works alla time. What am I suppos' ta do?"

She lowered her face to her hands.

Garven sat beside her. The sea of black and brown faces turned towards him. He put his arm around her shoulders.

"I'm his doctor. I will do everything in my power to help him. You need to trust me."

The people around him—the humblest of the humble—had never seen a white man convey tenderness to a person of color. They were touched.

Garven had one little problem. He had never done a lumbar puncture. He had seen a few, but that was a far cry from doing one. The other little problem was that he would have to have his intern agree, and Dr. Patton was so conservative, that that might not be forthcoming. He put the child down on the examining table and had the mother take off his clothes. The little fellow was clammy; his skin was now flaming hot. He had developed hundreds of little blood spots on his blue-black skin; some were coalescing into patchy collections under the skin. Garven set off to find the intern. Dr. Patton was off someplace to supper, the nurses told him.

"Where's Tom Atkinson?" he asked, referring to the ER resident.

"In the trauma room, got a train wreck in there," they told him.

They were speaking of a man who had fallen off a roof, sustained several fractures, and a ruptured spleen—a veritable "train wreck."

Dr. Atkinson did not have time to help a med student with a little LP.

Garven headed back towards Andrew and his mother feeling a little panicked. He asked the nurse to bring a pedi LP tray.

"You gonna do a spinal tap, Garven?" the nurse asked.

Her eyebrows were raised.

"Yeah, I really think this kiddo might have meningitis. Will you help me?"

The girl was only a nurses' aide, a Negro girl fresh out of the trade tech nurses' aide course. She looked around and confirmed her assumption that there was no one else.

"I guess so," she said with a conspicuous note of insecurity in her voice.

She had never seen the procedure done before. Fat lot of help she was going to be, she thought.

Oliver Wendall Harralsen walked across the ER hallway on his way to the second floor stairway. It was the shortcut to the surgical ward. Garven saw the neurosurgeon in his peripheral vision, and a ray of hope shot through his brain.

"Dr. Harralsen," he called at the top of his voice.

The message carried even above the background din of the emergency center.

"Hi, Garven, how goes it?" Dr. Harralsen called acknowledging the friendly greeting.

He wanted to get on with his work and get home to see the baseball game on TV.

"Hold up, please," Garven shouted.

He ran over to the staff man.

"I have a real problem, Dr. Harralsen, and I need your help."

"What's the trouble?" Dr. Harralsen asked.

Garven told him. He apologized for the possibility that he might be overreacting, particularly since the little boy did not even have a stiff neck, but he told the neurosurgeon that he needed his help to do a lumbar puncture anyway.

"Look, Garven. Lots of kids with very bad meningitis are just too sick to have a stiff neck. The pallor, fever, and hemorrhages in his skin sounds like the Waterhouse-Friederichsen Syndrome of meningococcal meningitis. You have made the right decision. There is a good neurosurgical dictum you ought to remember, 'If you even suspect meningitis, you need to do an LP'. Let's go get it done."

Garven heaved a mighty sigh of relief. He had broken into a bad smelling nervous sweat over the little Negro boy. The child did not flinch when Dr. Harralsen had the nurses' aide roll him on his side and into a ball so that his back stood out like a mad cat. He was complimentary to the nervous girl, and she responded with a genuine effort to please the attending staff doctor. Garven made a mental note of that little lesson.

Dr. Harralsen set up the tray and talked to Garven about the equipment and the procedure. He had Garven swab the lower spine with iodine solution, then encouraged him to instill a little local anesthetic.

"Most neuros don't bother with the procaine; but trust me, you'll get better cooperation and get more one-stick procedures if you do," Dr. Harralsen instructed.

He was the quintessence of calm. Garven's heart was thundering.

"Hold the needle with two hands, like this," the neurosurgeon showed Garven. "Now, stick it right in the midline. Try and keep it perfectly straight both up and down and side to side. That's it."

Garven felt bone with the needle tip. He withdrew the needle part way and looked at Dr. Harralsen. The little boy never flinched.

"Aim at a slightly more superior angle. That's better."

Garven felt the needle slide through the tissues of the small back unimpeded. It came to a firm but not hard surface.

"Take out the cannula; let's have a look," directed the senior surgeon.

Garven withdrew the cannula very carefully. Too slowly. But the neurosurgeon was patient.

"Nothing. Go ahead. Push it in a little more. You'll feel a little 'pop', and then you're in. After a while you'll get used to the feel."

Garven did as he was instructed, felt the 'pop', a rather satisfying, albeit faint, bit of sensation. This time when he started to withdraw the cannula, Dr. Harralsen stopped him.

"Put in the manometer, first. Get the pressure. The pedipods and the neurology nerds never do it, but now is the only time you can ever get an accurate CSF pressure. You don't want anyone to think you are a pedipod, do you?"

Of course, Garven did not want any such thing; so, he inserted the manometer and watched the fluid climb rapidly up its hollow center.

"What's the reading?"

"Two hundred fifty millimeters," Garven replied eyeballing the meniscus of the fluid column. "Give or take a couple."

"Okay, get some fluid for the lab. Let's do our own smear."

The fluid was almost the color and consistency of milk.

"So, what's the diagnosis, Garven?" asked his mentor.

"Well, I never saw CSF before; but I think it's supposed to be clear."

"Should be crystal clear. Just like water," said Dr. Harralsen.

"So Andrew has meningitis," Garven said with finality. "I'll get this to the lab, then when the results come back, I'll check him off and start treatment."

"Wrong," said Dr. Harralsen.

His face had taken on a more serious expression.

Garven looked at the neurosurgeon questioningly. He was sure about the diagnosis.

"Forget about the lab results. They will only confirm your obvious clinical diagnosis. You might get busy; the lab might lose the sample. In any case, it will waste time. This is a true medical emergency. Get on with it. Let's get an IV started and get some penicillin into him," said Dr. Harralsen.

Garven understood and complied. He got the nurses' aide to fetch two more nurses. One he dispatched to the lab, and the other he set to work getting the penicillin. He and the aide put in the IV. That, in and of itself, was a fairly significant feat. The sick little boy's veins were minuscule. It took Garven two tries, but he was finally successful. In ten minutes, penicillin was coursing down the IV tubing and into Andrew's veins.

Dr. Harralsen said, "Good work, Garven. You're good with your hands. Not a bad head either. You ought to think about neurosurgery. We need the best and the brightest. You going to work for me this summer, again?"

"You bet," Garven said.

He did not need any further convincing about neurosurgery. He knew he had a bad case of hero worship, but he also knew that his admiration for the neurosurgeon had not clouded his judgment. He was clear about his own interests.

He and the doctor smeared out the purulent cerebrospinal fluid and Gram stained it. The oil immersion microscopic image confirmed the fact of the infection and the characteristic Gram negative diplococci that looked like the flat sides of biscuits stuck together—Neisseria meningitidis. The diagnosis was firm. They plated some out on chocolate agar and put the plate in a high humidity 36°C ER lab incubator.

Garven called the resident on the ward and told him about Andrew. The resident was none too happy that Garven had bypassed the entire chain of command and told him so. Nothing could put a damper on the feeling of elation Garven had. He knew he had saved that little boy. He had learned another important medical lesson: don't let the bureaucracy or anything else stand in the way of taking care of your patient. If nothing else, a doctor was an indomintable advocate for his or her patient. He was grateful to the neurosurgeon for that pearl.

Andrew was well the next morning, and his mother was weepingly grateful. Though tired, she looked alive again. His father worked the late shift; so, he was able to be with his boy that morning. He was a huge, powerfully muscled man, as black skinned as his son. He had strong black eyes and a serious, intelligent face. He was dressed in Maricopa County Refuse Control bib overalls.

"Ah wants to thank ya'll for what ya'll done done for my little boah. He's the onliest one Ah gots, an he is mighty precious to me. Ah owes ya, doctah. Ah thanks ya frum the bottom of ma heart!"

That was pay enough. Garven knew what it felt like to be a doctor. It had to be better than saving souls like the preachers did, or countries like the politicians did. 'Ah thanks ya frum the bottom of ma heart!', coming from a genuine man was a thing to remember.

Garven told the parents that Andrew would have to stay in the hospital several days because,

"He had the Waterhouse-Friederichsen Syndrome, and that's very serious. Understand?"

The father and mother nodded. As Garven left the waiting room, he overheard Andrew's father explaining to the rest of the family that Andrew had the "Westinghouse Refrigerator Sickness, and Dr. Specialist was going to take the best care of him. We all gots to pray for our Andrew and fo' the doctah."

CHAPTER
Twenty-Three

The summer of 1955 was a good one for Garven. He had ended the junior medical school academic year with good grades—all 'A's and had started the summer with a good job in the lab. He and Dr. Harralsen had kicked around a number of hypotheses about the function of their SupraPineal Arachnoid Body—such as its erectile tissue swelling up to form a mass that compressed the internal cerebral veins to control blood flow, and secretion of a hormone with as yet an unknown function. They were not much further along than René Descartes and his 'seat of the soul' theory in practicality. Since, of all the species they had studied, goats had the largest SPAB, they decided to use them exclusively. Another advantage was that they were cheap. The lack of a clear-cut working hypothesis made for a considerable amount of empty spaces in his day, and Garven was having a restful summer.

Because he had finished a year of clinical work at the medical school, Garven was eligible to do some hospital work in the city. The private hospitals of Phoenix, lacking house staff of their own, were eager to hire cheap "doctor" labor. Medical students were considered legal as long as their work was supervised by a licensed M.D. and their orders were countersigned by a staff doctor. Garven was fairly desperate for money; so, he got himself a night job at St. Catherine's Hospital. St. C's was a Catholic institution that had originally been called St. Catherine's Lying-in Hospital because of its emphasis on obstetrics, and that characteristic of the hospital had not changed. For Garven, one of the best things about the summer job was that he was paid almost as much as a nurse. His level of nutrition went up, but he still could not afford a social life.

As a matter of reality, there was very little supervision by staff doctors in his moonlighting job. Garven was surprised, pleased, and more than a little insecure with his sudden assumption of responsibility. At St. C's he was not a second class citizen. Many of the nurses did not know whether he was a student, a resident, or a young physician just starting in practice. They were so busy that they did not care, either; so long as the moonlighter did the work. St. C's had a moderately affluent clientele with far less serious illness than Garven was used to seeing at the university hospital. The ER was busy with minor fractures, lacerations, colds, bellyaches, headaches, and nervousness. After ten in the evening, Garven was the only doctor on the premises.

It was incumbent on him to learn fast. On his first night, the floor nurse called for a sleeper for Mrs. Thompson, a stool softener for the gall bladder in 256, something for pain for eighty-six year old Sister Agnes who was a post op radical mastectomy. Garven had brought a copy of the *House Officer's Handbook* with him to work; and after a pause, while he hurriedly rifled through the appropriate pages of that peripheral brain, he was able to respond appropriately. After a couple of nights, he had established a few favorite drugs and had verified with residents and interns at the university the dosages. He became comfortable with his routine, learned a few tricks from the nurses, and accumulated experience in general medicine. It was not until he had been there for a month that he ran into his first problem.

The night started slightly off key for Garven. He found four H&Ps waiting for him; they should have been done by the man whose place he was taking. He had wanted to watch *This is Your Life*, with Ralph Edwards, on the TV before starting to work, but there was too much to do. One of the patients turned out to be a beautiful and voluptuous woman who was scheduled to have a cone biopsy of her cervix the following morning. Her pap smear had turned out very suggestive, and a small biopsy of the cervix had been inconclusive for cancer. She was a fun loving vivacious woman who liked to display her charms in a teasing way. Ordinarily, Garven was not at all susceptible. He, like the vast majority of other students and doctors, had a reaction to the examination situation that automatically turned off that part of his brain that controlled desire and fantasizing.

The difficulty with this woman was that she wore a filmy nightgown with a neck line that made chest examination difficult. Garven's mistake was in being in a rush and failing to have the nurses put the patient into a back opening, dowdy patient gown. Another problem came from the nurses being too busy to stand-by during the examination. Finally, Garven was wearing a scrub suit without underwear, as he always did to prevent getting bodily fluids on the scrubs and through to his own underwear when he worked in the emergency room.

He had to fumble with the neckline to perform the breast examination. It was more like groping in the back seat of a car than his usual pristine professional technique, and he had to press close to the woman's warm body to get the job done. To his humiliation, he developed an erection and had to flex his middle to keep the lump from showing. Finally, he had had to turn away and get control of himself which made the patient laugh. He was embarrassed and more than a little disgruntled with himself for his failure to maintain his dignity during the exam by the time he was done.

He was in a bad mood when Mrs. Jacobsen, the night charge on OB called. Ordinarily, he did not have to deal with the obstetrics patients because their attendings took care of them from the time they entered in labor until the baby was safely delivered. Except for the occasional call for a sleeper, a renewal of the pain meds, or a laxative, they tended to leave him alone.

"Dr. Wilsonhulme."

"We have a big time problem up here, Doctor. We have a Mrs. Stenger with a major cephalopelvic disproportion and can't deliver her baby. Her attending—Jackson—wants you to come up and help."

"Do a C section?" Garven asked.

That was a rarity in that Catholic hospital, and even more rare for the obstetrician to call in a doctor assistant. Usually the nurses handled all of the assisting.

"No, something else. Come on up. Jackson'll tell you."

"Okay," Garven said. "Be right up."

It was inconvenient because he still had one H&P, late rounds, and several patients waiting in the ER. He dutifully went directly to the delivery rooms.

"Glad you're here," Dr. Jackson said as soon as Garven found the right room.

There were several nurses and more than the usual amount of paraphernalia in the crowded room. The patient was in the standard lithotomy position draped for a vaginal delivery.

"Hi, I'm Garven Wilsonhulme. What's up?" Garven said by way of quick introduction.

"Ted Jackson," the graying portly obstetrician said.

His hands were gloved; so, he did not offer to shake with Garven.

"We have a bad baby here. Head is all the way down, too late for a C Section; and anyway, it would be inappropriate under the circumstances."

"What's the matter with the baby?"

"Scrub up, and come over and have a feel. It's obvious," Dr. Jackson said.

Garven did as he was bidden.

He did the vaginal exam and found the expected full dilatation and efface-ment of the cervix. The woman was having regular hard contractions, but nothing productive was happening.

"I'm not sure what I'm feeling," Garven said.

His OB experience was very limited, and this was decidedly unusual.

"What do you think that is?" asked Dr. Jackson.

"I think I can feel a soft spot of the baby's head," Garven said as he exam-ined the open cervix one more time.

"Fontanel," corrected the obstetrician.

"Right, sorry, fontanel," Garven corrected himself. "Anyway, that can't all be head, can it?"

"I'm afraid so. That's while it feels so weird. The head is three or four times normal size."

"Oo-ooh, hydrocephalus," Garven said, pleased with himself for remem-bering the term.

"Yeah, we have a water head here, the worst possible, too, I think. I think we have anencephaly—just a big bag of water instead of a brain. It's a real tragedy."

The doctor was making no effort to keep his voice down. Garven was con-cerned that the poor woman in labor would hear, and it showed on his face.

Dr. Jackson caught his expression.

"Don't worry about Mrs. Stenger. I've told her all about it. Thank God she's not a Catholic. I'm sorry, Garven, you a Catholic?"

"No."

He was wondering what religion had to do with it.

"Good, because we have to do something altogether unCatholic, and I need your help."

"That's why I'm here," Garven said.

His curiosity was piqued, and a little alarm bell was tinkling in the back of his mind.

"We have to destroy the baby to get it out," Dr. Jackson said flatly and without any softening lead-in euphemisms.

"Whew!" Garven said.

He was not ready for this.

"Whoa. How come? Why not a C Section? You sure the baby won't come vaginally?"

"She's been in labor for thirty-six hours. The baby's head is just too big. It's too low for a C Section now; anyway, that's too much to go through for a vegetable baby or a dead one."

That was about the starkest picture Garven had ever faced. This was the most terrible decision he had seen in medicine so far. He did not like being in this position. OB was supposed to be fun—happy parents, cute baby, all that.

"Boy," Garven said. "That's a lot to chew on. What about the sisters? I see what you were getting at about the Catholic thing. Will the nuns give an okay?"

"Garven..." Dr. Jackson said softly, almost reproachfully. "You know better than that. They think the mother ought to be sacrificed; save the baby at all costs. They will have a hyssy fit if they find out. I'm going to see to it that they don't find out."

"What about the nurses?"

"Protestants. I know these gals. You and I don't have to worry about them."

Garven took note of how it was 'we' and 'us', not 'I' when Dr. Jackson spoke of medical responsibility for this thing he was proposing.

"It's the only way?" Garven asked.

"Only way."

"Okay, I'll help. I will probably regret it, but I'll help," Garven said.

"You catch the baby; I'll do the deed," said the obstetrician.

He did not look as if he felt overly distressed. He wore an expression of professional resignation. It was just something that had to be done.

Dr. Jackson took a huge long needle, like the biggest spinal tap needle from a nightmare, attached it to a 50 cc luerlock tip syringe, and made sure that it was locked in place. He then inserted his fingers into the vagina taking care to keep the sharp tip from touching the vaginal wall. He made sure of the position of the anencephalic monster baby's head then inserted the needle deep into the cystic cranial cavity. He withdrew over a liter of crystal clear spinal fluid in 50 cc aliquots which Garven, in his role as assistant, discarded.

"There," Dr. Jackson said when finally the withdrawn fluid started to show a little pink tinge of blood. "The head has collapsed. I am holding the fetus in the uterus now. When I withdraw the needle, it will shoot out. You catch it, okay?"

"Okay," Garven said.

He guessed that he was ready. He felt very tense. He had yet to deliver a baby the regular way and now this. It was a baptism by fire.

"Go ahead," he said with as much assurance as he could muster.

Dr. Jackson whisked the needle out with a deft smooth motion; Mrs. Stenger chose that moment to have a mighty contraction. The baby came whooshing down the birth canal with a rush of bloody mucoid fluid. Garven caught it as best he could. It was perversely slippery. It was all he could do not to drop the dead infant onto the floor. The baby was grossly malformed. Its head was the size of a tennis ball, and the top had imploded into the shape of a bowl. It had a cleft lip and pallet; both arms were so malformed that they looked as if they had been amputated at the elbows, and the fingers were rudimentary giving the limbs the appearance of being flippers. Garven turned his head away. He felt very nauseated. The lesson of that night was a concrete one: Obstetrics was not for him.

The baby was listed as a stillborn, nothing more. Dr. Jackson comforted the grieving mother and cautioned her and everyone else that this was not an event they could talk about. When Garven was questioned by the priest-administrator a couple of nights later, he said he had seen nothing out of the ordinary, no complications of the delivery other than that the deformed baby was born dead. The priest looked at him as if he did not believe what Garven was telling him; but there was also a look of relief on the man's face. No one wanted the circumstances of that delivery publicized. Garven, for a brief moment, thought that this may have been his second murder. But he rationalized that the death of Stanford's Dr. Simpkins did not really count.

Later, Garven heard rumors around the hospitals that Dr. Jackson was the city's clandestine abortionist. It was hard for Garven to think that any doctor could do such a thing; but several doctors with whom he discussed the subject of abortion concurred that while it was a loathsome business, they were going to be done; and every city had its one good clean abortionist. Ted Jackson was the one for Phoenix and was really a very moral man, Garven was told by several doctors and nurses. Every city had its dirty little secret regarding abortion, and Ted Jackson was the one for Phoenix.

Garven could not get rid of the feeling that, no matter how the idea was rationalized, the fetuses slated for abortion were living people, only as yet unde-livered into the breathing world. From the moment of conception, they were possessed of every element possessed by a neonate. Abortion was murder, no matter how justified the excuse for doing it might seem. He heard arguments for abortion for rape, incest, and to get rid of the shame of an unmarried preg-nancy. They all came down to murder in Garven's book. He had seen and par-ticipated in the only justifiable abortion he imagined he was every going to.

The Catholic doctors warned him that abortion for rape or incest, if per-mitted legally, would lead to abortion for convenience and a sort of perverse birth control. They made the ludicrous prediction that half a million or more abortions would be done if the procedure were to be allowed. Legalized abortion would lead to a desensitization towards promiscuity, the destruction of the fiber of family life, a weakening of the conviction that life is sacred, to infanticide and euthanasia, they asserted. Euthanasia would lead to depravity and eventual anarchy. Garven did not know what to think about all of that; he was convinced that they were being overly dramatic, and that the country would never allow anything like the wholesale abortions the Catholics fretted about. But he felt an innate sense of repulsion about abortion and towards those who performed them. He steered clear of Dr. Ted Jackson ever afterwards.

Dr. Harralsen came up with the break-through idea about how to investigate the STAB.

"What if it has an entirely different kind of hormonal action, Garven?" he asked rhetorically. "I've been thinking about it. It has cells consistent with gland function; maybe it secretes something that keeps us young and involutes in time allowing old age to take over. Or maybe it secretes a hormone that combats or helps to contain cancer. Whatever, let's get the biochemists to look it over. We'll collect some fresh specimens for their analysis. They can get us some extracts, and we can try it out on rats, see what happens to them."

Garven had something to contribute.

"One of the pathologists has grown a strain of rats that get brain tumors, more than half of them. We could use it on the ones with the tumors and have those without the cancers as controls."

"Huumm. I think you may just have something there. Maybe that head of yours does more than keep your ears apart. Can you work on getting us some of the rats? I'll give the biochemists a purpose in life."

"I'll get on it today."

At least it was something purposeful to do in the lab besides drinking coffee and listening to ball games.

By the end of the summer, they had an extract, presumably a fairly crude one; and they started giving it to rats. The rodents with the tumors seemed to remain more active, and some of those sacrificed several weeks after receiving the extract appeared to have smaller tumors. The summer season ended with the start of Garven's senior year in medical school and before the project could be followed long enough to get any definite and reproducible results. Dr. Harralsen was too busy building his clinical university neurosurgery practice, and he had to shelve the study for the time being.

168

CHAPTER
Twenty-Four

As a junior-year clinical extern rotating on the medicine service, Garven started on obstetrics and gynecology that fall while the rest of his class divided up into sections going to the psychiatry services and to the surgical and medical subspecialties. He counted himself lucky to have avoided the quarter's first brouhaha. A surgery service intern, who failed to recognize that Dr. Cartral was essentially the fourth member of the godhead, misunderstood the significance of the venerable daily rounds. Medical rounds were conducted by Dr. Maxwell Cartral, the man himself, who always walked first, followed closely, in single file, by the staff, then the residents, then the interns, then the students in a rank order as carefully adhered to as the protocol at a state dinner. Dr. Cartral held full sway. When he spoke, it was *ex cathedra*—right from the lips of the pope; and people listened. To make sure there was no interruption to the flow of wisdom from the great professor's mouth, an intern was assigned to walk ahead in order to open the upcoming doors. Dr. Cartral and his entourage then swept through with the scintillating conversation uninterrupted.

The habit pattern had become so ingrained that Dr. Cartral took the door opening entirely for granted. He did not deign to look ahead for obstacles, and had the intern not been fully responsible, the eminent professor would have walked right into a closed door. The surgery intern, a man who had gone to medical school elsewhere, and thus perhaps had not been able to become fully imbued with the grandeur of the procession or the luster of the eminence at its head. Nor, apparently, did he understand who could be and who could not be the butt of a joke.

It was his day to hold open the doors for the head of medicine—the *eminence rouge*—for the *eminence grises*, and for the lesser lights of the procession. He did not take the task seriously despite careful instruction by the chief resident. As the entourage swept onto the geriatric floor, young Dr. Kirkpatrick efficiently opened the doors and let Dr. Cartral and about six others walk into the broom closet. Then he closed the door and stepped quickly to the back of the line. The practical joke was not well received, and there very shortly became a marked increase in the amount of work that fell to the residents and interns. The medical service house staff was one man short; Dr. Kirkpatrick returned to the surgery service where he belonged. There was a great deal of teeth gnashing and expressed pain, but the episode was the stuff of legend; and Garven wished secretly that he could have been the perpetrator (and could have gotten away with it.) However, he observed that he was getting a great deal more cautious in his old age (twenty-four).

The senior year was characterized by several changes. There was considerable independence in choice of clinical services because it was impossible for any one medical student to spend time on them all. Only psychiatry and obstetrics were mandatory. Secondly, post graduation plans became a consuming interest. Fall quarter was the time to make application to the National Intern Matching Plan, a program started three years before, in 1952, to bring order and common decency to a previously chaotic and cliff-hanger quality method of choice of internships by students and hospitals. Prior to the matching program, students applied willy-nilly to the hospitals of their choice with the most sought after hospitals being able to wait their own sweet time to get the young doctor with the most potential, as they judged him or her. Students reneged on their commitments to lesser hospitals when the more prestigious ones made a belated offer of a position. That meant that all of the potential interns and most of the nation's hospitals simply had to bide their time, and hope that the nation's medical school seniors would finally filter out to fill the slots available across the country.

With the matching plan, students made application to several hospitals in the fall and their academic record was sent only to those hospitals. In the late winter and very early spring, the students were interviewed by the hospitals, then in the spring the students and the hospitals listed their preferences from most to least preferred and submitted that official list to a central office.

Computers that filled whole buildings whirred and matched students and hospitals with the one highest choice possible on their list, and the hospital offered the student a position.

Garven submitted a list of ten hospitals, some of the names learned from scuttlebutt from other students; and, more importantly in his case, from Dr. Harralsen who suggested hospitals with good programs of neurosurgery. It was more than common sense to expect that Garven's chances of getting a neurosurgery residency would be improved by being a known quantity in the hospital where he most wanted to train. He had made a firm decision to pursue brain surgery, and Dr. Harralsen's recommendations carried the most sway.

Garven sent off a letter of application to Harvard—the Massachusetts General Hospital—even though the neurosurgery program was not felt to be all that good by the neurosurgeons Garven queried. Virtually every student in the U.S. applied to the Mass General on the off chance that he or she would be picked by the most prestigious of all training programs. Garven's other choices—his real choices—in order of preference in his mind at that point, were: University of Texas, Southwestern Medical School in Dallas (Parkland Hospital), University of California (Los Angeles Osterlund Memorial Hospital), state university hospitals in Minnesota, Texas (Houston), Pennsylvania, Cornell, Stanford, and Utah. He applied to the Seventh Day Adventist school in San Bernadino, California (White Memorial Hospital) only because he had heard that anyone could get in there and could get a residency, not a good one, but a neurosurgery residency nonetheless; and he wanted a bit of insurance. He set about to do his work on obstetrics while he waited for the formal application materials to come in.

Obstetrics and gynecology was a peculiar career field to Garven's way of thinking. In a specialty that served women, it was the nearly exclusive province of male physicians. You either liked it or not, and Garven did not like it. His fingers were too short to be able to do a vaginal examination well and reliably enough to reach the ovaries. In fat women, he had no choice; and found himself faking the findings most times and worrying about some woman sometime coming up with an abdominal, or especially an ovarian mass, that he had missed. The women in the indigent clinics were all too often very obese and very unclean. Their diseases, even their normal functions were messy and smelly. He found himself in daily dread of going to "dirty-bottom" clinic.

Garven was celibate for the time being, more by lack of opportunity and the press of his busy life than by any overriding moral consideration. The experience on gynecology might have been enough to turn him off women altogether; and indeed, he adopted a rather diffident, almost clinical attitude towards women as a result of the exposure to the specialty.

Women came in with purulent Vaginoses—bad smelling, itching and damp. They presented with their bottoms drooping—pelvic floor laxity with the cervix visible in the lower vagina. Others had the putrid green pus of gonorrhea for him to see and complained of severe abdominal pain from their pelvic inflammatory disease (PID). They had lumps, e.g. Bartholin's cysts, and bumps, e.g. condyloma acuminata—venereal warts, that disfigured their most private parts. Garven had to learn to separate himself from the nakedness he saw constantly, not because of any tendency to prurient interest or arousal; but to allow himself to hope to be allured by a woman some day in the future. Garven was a convinced celibate during his gyn—pronounced 'gin'—rotation.

The thing Garven disliked most about the specialty of treating the diseases of women, however, was their emotional response to their problems, real and imagined. Some of them misinterpreted the necessities of the finger examination as personal; some of them were aroused, some frightened, some made indignant, and Garven had to contend with all of those feelings and responses which only prolonged an examination that should have been brief and perfunctory. He could do a normal pelvic examination, the bimanual and speculum exams and a Pap smear and include the breast exam in about three minutes if he did not have to talk to them. Talking to the women was the worst part of the whole thing to Garven as it was to most of the senior medical students.

The gyn clinic was overwhelmingly busy; there were always more women waiting for their turn in the stirrups; women complaining of honeymoon cystitis—at the age of thirteen—women with impacted tampons, women with venereal warts, women with various types of vaginitis. The interns and residents moved swiftly from woman to woman scarcely noting their existence. It was not rare to forget and leave a woman in the uncomfortable position of the pelvic exam and fail to tell her that she could get down. Occasionally, Garven and even house staff men would not only leave the woman in position, but failed to remove the vaginal speculum as well. When that happened, Garven had a stock response that worked every time.

First, the woman would holler, "Hey, doctah, this here's been in ma stuff foah more'n half a hour. Ain't it about time to git it out?"

Then Garven would return to her examining table fighting to keep a chagrined look off his face.

"You say it's been in there for thirty minutes?" he would ask.

"Yes, suh, doctah, sure has."

"Excellent," Garven would respond without hesitation, "I think the treatment is complete. You ought to feel a lot better. You can go home now. No baths for a month, and no sex for the rest of your life."

The woman would laugh with the doctor at his little joke. Garven would remove the speculum, and the woman would go home feeling better after having spent five hours in the clinic.

The saving grace on gynecology was the surgery. Garven liked the abdominal procedures—hysterectomies, appendectomies, removal of tubes and ovaries, going after sometimes absolutely huge tumors, removing portions of bowel with the reproductive organs to get out cancers, and procedures to correct incompetent pelvic floors brought on by obesity and too many pregnancies. The residents maintained their sanity by becoming proficient at doing hysterectomies, knowing that their future livelihoods depended, in large part, on that skill. Garven tried to learn the indication for doing a hysterectomy from them.

The standard answers were: "The only reason for the existence of a uterus after menopause is to grow cancer." Others, less sensitive to the emotional investment that women had in their uteri, listed the indications for hysterectomy as:

1. Presence of a uterus
2. Presence of insurance
3. Haven't done one for a while
4. Mortgage payment is due

The other half of the students' time was spent on obstetrics. Each morning, five days a week, they had a class; then they delivered babies in the indigent women's delivery rooms for the rest of the day; and when they were on call, they delivered babies all night as well. Two days a week, they took outservice call and were sent out with a nurse and a case of obstetrical tools to deliver babies of women who, for one reason or another, could not make it to the hospital. The most common reason was that the women were too poor to come up with cab fare; other reasons included simple procrastination and plain ignorance ("Ah cain't be preggers"). In the university hospital the students were more or less supervised by the OB residents; but on the outservice, they were on their own. It was a regularly humbling and often self or school imposed chastening experience to travel into the poorest sections of Phoenix.

Garven put on his white scrubs his first day on OB and very soon wondered why that color had been chosen. Every where else in the hospital the scrub suits were easy-on-the-eye green. In a matter of minutes on the service his whites were blood specked, and by the end of his shift they were completely bespattered with blood, amniotic fluid, urine, and vernix caseosa.

When he asked about the choice of color, one of the residents explained, "We are distinct, and the color sets us off. We are cleaner; so, we wear white. We have our own terms, our own ways. The color difference makes that apparent. The women of Phoenix have come to expect and to be comforted by the white color over the many years it has been used; so, it is an important tradition."

Much of what the obstetricians did and taught was 'tradition', it seemed to Garven. 'Stand this way'; 'estimate size this way'; 'use—old fashioned sedatives like—mag sulfate', 'use catgut for everything' even though the incisions always spread and left a much bigger than necessary scar; and 'always make an oblique episiotomy' even though the midline incision was safer, simpler, and much less painful. It did not take Garven long to learn to keep his mouth shut about those things he thought might have been done better. Obstetricians had a tradition to cover every eventuality, and they held those traditions in great and obstinate reverence.

There were between ten and thirty deliveries a day. The residents were completely jaded by their body and mind numbing work and were easily willing to allow the students to do the uncomplicated deliveries and to come in only when there was a problem lie (position) or dystocia (slow and difficult delivery). In a week, Garven was averaging ten or twelve deliveries a day by himself. He became quite facile with the mechanics of normal deliveries—estimating the degree of dilatation of the cervical opening and the amount of effacement or thinning of the cervical wall and learning what that meant, on the average, and the station (degree of progress into the birth canal) of delivery. Having rather short fingers, he never really trusted what his fingertips were telling him, but he could make a pretty good guess about what position the baby was in as its head pressed against the upper end of the birth canal. He hoped every time to feel the occipital fontanel (posterior soft spot) which indicated a routine vertex presentation. He was not as confident about the direction the baby was facing: Occiput, Left Anterior (OLA) Occiput, Left Posterior (OLP). His second patient failed Garven, and he took it personally. His fingers contacted the baby's chin, and Garven had to admit that he was faced with an abnormal lie and had to summon the resident. The resident handled the problem position as if it were perfectly routine.

"I was impressed," Garven told his resident. "You almost climbed up into the birth canal. You moved everything around; and then you brought that kid out like it was nothing."

"This was not very tough, Garven. Tell me, have you felt a breech presentation? Let me tell you that gets a lot tougher. You aren't sure what you are feeling when the baby's butt is the first thing your fingers touch. Then comes the hardest delivery you ever see, most times."

"Doesn't sound hard to me," Garven said with a smile.

The resident raised his eyebrows.

"Yeah, piece of cake," Garven continued. "I just call the resident. No problem."

"Unless you are on the outservice, and it happens."

"Oh, yeah," Garven said, recognizing that he might have anxious times to come.

CHAPTER
Twenty-Five

Garven's first breech birth, the first he ever encountered outside of *Williams Textbook of Obstetrics*, occurred during his fourth week as a student obstetrician in his senior year. The frightening case could have occurred during a weekday in the university hospital when everyone was rested and when the house staff, the OR, and the full complement of emergency facilities were available. It could have, but it did not. Garven was on call for the outservice when Gladys Strother went into labor with her fifth child. She was a week early; and her husband Carl, an independent trucker, was on a long haul when the surprise came. It was all Gladys could do to make the phone call.

Garven was on call with Sarah-Lee Griffith, a big, strong, no nonsense, Negro RN. who had been a midwife before getting her formal training. The only reason she had left midwifery as a profession was that the hospital pay for an RN was better. They wheeled the white delivery van, with the sign "University of Arizona Faculty of Medicine, Mobile Outservice Obstetrical Unit" emblazoned on its doors and a large red cross painted over the hood, into the poorest, meanest section of town where Gladys lived. The mother-to-be did not have an address, just a box number. The streets in the area were unapproved by the city of Phoenix or by Maricopa county, were dirt, not even gravel, and were haphazardly directed and in execrable condition. It was an area where real old-time bandits still roamed, where cops went only in pairs, and taxicabs would not go at all. The purpose of the white paint with the red cross on the truck was to identify the vehicle as one to be left alone, even protected.

The citizens and denizens of the Hatchlo Project were acutely aware that their source of emergency help was the county facilities in the form of the university hospital. As ruthless as they might be, even the bandits had a soft spot for their children, and the OB van was vital to the care of their women in labor, and therefore, their infants. No one ever molested the OB van or ambulances, night or day. Even the drug addicts who might have been tempted—being devoid of all of the rational thinking of human beings and would sacrifice their mothers if need be for a fix—left the university hospital people and their vehicles alone for fear that the people and the bandits would tear them into pieces if they interfered in the good work.

Garven and Sarah-Lee made their way through the meandering by-ways striving to locate the landmarks Gladys had described as the means of identification of otherwise unnamed and unmarked streets. They entered the Strother residence without knocking, knowing they were at the right house because of all the screaming coming from inside.

Gladys was in bed, smothered in covers. Her abdomen was huge and tense, much more so than Garven had seen in other mothers at term. He donned rubber gloves and did a quick finger examination for an initial assessment. It did not feel right. He probed around trying to locate the fontanel or the chin or a shoulder; but each time he tried, he came away with the sobering conviction that he had to be feeling the unborn infant's soft behind. Four younger children peered into the room, frightened by the noise being made by their mother.

"Check her, Sarah-Lee," Garven asked the nurse. "Something's not kosher."

Sarah-Lee put her practiced right index and third finger into place and probed for half a minute.

"Breech," she said. "We are in some luck here. She has polyhydramnios."

She looked at Garven and shook her head when he looked as if he were going to speak. She was afraid they would scare Gladys to death.

"Big bag of waters. Makes it so we can move the baby around," she whispered.

"I can't hardly get at her in the bed. What do you think about moving her?" he asked Sarah-Lee.

"Yeah. No sense ruinin' our backs doin' this," she said. "I'll get some water on to boil; so, we can clean her up. How 'bout you settin' down some papers on the kitchen table."

It was fine with Garven.

"Why the newspapers?" he asked.

"They're pert near sterile, Doc. I thought you big doctors knew all of that sort of thing."

"I'll take your word for it," Garven said and went about his work while Sarah-Lee started a teapot of water.

They carried Gladys—who was, luckily for them, quite diminutive and thin—to the kitchen table and did their best to place her in a lithotomy position. Garven had done his reading in *William's*. He listened to the fetal heart tones, still strong and rapid—160 per minute.

He reached in and moved the infant's bottom. It was not fixed in position; that was good; but the mother could not stop pushing down every time a contraction occurred; and that made things more difficult. Garven was trying to shift the baby by external version—manipulating its position with his hands on her abdomen. He could only work between contractions, and they were coming every two minutes. He moved the baby well up into the uterus but could not get it to make a full turn so that the head presented. He could not even get the baby in position so that both legs came into the birth canal as a second choice. His hands were cramping, and he was beginning to tire from the effort and the psychological strain. Sarah-Lee Griffith looked on patiently. Garven was feeling testy towards the imperturbable nurse.

Finally, Garven rotated the baby, and it made a major shift in presentation. It would not or could not proceed down into the birth canal. Now, as he did an internal examination, Garven was unsure what he was feeling, what part was presenting. He swallowed his pride and turned to Sarah-Lee.

"Okay, I give up. I can't tell what's going on now. Have a feel."

Sarah-Lee smiled and shrugged her shoulders. Behind her expression of equanimity, she had been growing nervous. They had to get this baby out. She stepped into Garven's place between Gladys' thighs. Her fingers were long and slender, and she had thin wrists. Her hands were strong and sure.

She made the examination and said, "You got a neck and shoulder here. This little one won't come out in a month of Sundays."

Sarah-Lee continued to work. Her arms moved, and she put considerable body English into it.

Finally, she did a quick vaginal exam; then, she broke out into a big smile and announced, "Got it. OLA now. Gladys, you can push to your heart's content now, girl. You are gonna have a baby any minute."

Delivery proceeded rapidly now. Shortly, the head was crowning. Gladys was yelling in pain.

"Hey, doc, how 'bout gettin' us an episiotomy done, huh?" Sarah-Lee asked.

Chapter Twenty-Five

Garven shifted into the position of the deliverer.

"Hand me some local, Sarah-Lee," he asked.

"You don't need it. Just do a midline cut with the scissors. Just a snip. She won't feel a thing."

Garven looked at the former mid-wife very questioningly. First of all, he could not see how he could cut her introitus with scissors without it hurting the woman, and second of all, he could not bring himself to make anything but an oblique episiotomy as he had been taught innumerable times.

The baby was pressing hard. Gladys was laboring. Sweat poured from her face, and her neck veins stood out in bold relief. Her arm muscles were straining from her hold on the edges of the kitchen table.

"Do it!" Sarah-Lee ordered.

The pretense of who was boss was dropped. Garven took up the scissors and made a midline snip.

"A little more, Garven. That's it," Sarah-Lee said, satisfied.

Now the baby slowly appeared.

"Don't push hard now, honey," Sarah-Lee told Gladys. "Don't want this little one to come a rushin' out. Might tear your bottom up."

Garven was carefully manipulating the head. It was all the way out, then one shoulder.

"Okay, Garven, ease that other shoulder out; so, it don't spread her too wide. Good."

Now Garven's problem was to keep the baby from squirting out. It was as slick with blood and vernix as if it had been greased. Garven juggled it as the little baby made its full appearance in the world.

"Hey, doc," Sarah-Lee said quietly. "Don't go droppin' that kiddo now. Spoil your record."

Garven got a good grip.

"Nice job, doc. You surely oughta go into OB; you got the feel for it."

Garven had believed everything the steady experienced nurse had said up to that point. Now he knew she was just shining him on, but he liked it.

Sarah-Lee took the baby and wiped it off. She laid it on Gladys' chest.

"It's another boy," burbled the exhausted woman.

She was well pleased with her work.

Sarah-Lee told Garven, "Better get that episiotomy sewed up while she's still got an anesthetic bum. Do a nice job, and throw in a good tight 'husband stitch'," she grinned at Garven who blushed.

He knew that she meant that he should tighten up the introitus or opening of the vagina for future sexual pleasure of the couple. It embarrassed him to hear it from the nurse. He was more old fashioned than he had thought.

Mrs. Strother thanked Garven and the nurse profusely, wishing she could give them more than just the verbal assurance of her gratitude.

"That's all right, Mrs. Strother. We're happy to be able to help. Look after that baby now, you hear? And have a care for yourself. No heavy work and no sex for six weeks," Garven said.

Sarah-Lee handed the new mother the birth certificate form.

"This has to be filled out and into the state in one week, okay? Don't forget."

"I don't know what to name the boy," Mrs. Strother said.

She was a simple woman used to following directions. The decision probably was beyond her.

"Why not name him after your husband?" suggested Sarah-Lee.

"Already got one of those," Gladys Strother said.

She had a somewhat defeated look. It seemed like too much effort; thinking and deciding was a very taxing business.

"How about some other man in the family, or somebody famous—you know, like George Washington?" asked Sarah-Lee, willing to make one more try.

"Don't care so much for the men folk on either side, mostly shiftless. I want to give this boy more of a start. Maybe I could name him after you, doctor," she said shyly and looked furtively at Garven.

"How about that, Garven?" asked Sarah-Lee who was controlling an insistent smile with difficulty.

Garven paused for a moment.

"I have a better suggestion. The head of our department, the man who makes all of this service possible, is named Sidney Alfred Caesar. That would be an important name. People know that name."

Mrs. Strother could tell that Garven was in earnest.

"Okay, if that's what you think. Now that I say it over in my mind; it sounds good... 'Sidney Alfred Caesar Strother'... Kinda long... But I like it. Okay. My little boy will be Sidney Alfred Caesar Strother. Thanks again."

"Our pleasure," Garven said as they left.

Once safe in the van and on the way back to the hospital, Sarah-Lee started to laugh until there were tears in her eyes. Garven did not have to ask why; he laughed with her.

"That was mean, Garven," she said between waves of laughter.

"Why mean?" Garven asked trying to hold an innocent expression.

"You know all of the residents on OB and surgery hate Caesar. He can be a real monster. They have been getting back at him for years by having the silly little mothers name their babies after him. There must be five hundred little white, black, brown, and Asian kids in Arizona with the name of Sidney Alfred Caesar Jones or Sydney Alfred Caesar Smith or Sydney Alfred Caesar McDonald. Just think of the initials of this kid—SACS. Poor little thing."

She was still laughing as they parked the truck in the hospital vehicle parking zone.

Garven took some heat from the staff about the midline episiotomy, but no one could quibble that much with success. He was warned that he was too independent for the OB service, the kind of guy who thought he could make a better mousetrap, the kind of thinking that got medical students, and doctors, for that matter, into trouble.

"I'll be watching," said Dr. Caesar, the head of OB.

CHAPTER
Twenty-Six

Garven's comeuppance for his daring-do with Gladys Strother came in the middle of the next week. A sickly Mexican woman who had crossed the border so her child could be born in the United States and thus become an automatic US citizen, was rushed by her cousins into the ER and in turn to the delivery suites. She was having a precipitate delivery. Garven was on call and rushed to her. He and the nurses cut off the woman's clothing and swabbed her with disinfectant as fast as they could. The head was already crowning. Before Garven could get a good purchase on the head, the rest of the baby came rushing out with a splash of blood, meconium, and amniotic fluid. The nurses took care of the infant who had an Apgar score of three, well below the desirable seven or eight, and the ideal of ten. Garven started to work on the mother.

He started to put in the chromic catgut sutures in the spontaneous tear in the vagina. To his horror, he saw feces in the vagina, back of the openings of either canal. Air bubbles welled up from the rectal side of the tear. She had a huge recto-vaginal tear. Garven knew when he was beyond his limits of expertise.

"Get Dr. Hansen. Right now," he ordered.

One of the LPNs left on the double.

The tear was extensive enough that the resident, Dr. Hansen, decided to take the Mexican woman to the OR and to repair the damage under general anesthetic. He shot Garven a deprecating look.

"Hold down the fort while I'm in the OR. Try not to screw anyone else up for a few minutes."

That stung. Garven was about to protest his innocence against the unfairness of the accusation. The precipitous delivery had been out of his control. But he knew he would sound petulant and immature if he did; so, he elected to keep quiet and to seethe.

It took four days for Garven to hear about the extent of his sin. When the delivery was discussed in Mortality & Morbidity (M&M) conference, and to throw salt into the wound, Garven had to present the case. Dr. Caesar gave a long and nasty lecture on the care and attention all of the university's patients deserved and how daydreaming students needed to wake up and to recognize their responsibility. There had not been the slightest question about whom the references were made, and Garven felt as low as a snake's belly in a wagon rut. After the conference, he was approached by the resident, Dr. Hansen and by Dr. Caesar himself.

As the head of the OB-Gyn department spoke, Dr. Hansen looked on with a self-righteous serpentine expression. Garven half-expected to see the man's neck inflate in a pre-strike flare.

"Young man," Dr. Caesar said. "You are at strike two. I will personally monitor your progress. One more foul-up, and I will recommend that you repeat your tour on OB. Now get out of my sight until tomorrow, then meet me in my office at six o'clock; and we will spend the day delivering babies. I will see if you have learned enough to stay on with your group."

He made a near military about face and marched off down the hall with the cobra, Dr. Hansen, in tow.

The next three days were nightmarish. Every move Garven made was scrutinized and criticized. He was brought up short for examining a post partum without having a nurse present. She had not complained; and there was no impropriety; and the nurses were always too busy; but it was Garven's turn in the barrel; and he had to take it. He gave Pitocin too soon or too late; he had the mother push when she should rest and rest when she should push; but the criticisms were all picayune; and Dr. Caesar realized that. Garven did a good job on his deliveries. He was calm and collected despite the carping criticisms; and that was not lost on the department head. He did not deign to let Garven know that he held any sense of approval of Garven's work. Only the resident, Dr. Hansen, remained friendly.

"Don't sweat it too much. We all have to take a load of crap at times in this business. Can you imagine what I went through after my first delivery? I let the infant squirt out, through my fingers, and onto the floor. You'd think I was Attila the Hun the way everybody reacted. Kiddo wasn't even hurt. Took me a year to live it down. Hang in there. 'This, too, shall pass away', as my sainted mother used to say," Dr. Hansen reassured Garven.

On the third day came the riskiest situation of all. One of Dr. Caesar's private patients came in to deliver. Beatrice St. Javier was the wife of the owner of the Camelback Inn, and nothing was spared to make her stay comfortable and free of problems. She was given her own private room. Two nurses were taken from the indigent suites to attend Mrs. St. Javier even though her needs were minimal. Her pregnancy had been uneventful, and her prenatal care had been the best the university could offer. Mrs. St. Javier was a very pleasant and undemanding woman for all the fuss that was made over her. Garven resented her, nevertheless, because he knew that the poor women would receive less than their usual barely adequate care from the overworked nursing staff. Although he did not express his negative feelings in any way, Garven nursed his ill-feelings up until the time of the delivery.

"I will deliver this baby, Mr. Wilsonhulme," Dr. Caesar said, as if Garven had expected anything else. "You might learn something about technique. And for that matter, your bedside manner could use some improvement."

There was apparently nothing he could do right. Garven had to admit to himself that his feelings towards the privileged woman may have inadvertently crept out. He would have to learn the lesson of being dispassionate and objective if he were to survive in this competitive world.

The delivery was as routine as it could possibly be until the entire head appeared out of the woman's introitus. Then Garven got the worst shock of his young life to date. The face was a monstrosity. The head was low browed and almost flat. The ears were large and flapping. There was a huge cleft lip and cleft face that extended all the way nearly to the eyes. The limbs, when the baby was all of the way out, were seen to be shortened, something like flippers. A large hole in the abdominal wall had a thin translucent membrane over it through which the intestines could be seen. The baby's cry was pitiable, sounding more like an animal's squawk than a human sound. It was a very vigorous infant for all of that congenital abnormality.

"What is it?" questioned Mrs. St. Javier when it seemed to be taking too long. She knew the baby was fully delivered.

The nurse at the recording table asked, "Apgar score, Dr. Caesar? Sounds like a ten to me."

She had not seen the baby, and wanted to do Dr. Caesar the respect of giving his baby an Apgar of ten. It was a form of brown nosing, Garven realized. He was mesmerized by the fetal monster lying in Dr. Caesar's hands. He took back all of the unpleasant thoughts he had harbored for the woman of privilege and pitied her.

"Mrs. Danielson. I will take care of the Apgars. Please see if the patient needs anything.

Garven looked at the department head's face. It was completely impassive. He could have been looking at a perfectly normal infant or a puppy or even a Christmas doll for all the emotion he displayed.

Garven started to ask Dr. Caesar something like, "Now what do we do?" but his words caught in his throat unuttered.

The obstetrician very swiftly and smoothly broke the baby's neck. It had been crying weakly, and now it was silent and limp. He covered it with a draping towel and placed it in one of the empty stainless steel instrument bowls. Garven was thunderstruck. He turned pale. Dr. Caesar glared at the medical student quickly forestalling any utterance. He looked over the drapes at the mother's expectant face.

"I have some bad news for you, Mrs. St. Javier."

"What is it, doctor?" came the sad voice.

She knew there was something amiss when no one had shown her the baby right off.

"I'm afraid the baby was born dead," Dr. Caesar said in a soft avuncular voice.

There was little else he could do to soften the blow. Garven felt as if he had been struck in the chest with the end of a six by six. Another murder. This time, he was only a witness.

"But, I thought..." stammered the mother. "Oh, how dreadful," was all she could think to say.

She had turned dead white, and her eyes had a far away look. She clutched her rosary to her chest.

The nurses swiftly removed the dead infant and cleaned up Mrs. St. Javier; so, she could be taken back to her room. Garven then watched a master at bedside manner deal with the bereaved woman and her stricken husband.

"It was for the best," Dr. Caesar said to his patient and her husband. "The baby was badly deformed. It could never have lived. It would have been in misery, would have been severely retarded, and its g-i tract would never have functioned. You are all better off this way," he convinced them. "You can try again. No reason why this should happen again. None at all. Let's get Beatrice over this; maybe go to Europe like you've been wanting to, and then try again. She's young and healthy. This sad episode will pass, and one day you'll have a healthy baby. Try not to think overmuch about it."

Later, to Garven he said only, "Young man. There are some things in medicine we do not talk about. Do you understand?"

"Yes, Sir."

What else could he say?

For a few days, Garven ruminated over what had happened. His thoughts ranged from the radical end of the continuum that he might inform the police or someone, to the medical stick-together white shield end that told him that the baby could never have survived and could never have had a remotely decent life. He wondered endlessly what he would have done, how he would have approached the parents. He came up with no good explanations, made no real decisions, just decided, by default, to do nothing more than to ruminate on it. He was not at all sure what lesson he had learned. Maybe it was that doctors did have to play God. Some of them. Sometimes. He was not sure. He was sure that he was not in a position to cast the first stone. Nonetheless, he took time to record the incident in the spiral notebook where he kept his most secret observations, right under the note about Ted Jackson. He was unsure why he did it, but it seemed prudent for some reason.

Nothing more was said about Garven's obstetrical sins or that he might be punished by being made to repeat the year. He had, in fact, been a good student on the service, and everyone seemed to let it go. He delivered babies well enough to be given the one prize awarded by the vote of the faculty and the residents. He was one of two chosen to work their final week on OB at Gilmer Memorial Hospital on the north side. Gilmer was a strictly private, very posh institution that catered to the rich and not-too-sick. They had the busiest obstetrical service in the private sector. The hospital was run with an iron grip by the general practitioners, including OB, and they were not in the least inclined to the changes they saw around the country wherein specialists were gaining the upper hand in hospital politics because of their greater degree of training. The GPs liked having medical students; they did the scut work; they were good listeners to the old war stories and heart felt dicta. If they were good, the students could deliver a baby or suture a laceration as pay. The students liked the rotation because the food was excellent, and the GPs treated them to theater and sports events tickets and generally provided them with what amounted to a vacation.

The Saturday before he was to go to Gilmer Memorial, Garven received answers to his requests for internship interviews. He was offered interview appointments by nine of the ten hospitals; only Mass General turned him down. The premier Boston hospital maintained a nearly perfect record of rejecting everyone west of the eastern snob line that ran along the western border of Pennsylvania, Garven was told by the rest of his classmates. He was not at all sure of their information, but he took the slight solace he thought he needed from the self-serving statements. Garven's problem was money. There was no way on earth that he could afford to travel to nine cities to interview. He had to narrow the choices down to three, and he would have to take out a student loan to be able to do that. His only other alternative seemed to be to marry a rich woman, but that seemed like a pretty remote chance at this juncture of his life.

He selected Parkland Memorial Hospital in Dallas, the University of Minnesota Hospitals in Minneapolis, and Osterlund Memorial UC Hospital in Los Angeles, and reluctantly round-filed the rest of the responses. He had pangs of concern; what if he had thrown away the place that really wanted him while the ones he chose rejected him? What if he had discarded one of the prestige school applications that would have made him rich and famous? Garven knew that he was not very good at 'what ifs', and he put the questions out of his mind. He was refreshed and ready for the OB service at Gilmer Memorial on Monday morning.

After the busy indigent service at the university hospital, Gilmer was so quiet that it was boring. The OB service delivered an average of six babies a day, and Garven and his fellow student, Kent Cochran, were not even allowed to help on all of them. Some of the G-Ps were more paranoid than others. They refused to let anyone but themselves and the nurse into the delivery suite. Others, like the chief of OB, Dr. Carleton, allowed the students to observe and occasionally to deliver the baby if the woman was sedated. and her line of sight was behind the drapes. Still others—actually only one other—went so far as to allow the husband to be in the room sitting by his wife's head if he promised not to go down by his wife's perineum. It was well known that husbands could not bear to see the blood around the perineum much less the intensely exciting birth of the infant. That was for doctors and nurses only. The fact that the young man allowed husbands in the room was a matter of strong debate in hospital staff meetings, and the jury was still out on the decision whether or not to allow the practice to continue.

The oldest physician on the staff at Gilmer was Leonard Cartelini, age seventy-six. He was a true general practitioner of the old school. He delivered babies, took care of infants, children, adolescents, adults, and the elderly. He prescribed their medicine, did their surgery, and gave them counsel—cradle to grave and across all specialties. His comment about specialists was delivered with a hearty short snort.

Dr. Cartelini loved to teach. And if the truth were known, he liked to have the medical students with him because they could stand longer. He liked to give nitrous oxide to all of his patients, and with the students to do the easy part, the baby catching, he could administer the N2O and give the medications. Garven and Kent were called by the head OB nurse when one of Dr. Cartelini's patients went in to active labor and was being taken to the delivery room. He wanted both of them to help.

Mrs. Danielle was a young primip, age eighteen. Her baby was a week late, not particularly unusual for primiparas women. She was a very sheltered Catholic girl, and no one had told her anything about what would go on with the delivery of her first baby. Her fear caused her to tolerate the labor pain poorly, and Mrs. Danielle started to panic.

"Shall I set up the nitrous, Dr. Cartelini?" asked the delivery room nurse.

She already knew the answer and was bringing the oxygen and nitrous oxide tanks into position. Dr. Cartelini gave nitrous at the slightest provocation.

"Please do, Mrs. Acton," the old obstetrician said. "Boys, how about you going down to the business end and take care of matters there. I'll manage the anesthetic. We have plenty of help, Mrs. Acton. You can go about your work someplace else, if you wish."

Mrs. Acton was chronically busy; so, she accepted the reprieve offered by Dr. Cartelini.

Labor was progressing well, and all Garven and Kent had to do was wait. Dr. Cartelini placed the mask on his patient's face very gently. She moved her face from side to side trying to get away from the rubber cover over her mouth and nose.

"Try and relax, dear," Dr. Cartelini said soothingly. "This is a little something to make you relax. Takes away the pain for a bit. Before you know it, you'll have a big bouncing baby. There now, that's it."

The kindly old doctor's hypnotic voice was almost as soothing as the anesthetic itself. Garven was surprised to hear the patient begin to laugh. It seemed very much out of place.

He poked his head over the drapes, looking from the bottom up.

"Now you know why they call it laughing gas, young man. I understand that the specialists don't use it at the big university. Shame. Good for you to see some different ideas, to my way of thinking."

Mrs. Danielle settled down, stopped struggling, and the room became peaceful.

Dr. Cartelini and the two medical students chatted amiably about the weather, the relative advantages of the western over the eastern U.S., and about how much harder medical school was back when Dr. Cartelini was a student.

Kent whispered to Garven, "You see any action?"

He was referring to the progress of the delivery.

Come to think of it, Garven could see that they had not made any progress since the patient had gone to sleep.

"Nope," he said. "I read about nitrous in *William's*. You can expect delivery to slow down. That's one of the reason's it's not popular at the U."

After a few more minutes of inaction, Garven asked Dr. Cartelini if it was all right to use forceps.

"You know how, boys?" the elderly doctor asked.

"Yes, Sir. Do it all the time at the U. We get lots of pregnant little girls there," Garven told him.

"Do what you think's best, boys. You're down at the business end. Got to learn to make the big decisions sometime. That's part of the education they don't tell you at the U. Always got some big professor to back you up. This is the real world. Go ahead."

Garven leaned from his seat and picked up a pair of Simpson forceps. The instrument was disarticulated, and Garven inserted one of the blades, which had a pelvic curve and a flattened cephalic curve, as gently as he could around the baby's face. The head was still high in the canal, and placement was tight and difficult. He put the second blade on the cheek bones because he could not get either blade well situated around the lateral bossing of the head. He began to move the forceps gently to and fro and back and forth. There was very little movement of the infant. Garven was sweating.

"Think the Elliots would be better?" Kent asked.

He held up a different pair of forceps, this one simpler and with a rounded cephalic curve.

"No. I'm making some progress with the Simpsons. It's a slow go. Mrs. Danielle doesn't seem to be doing anything."

A small light turned on in the dark recesses of Garven's mind. He had a bad thought.

"Hey, Kent. Take a look at her skin, okay?"

Kent pulled back the drapes. "Jeez!" he said, hissing the word almost under his breath. "She's blue! Almost purple!"

"Oh, no," Garven moaned.

His worst fears were realized.

"Get up to the head and see what's going on. She's not getting any oxygen."

Kent leaped from his position as an observer at the bottom as if he had been propelled from a cannon. The movement startled old Dr. Cartelini who had been dozing nicely as the two medical students did the hard work of the evening.

"Wha... What? What is going on, young man?" the doctor asked.

Kent was at his side. He ran his fingers from the mask on Mrs. Danielle's face to the tank. To make sure, he ran his fingers along the tube from the green oxygen tank. It lay innocuously on a side table. The tank was slowly emitting four liters per minute onto the table top.

"Garven!" Kent shouted, ignoring the doctor. "She's been getting straight nitrous. I haven't got a clue for how long! Jeez! What are we going to do?"

Dr. Cartelini looked dumbstruck, bemused. He could not articulate. The gravity of the situation had penetrated fully, and he was now living out his worst medical fantasy noir.

Garven became more calm and thoughtful as his medical school partner became more excited and as he fully comprehended what had happened. Nitrous oxide should be given in high concentrations only in the early induction phase of anesthesia then the patient should receive mostly oxygen with only occasional whiffs of nitrous to supplement the initial anesthetic dose. Some of the physicians liked to run a very dilute flow of the anesthetic along with the oxygen to keep the anesthesia smooth. No doctor ever wanted a patient to receive pure nitrous oxide for a prolonged period.

"Listen to me, Kent, Dr. Cartelini. She's anoxic, probably hurt real bad. We need help. Get Mrs. Acton in here. We need an anesthesiologist stat! Get rid of the nitrous tank altogether so there can't be another mistake. Turn up the O-twos to fifteen liters a minute. It's our only chance."

By default, Garven was now in charge.

Garven set about to deliver the baby as fast as he could. Kent ran for the nurse. Dr. Cartelini held the mask to Mrs. Danielle's face. His face was contorted in an agony of remorse, and he was praying.

Everyone stayed where they were until the baby was delivered—dead—and until the anesthesiologist said they could get the mother over to the ICU. She had a heart beat and a pulse, but no respirations. The anesthesiologist had intubated her trachea and was giving her straight oxygen from an automatic machine.

In the ICU, when the patient was settled in, the anesthesiologist took Dr. Cartelini, Garven, and Kent aside and said, "Look, this is bad. The worst. She probably had no O-twos for half an hour or more. She's gorked if she's gonna live at all. Probably be best for all concerned if she doesn't make it. Leonard, you better get neuro down here. Got to spread this as far as you can. You'll get the straight skinny from whichever one of the neuro guys is on call. You better have that to tell the husband. Might want to have one of them see the family with you; the neuros are good at this sort of thing. They see death and people being made into gorks all the time. They know what to say."

Leonard Cartelini's face was the color of yesterday's ashes. He truly looked ill.

"Yes... I'll get Stridell or Knox in. They'll know what to do," he said quietly.

His voice was lifeless. He had aged twenty years in the last hour, and he could ill afford it.

"I never had an OB death before. This is awful, just awful."

He sagged into a chair.

"You guys get hold of Stridell and Knox. They need to get here stat. Tell them this is a touchy one; they'll have to help handle the husband," said the anesthesiologist. "Nothing more I can do. Good luck. You'll need it."

Kent stayed with Mrs. Danielle. Garven called the answering service and got hold of Dr. Knox, the neurosurgeon, and explained what had happened.

"Anyone said anything to the family yet?" Dr. Knox asked.

"Not yet."

"You go out and tell them there's been a problem in the delivery room and that Mrs... what is her name?"

"Danielle."

"Mrs. Danielle is having some difficulty. Don't say anything more and nothing less. Understood?"

"Yes, Sir."

"And you do it. I don't think old Cartelini is up to it. He should have retired a long time ago. I guess I'll have to do something about it. I was hoping he would get the hint and fade away. Anyway that's a problem for another day."

"Okay. Boy, I'd give my left arm not to have to, but you're right, Cartelini is in no condition at this point."

"Better get used to it. This is why people with any sense don't become doctors, especially neurosurgeons. But somebody has to deal with the bad stuff. And..."

"Yes, Sir?"

"Get an arterial blood gas. Let's at least find out where she is now. Know how?"

"I've done a couple," Garven said with well warranted humility.

"Good. That's almost a series. You've seen one, done one, and now you'll be ready to teach one."

Garven seemed to remember hearing that line before.

The arterial oxygen saturation was 300, about triple the normal value. They certainly were giving her enough O2. He gave the family the exact message Dr. Knox and told him to communicate. Dr. Knox was in the ICU in fifteen minutes.

"Hello, I'm Dave Knox," the neurosurgeon said as soon as he had checked over the labs. "Let's look at the patient. You Garven?"

"Yes, Sir," Garven said to the tall authoritarian looking physician.

Despite the lateness on the hour—it was one-fifteen in the morning—he was dressed in a dark suit, fresh starched shirt, and a regimental tie in obvious contrast to the bedraggled appearance of the two medical students and the exhausted elderly physician who remained slumped on the ICU chair with his head in his hands.

It took Dr. Knox less than five minutes to run through a thorough neurological exam.

"So tell me what you see, Garven," Dr. Knox said when he had finished his evaluation.

"Oh, this is Kent. Kent Cochran, Dr. Knox."

Kent had joined the two men and the ICU nurse who was listening to the conversation.

"Kent," the neurosurgeon said and extended his hand.

"Anyway, she has pinked up; vitals are okay. She doesn't react much. Pupils are dilated," Garven said in answer to Dr. Knox's question.

"That's pretty fair," the neurosurgeon said. "What year are you guys?"

"Seniors," Kent answered.

"Then you ought to be able to do a little better. Does she react to external stimuli?"

"I couldn't get a response," Garven said.

"Did you do this?"

He gave Mrs. Danielle's nipple a very hard pinch and a twist. She did not move in the slightest.

"Oo-oh, Dr. Knox, I wish you wouldn't do that. It makes me hurt," said the nurse cringing.

"Here's another way. Pinch like this."

He used the tips of his fingernails to crimp the skin. Nothing. The pinch left a clearcut mark.

"I was taught to push a knuckle into the sternum. Is that a good way?" asked Kent.

"Nope. Makes a big bruise. It's a good enough stimulis, but the mark makes you look like Thoralf, the Visigoth. You never want to have the family think you are hurting their loved one. Just one of those little pearls," said Dr. Knox.

Garven was taking in the pearls of wisdom as much and fast as he could. His head was fuzzy from the late hour.

"Turn off the respirator," Dr. Knox said to the nurse.

"Don't you want an EEG, doctor?" the nurse asked the neurosurgeon.

"What for?" he asked.

He took the respirator connection off Mrs. Danielle's endotracheal tube himself. She did not breathe.

"Her brain has been destroyed. She will never live off the machine, and that's no life. She'll be gone in ten or fifteen minutes. We'll wait."

"Don't we need to talk to Dr. Cartelini or the husband or maybe the medical examiner first?"

"Nope. Relax Jennifer. I know this is a tough one, but you're in the ICU because you're smart and tough. She's gone, and you can't let it eat you up. You'll have to let it go. The poor husband will have plenty on his plate not to have to deal with the decision about unplugging her. That's what I'm here for. Someone has to do the hard things, and I just did it."

"I know you're right, Dr. Knox; but it's just that she's so young. It's her first baby. It's ghastly. I hate this," Jennifer said.

She was near to tears.

Dr. Knox put his arm around her shoulders.

"Try and forget it. It's terrible, and there's nothing we can do now. We'll just have to put the best face on it we can, and go on. Is the husband in the ICU waiting room?"

Jennifer nodded, 'yes'.

Dr. Knox talked to Dr. Cartelini separately and very calmly and gently. The old man looked as if he would collapse, and the neurosurgeon treated him as if he were one of the patients, which, in a sense, was true.

"I'll do the talking. Be very careful what you say," Dr. Knox told Garven and Kent.

The two medical students, the G-P, and the neurosurgeon approached the young husband.

For the next thirty minutes, Dr. Knox talked to Mr. Danielle in a calm soothing fatherly voice. He explained that there had been an anesthetic complication—no one's fault, just one of those things. He discussed the damage to Mrs. Danielle's brain—irreversible damage caused by no oxygen. He made it plain that there was nothing on earth to be done. She had died peacefully never knowing that she had trouble, and she was now in a better place. Dr. Knox said that it would have been worse had she survived because she would have been a complete mental cripple, a vegetable; and she was too fine a woman to have wanted that.

Mr. Danielle agreed. He broke down and sobbed. Dr. Knox put his arms around the portly young man and let him cry it out.

"Nothing to be ashamed of. Let it all out," Dr. Knox soothed.

When they left, the neurosurgeon called Bert Duxton who was on internal medicine call and told him he thought Dr. Cartelini should be admitted to the hospital.

Before he left Dr. Cartelini, he said, "Now, I took care of this mess, tonight, Leonard. But you have no business in OB from here on out. Understand?"

Dr. Cartelini just nodded. He knew that he was defeated. It was a terrible way to end a medical career. His heart cried out in protest, but his rational mind had returned and overruled his emotional side. He knew that Dr. Knox was right. He would be lucky if they let him retire without something dreadful like a malpractice suit happening. That would be the last great ignominy. There had never been a malpractice suit in the entire history of the hospital. He offered a silent prayer that he would not be the first.

Garven made a short pointed note in his secret journal, naming names. For Garven Wilsonhulme two things came out of his assignment on obstetrics. If Garven had ever given a moment's consideration of OB-Gyn as a career, his medical school experience had dispelled that notion forever. Secondly, he was now inalterably set on a course that would lead to his becoming a neurosurgeon, and he would let nothing get in his way. Everything else, careerwise, seemed insipid and superfluous. "*Alea jacta est,*" he said to himself, "The die is cast."

CHAPTER
Twenty-Seven

When Garven scheduled interview trips for his internship applications in November, he realized that his finances were beyond the difficult. They were fast approaching the crisis state. He would have to fly to the cities for the interviews because there was not enough time to drive on the two day weekends he could afford to be away from school. He could not moonlight much because he was on call most of the time, and his days were routinely sixteen hours long. Even he had to sleep sometimes. He felt desperate.

There were beginning to be comments made about his eating from patient trays, and between quarters it was difficult to justify his presence on the wards at all. His hidey-hole living quarters were as yet undiscovered; that was the saving grace in his day-to-day existence. He broke down and got a student loan. He felt almost as if he had applied for welfare. Somehow, he sensed that there was a stigma to getting the loan, that the admission that he had no money was like a confession of laziness or failure. Furthermore, the interest rate was high, and even if he filed for bankruptcy someday, he would not be able to discharge the student loan debt. It gave him a sense of powerlessness that he hated. Whatever it was, Garven did not like the feeling, and grew angry. He was determined to change his fortune.

Garven spent Christmas with his mother. She was now living in a small two bedroom house provided by the school district; and by dint of her industry, had made the house into a pleasant homey place with her decorating stamp on it. For supper the first night of his short vacation Garven ate his first steak in two years, then slept for eighteen hours. He did not get to Emmett to see

Dr. Wilsonhulme. Rachel told her son that the doctor was showing his age rather markedly. His years of smoking had caught up with him, and he was suffering from emphysema to the point that he kept to his home much of the time. Garven had to be back to his autopsy job by the third day.

"You look pretty thin, son," Rachel said as he left. "I know you're busy, but you'd better take some care of yourself, can't afford to get down sick at this point."

"Rest and good food are in short supply, Mom. I need you to come up and cook for me," Garven said.

"It's about time you found a wife, Garven. You truly look like you could do with what a wife can provide. Can't you find some rich girl that loves to cook and keep house?" Rachel asked with a smile.

"Somebody told me the girl to look for, something like what you're suggesting: 'My perfect girl and who could ask for more; deaf and dumb and beautiful and owns a liquor store'. I think a wife who wants to support me is another item in short supply," Garven answered.

He kissed her good-bye.

Perhaps it was the mother and son talk, or perhaps it happened because Garven was explicitly looking; but it was serendipity either way. Garven met the girl of his mother's description and of his most serious needs at a party the Saturday after Christmas. The party was at his friend Gordon's. His parents, the Fitzpatricks, were the only people Garven knew who had enough money to have a party. Garven saw her because she was standing alone for the bulk of the evening and appeared somewhat unhappy. He would not have paid her any attention, either but for a chance remark by Gordon Fitzpatrick.

Garven was enjoying himself.

He said to Gordon. "I appreciate the invite. Good booze, good food, the whole schmear. I am going to remember every crummy little sacrifice when I get done with med school and go out and make me a bundle and not pay a second's attention to anyone who gripes that I'm rich. It must be nice. Your folks have it made."

He did not say it with envy; he was in simple agreement and was waiting his turn.

Gordon said, "You should do it the easy way, Garven. Do you know who that is over there."

He pointed at the girl who was standing by herself.

"No idea. Who?"

"She is hands down the richest girl in Arizona, probably in the entire western U.S. Her dad is the 'Fletcher' of 'Meredith, Fletcher, and Daniels'," said Gordon.

"The MFD grocery store chain Fletcher?"

"The same."

"How come she's standing there all by herself? How come she's not married, for that matter?" asked Garven.

"She's kind of funny. I don't know, just not very appealing in the personality department. Not a real looker either," Gordon said. "I've known for a long time; she's kind of fragile in the emotions department."

"You could put a sack on her head and avoid long and deep conversations," Garven joked.

"And I guess her old man is a holy terror on all of her dates. Thinks everybody is a gold digger out after his dough. From what I hear, that hasn't been far from wrong," Gordon told him.

"How come you haven't given her a tumble, Gordon? No one would accuse you of being a fortune hunter," Garven asked seriously.

"Oh, that's impossible. Elizabeth and I are pals, childhood buddies. We grew up together. It would be like kissing my sister. She would have a heart attack if I made a pass at her. I really like the girl, but not in any kind of a romantic way."

Garven was calculating and hoped it did not show in his face.

"She looks kind of forlorn standing over there all alone."

The light bulb came on over Gordon's head finally.

"Hey," he said, "you want me to introduce the two of you?"

"That would be great. I don't seem to be wallowing in companionship, myself," Garven said, glad that his friend had gotten the message at last.

Elizabeth Fletcher could generously have been described as plain. She did not augment her plainness with much in the way of make up, eschewing it from a semi-religious, Episcopalian, viewpoint. Her face was long and angular, "high cheek bones," her mother said; "horsy," her girl friends said—behind her back. She was thin and tall and accentuated her longness by wearing ankle length plain skirts and dresses of the richest plain woolens in the fall and winter and cottons in spring and summer. For some perverse reason she was fond of long dangling earrings, long strands of beads, and Indian belts with hanging strands of beads or silvered thongs. The effect was that of stalactites hanging from a thin white cave column.

Elizabeth had had the best education that money could buy, including a year in the *Le Manoir Ecole pour Jeunes Filles*, a finishing school for girls in Lac Neuechatelle, Switzerland. She had been placed, one time or another, in the company of the sons of most of the Fortune 500 executives, European princes and pretenders, Olympic athletes, English high churchmen, and even the nouveaux riche of New York City. She could tell a confidant about her friends the Cabots, Lodges, Astors, Gettys, and Hunts. But still, she was shy to the point of being "retiring", as her mother put it delicately, and of being a "wallflower" as her friends described her—again behind her back. That was why she was standing alone and having no fun when Gordon and Garven strode up to her.

"Hi, Lizzie," Gordon said in his most sprightly party voice.

"Oh, hi, Gordon," said Elizabeth.

She had been lost in thought, and Gordon's voice had startled her a little. She could not avoid a frown. Gordon knew that she hated to be called Lizzie.

"Having a good time?" Gordon asked.

"Oh, sure," she answered perfunctorily.

"This is a friend of mine. I'd like you to meet him. This's Garven Wilsonhulme. He's a med student with me. I think you'll like him, Lizzie; he isn't anybody important, or rich; and he doesn't know any of the snootin' groupers."

The latter phrase was his and Elizabeth's for the stuffed shirts of their mutual acquaintance.

"Hello, Garven," Elizabeth said and extended her hand.

It was soft, thin, and dry. Garven bet himself that she had never held a broom or done a dish.

"Garven, may I present my old kindergarten friend, Elizabeth Fletcher," Gordon said and swept his arm in a theatrical mime of a bowing musketeer.

"Elizabeth," Garven said and nodded his head in a very brief little bow of his own.

"Thank you for not calling me, Lizzie. Gordon knows I hate that corruption of my name; that's why he does it all the time."

She chucked Gordon in his ribs.

Gordon looked up abruptly.

"Hey, there's the Hathaways. I have to say hello to them. See you guys later."

He left Garven and Elizabeth alone, standing in the middle of the room.

Garven looked around and smiled shyly.

"We're sort of on display out here. Mind if we find someplace more private and talk. I don't get to talk to smart nice girls that much. Would you mind?" he asked.

He had an air of innocence that was fetching to Elizabeth. She knew the house and led him to one of the sitting rooms where they could get away from the noise and chatter.

Garven found that he genuinely liked Elizabeth before the evening was over, despite all of her riches, quirks, and frailties. He accomplished three things that night: He made her laugh; he drove her home; and he secured another date for the next weekend. Unknown to Garven, Elizabeth was twenty-eight, had not had a real date for two years, and the last date with a boy she liked was more than five years ago. She would have broken his arm if he had not asked her out again.

CHAPTER
Twenty-Eight

Psychiatry was the main clinical service for winter quarter for his third of the senior class. He also had short courses in cardiology and electrocardiography, the medical subspecialties, and clinical pharmacology. For practical purposes he lived on the psych ward for three months.

Psychiatry was going through one of its periodic upheavals. Whereas previously, psychiatrists bristled when another doctor or a patient compared 'psychiatrists, and real doctors', and especially when the neurology and neurosurgery residents made disparaging remarks about pseudoscientific mental masturbation being the core source of the psychiatry discipline, now the psychiatrists had become afraid that traditional medicine was a source of their patient's symptoms. The fall before Garven came on the wards, they did away with physical examinations, stating that the hands-on familiarity entailed could be interpreted as an assault to those of fragile psyche. When Garven admitted a patient to the psych ward, he had to get a medicine intern or medical student to do the physical. This caused him acute embarrassment, and the doc who had to do his scut work was invariably nasty about it. It did no good to try and explain.

Garven quietly observed the psychiatrists as much as he did their patients. Sometimes—no, often—he was not so sure he could tell which was which. The psych residents and staff lacked senses of humor, for one thing. It was out and out foolhardy to refer to them as 'head-shrinkers' or just 'shrinks' since that was an insult to the scientific basis of their specialty. And to hear them talk, you would have thought that psychiatrists invented the very idea of the scientific method or at least were the last great bastion of objective scientific thought. He wanted to get along well; so, Garven was careful not to mention the word 'voodoo' either.

On his first day on the ward, Garven learned to take the discipline of psychiatry seriously or at least not to make light, publicly, anyway, of the intense feeling of pride the shrinks had for their specialty. He told a joke to one of the other students and was overheard by a staff psychiatrist.

The joke Garven told was: "A rich woman went to her psychiatrist for five years, one fifty-five minute hour every week, without fail. Finally, the doctor told her, 'I am pleased to announce that you are cured, and I am marking your case closed.' Instead of rejoicing, the lady frowned and developed very sad eyes. 'What could be wrong, Mrs. Vanderbilt?' asked the psychiatrist. 'I would have thought you would be thrilled at my diagnosis and prognosis.'

"'Well,' she said, huffily, 'that's what you psychiatrists would think. Five years ago, I was the Lady Godiva, and everyone stared at me. Now what am I?'"

The lecture from the senior psychiatrist had started much like those Garven was used to hearing from as far back as prep school, maybe even further, "Young man, perhaps you do not realize the significance of such ideas to our patients. We consider them serious and to laugh at their mental aberrations is an unprofessional insult."

Garven had fallen all over himself to apologize. He all but put on sack cloth and ashes and was finally forgiven. He promised himself not to tell any more jokes during his stay on psychiatry or even to listen to them. He knew it would keep him out of trouble. It was probably the most difficult thing he did the whole time he was there.

Schizophrenic women were known as having the 'hairy leg syndrome' which included a high degree of inattention to armpits as well. Someone explained to Garven that the condition was different in French women; they just did not know about the pleasing hygiene of leg and armpit shaving. The medical students assumed that the schizophrenic women must have spent their time reading up on how to be ugly, because none of the men could ever recall seeing a schizophrenic that was the least bit attractive. They took care of them without prejudice, but the medical students put in three months of longing to see at least one good looking woman on the wards. The joke was that a very unlovely middle-aged woman sat in her psychiatrist's office and complained, 'I am depressed and lonely. No one talks to me, looks at me, or touches me. Some men even laugh at me. Do you think it could be because I am ugly? Is there any way you can help me accept my life as an ugly woman?'

The psychiatrist answered kindly, 'I am sure psychiatry can be of be of help to you. Please go and lie face down on the couch; so, we can talk.'

Garven had to wait six weeks before a beautiful girl was admitted to the ward. And she was worth waiting for—crazy as a bedbug, completely uninhibited, and as gorgeous as any Hollywood starlet. Garven first encountered her in group therapy. She had taken it upon herself to keep one of the young men in the group as crazy as possible and persisted in molesting him despite all efforts by the staff to get her to cease and desist. It was the new concept to have group therapy in the first place, and someone wrote a scientific paper that proved that sitting in a circle was more beneficial than sitting in rows or standing. Every group session, the girl made sure she sat directly opposite the pathologically shy boy of twenty-two. She came dressed in a blouse whose top buttons seemed incorrigible, and in a skirt much shorter than the norm—a sure sign that she was crazy.

As the group session progressed, and members unveiled their innermost repressed sexual hang-ups to one another, the girl would lean over and display her chest or accidentally on purpose flip up her skirt to reveal to the shy boy with dementia praecox—schizophrenia in the young—that she did not wear panties. About ten times in each group session the boy would let out a yelp or go into a paroxysm of embarrassment. Garven thought he would have a stroke from suppressing his own inner merriment. He did note that group therapy seemed to benefit the young man. At least, the boy's attendance was one hundred percent.

Garven tried to be fair about the discipline. He had to admit to some usefulness of psychiatry. Two cases convinced him of the value of clinical mental health treatment in some patients' lives although not as a field of legitimate endeavor for himself. The first case was on the private service of the chief of the department, Dr. Hyman, Claus Hezekiah Hyman. Garven was assigned to accompany a staff man three mornings a week in his psychotherapeutic sessions. The patient who impressed the medical student was the fifty year old wife of the professor and chairman of the department of fine art at the University of Arizona, the medical school's parent university. In all respects, except one, she appeared to be perfectly normal. She was thin, elegantly dressed, and haughty, exactly as Garven would have imagined the wife of such a luminary to be. She was articulate and spoke with an unaffected Bostonian accent. She was educated, urbane, well-traveled; and she saw things that were not there.

"Come in and take your seat, Mrs. Fairclough," Dr. Hyman invited as soon as Mrs. Fairclough came into the office.

She had been coming to therapy for months and, as a matter of habit, sat promptly down on the couch.

"This is our new student for the next couple of weeks, Mr. Wilsonhulme. I hope it is all right with you that he attends our sessions."

"Fine with me, Doctor. How do you do, Mr. Wilsonhulme?" Mrs. Fairclough asked politely.

"Fine thanks, Mrs. Fairclough. I am pleased to meet you," Garven said.

From that point on, three times a week for six weeks, she ignored Garven. It was as if he were one of the lamps or chairs in Dr. Hyman's office.

"Tell me about your weekend, Mrs. Fairclough," asked Dr. Hyman to start the morning's session.

"Routine, I guess," she said. "We had a small party for some of Henry's junior faculty and their wives. I handled it fairly well, I thought."

"I'm sure you did. Any further visions?"

Garven was surprised at the abruptness of the question. Mrs. Fairclough did not seem the least bit perturbed at what would have been a most improbable question for anyone else.

"Yes, doctor. Twice. The Virgin came again. To my bedroom."

"Did she speak?"

"Yes, for a long time."

"About what?"

"I can't recall everything, but the gist of what she said was that I was the chosen one, the vessel for ushering in the millennium. She gave me instructions for changing the catechism and several of the holy sacraments; so, we could be prepared for the coming of her Son."

The delivery of her statement was perfectly matter-of-fact, as if she were describing gossip during a bridge game.

"Was this real, Mrs. Fairclough?" asked her psychiatrist.

"As real as the ring on my finger," she replied without the slightest hesitation, holding up the fourth finger, left hand. "I know what I saw. I know I saw a vision, and I know that God knows. Who am I to deny what God knows and what I know he knows?"

"Did you touch her?"

"No, Doctor. She is the Mother of God."

He should have known better.

Mrs. Fairclough told of hearing voices coming from her husband's ham radio set, directed at her. She related a second vision during the weekend in which she was visited by Queen Victoria. She had been created a Lady in Waiting with the special function of declaring the imminent approach of One Greater Even than the Queen. This was a follow-up to the visit of the Virgin Mary. Mrs. Fairclough was a devout, even mystical Catholic, but ecumenical in her social acquaintances, evidently, thought Garven.

They were nearing the end of the fifty-five minute hour. Dr. Hyman summed up and gave his clinical therapeutic admonition.

"I trust that you did not share these experiences with anyone else, Mrs. Fairclough. You know they would not be accepting of such confidences, and you could be embarrassed by them broadcasting what you tell them. It is best that you remember to confine your telling about the appearances to me. We can talk about them freely here, but please be very careful to keep them to yourself otherwise. They are of too personal a nature to share outside this room. Will you remember that, no fail?"

"Yes, Doctor," the patient replied.

She seemed perfectly satisfied with the arrangement.

After Mrs. Fairclough left, Dr. Hyman told Garven, "The patient has a very entrenched delusional system. She has visual and auditory hallucinations that she is wholly convinced are not only altogether real, but purposeful. Fortunately, she seems to function just fine otherwise. As long as she keeps from telling other people about the visions and such, she does well and maintains her position in society. I don't have to give her any sedatives. I can't let more than three days go by without having her tell me about her subconscious events, or she will hire a sound truck or some other awful way of broadcasting her delusions."

"That makes it difficult for you to get away, doesn't it, Dr. Hyman?" Garven asked, thinking for the first time of the consequences for the therapist.

"I feel like the prisoner of Zenda. Medicine is a jealous mistress, Garven. No matter what area you choose. Bear that in mind."

"I can see that, Dr. Hyman. I'll keep your advice in mind," Garven replied.

"So what's the diagnosis, Mr. Wilsonhulme.

"Paranoid schizophrenia. Classical," Garven answered.

"Good boy. Even though she doesn't express any fears at this point in the course of her illness, she has a compartmentalized, complex, and intelligently presented delusional system, hallucinations, and ideas of reference that are indeed classical. I'm afraid that she will deteriorate mentally in the future.

We'll keep a close watch on her. You have done a good job on the service and seem to have an aptitude for psychiatry. Are you interested in pursuing a residency in our specialty?"

"I've been giving it considerable thought," Garven lied.

It was always best to let the current professor believe that his or her subject was the greatest thing since proverbial sliced bread and that you were on the very verge of committing your life to the study that the professor found so fascinating. Garven had not the slightest inclination even to think about psychiatry as a career. Most psychiatrists were touched in the head, so far as Garven was concerned.

The second patient who convinced Garven of the relevance of psychiatry was a young man who entered the hospital during the second to the last week of Garven's stay on the psychiatric service. Garven was taking ward call. That meant that he was responsible for doing the admission history, including the very extensive mental health survey. He had to find a medicine resident to do the physical exam, which still galled him more than it did the psych residents.

Tommy Lee Gainer came onto the psych ward between a graying middle-aged man and one of the burly psychiatric aides. Even at a distance, Garven could tell that something was gravely wrong. The boy was disheveled, dressed in mis-matched clothes, and his hair was uncombed. The man accompanying the boy, obviously his father, had been crying, and appeared pale and frightened. He had obviously come from work. He was dressed in an expensive three piece suit. He wore a Phi Beta Kappa key on a gold chain and had a signet ring on one pinkie. The boy was red-faced and excited. Like his father, he appeared to be frightened—more accurately, panicked.

"Here's a new one for ya, doc," said the psychiatric aide and drew the boy up near Garven by pulling on his arm.

The boy was resisting and seemed to be afraid of Garven.

"Thanks," said Garven. "I'll handle it from here."

"Best I stay for a while, he's been actin' up," said the aide.

As if to give credence to the aide's statement, Tommy Lee chose that moment to take an erratic and poorly aimed swing at Garven's head. Garven ducked and stepped back. He need not have. The attack was like shadow boxing with a blind man. It was as if the boy could not see Garven. As Tommy Lee made threatening motions, he busily muttered to himself. His conversation, like his hostile swing, seemed to be coming from another dimension. Tommy Lee had the wildest, most haunted look in his eyes that Garven had ever seen. Garven was not a believer in angels or devils, but the feeling he got from looking into those psychotic eyes gave him empathy with religionists who described persons possessed by demons.

"Let's go in a room and talk," Garven said to the boy, whom he judged to be around seventeen or eighteen years of age.

The young man looked at Garven as if he were speaking a foreign language. Garven tried several more times with the same result then gave up. He and the aide led the boy to the holding room.

"Get the nurse. I'll stay with him," he told the aide.

"Yes, Doctor?" the floor nurse asked when she came into the holding room five minutes later.

Garven was annoyed at her.

"Two hundred of Phenobarb, IM," Garven ordered.

"Two hundred?"

"That's right."

"You want to knock him out?"

"That's it exactly. Maybe someday we'll have a sort of 'tranquilizer' that stops people from being crazy without knocking them out, but we don't have it yet. Let's get on with knocking him out; so, we can do something besides just standing here."

The nurse complied, glad that the doctor was in charge. She did not like these new admits with the crazed look. She was afraid that she would be alone one day and get hurt. She was going to transfer to peds in a couple of months. It was the kind of nursing she intended to do when she first started nursing school and not this odious tour of duty with the loonies.

Tommy Lee wound down after about an hour of fighting his internal demons and the affects of the sedative. He finally fell sound asleep. Garven had protective pads attached to the bed, then he went out to talk to Tommy's father. The boy's mother had joined the father in the meantime.

"How is Tommy?" asked Mrs. Gainer the second Garven entered the room and before he could even introduce himself.

"Better. He's asleep now. I am Dr. Wilsonhulme...on the psychiatric service."

"Oh, thank goodness you're here; we are about at our wit's end. This has been the worst day of our lives!"

She was very excited and appeared confused and exhausted.

"Take it easy," Garven soothed.

"Tell me what's wrong with my boy, doctor?" demanded Mr. Gainer.

He was nervously wringing his hands and could not look directly into Garven's eyes. The stress of another direct confrontation, even a helpful one, was too much for the man.

"Tommy Lee seems to have had a psychotic—that's crazy—break."

Garven regretted his intemperate use of the inflammatory word the second it left his lips.

"It is a problem of young people his age," he hurried on to cover his *faux pas*. "called Dementia Praecox."

"Is our boy mentally ill? I mean really crazy, doctor?"

"He has a mental illness. It is too early to tell how severe it is going to be. Many people can live pretty normal lives with it."

Garven's extensive experience with one young patient hardly qualified him to pronounce such a judgment, but he ignored his ignorance and made an effort to give the parents a ray of hope.

"We'll take care of him here, and I think you will have better days to come."

"Thank you, thank you, Doctor," gushed Mrs. Gainer.

She looked at Garven as if he were an angel who had just descended into the room through the ceiling. Garven had to confess to his secret self that he rather liked his moment of adulation.

"Could we take a while and get a history. I need the information; so, we can develop a treatment plan."

That phrase was one he borrowed from the nurses, and he quite liked it.

Garven started out with the interminable questions from the mental health survey but soon found the irrelevance of most of the questions to be hampering the conveyance of useful history.

"Why don't you just tell me what happened?" Garven finally asked when he thought the parents might get up and leave out of sheer frustration.

"Finally!" said Mr. Gainer.

He had been bottling up the events of the day in his mind for too long.

"My wife wasn't there. I'll tell you what I saw."

"Start right from the beginning, okay?" Garven asked.

"Yeah. That's right. That's what I should do," said the young patient's father. He launched into his narrative, "The first thing odd that I saw was that all through the fall, Tommy spent a lot of time, too much time, with our neighbor. They were alone alot."

"I always thought he might be kind of funny, one of those kind, if you know what I mean," chimed in Mrs. Gainer.

Garven was pretty sure that he did know what she meant. This was getting sticky.

"Anyway, we didn't like Tommy Lee to hang around with this older man so much, to be alone with him so much. When we tried to talk to him about it, he'd get huffy. You know, clam up, and walk off. We never mentioned our suspicions about the neighbor's, you know, "inclinations", I think they say," said Mr. Gainer.

"Until today," blurted Mrs. Gainer.

"Yeah, today. I had to go an open my big mouth. It's all my fault."

Mr. Gainer was wringing his hands. Garven had never seen anyone do that before. He thought it was just a literary expression.

"I came right out and asked Tommy Lee if there was something funny going on. He got real bent out of shape, yelled at me, said I was crazy, I didn't understand, stuff like that and ran; I mean, he ran, out of the house and slammed the door. That was in the morning. At one o'clock, I got a call at the office that our boy was acting up at school. Man, that wasn't the half of it! Seems Tommy Lee was creating a disturbance. His English teacher told me Tommy Lee overheard one of the kids in the class telling a joke about homosexuals. Our boy burst into tears for no reason, started laughing the next minute, then got hysterical. He threw his fists around, yelled, swore; and believe me, Doc, we never heard him take the Lord's name nor anything else in vain before. He ran out of the back door of the school and hid down in the gully behind the building. That's when I got there."

Mrs. Gainer had her head in her hands as if to hide her eyes from the scene that she could envision from her husband's description. She was crumpling her dress with her hands, oblivious of what she was doing.

"It was like hell. Like listening to hell. Possession by devils. I could hear Tommy Lee's voice. He was yelling, growling, howling, like some kind of trapped animal. He swung at the cops and me when we tried to get him in hand. And the stuff that came out of that boy's mouth. I never heard worse in the marines. He called me every bad word in the book. It was terrible. I have seen some bad things, but I don't mind telling you, I was scared. Finally, you couldn't understand a thing he was saying. Gibberish! The cops had to wrestle the kid to the ground. He didn't know what he was doing!"

Mr. Gainer paused in his narrative, thought a moment, then decided that he was done. Garven had let him vent the steam that had built up during the entire fall and especially that day.

Now, he said to the father and mother, "I think this is what is called a 'homosexual panic'. That doesn't mean that Tommy is like that; it more likely means that he felt threatened with the possibility and that set him off. This dementia praecox is a strange business. He had the mental problem smol- dering underneath the surface for a long time, and this was just the catalyst, the spark, to set him off. I am going to work on him today. Why don't you get some rest and come back in tomorrow?"

The parents were relieved at the suggestion and that someone who knew what was going on was now in charge. Garven recognized what they were probably thinking, and allowed himself the flattery that it was all true in his case. He did not have the slightest inkling what he would do when Tommy Lee woke up. He would leave that problem for later; hopefully by then, it would be someone else's watch; and he would not have to deal with it.

The following day, Garven got a rasping from the psych residents. They were upset that he had taken the whole project of Tommy Lee Gainer on himself instead of calling them at home. Not that they had any complaints about how he handled the case, but they did not get to see a homosexual panic or an acute psychotic break in a youth very often. They needed to see these kinds of cases, and Garven had usurped their prerogative. It had never occurred to Garven to share.

CHAPTER
Twenty-Nine

G arven encountered neurosurgery four times that quarter prior to his formal short rotation on the service that occupied a week during Spring Quarter. All of the encounters served to solidify his determination to be a brain surgeon. During winter quarter he was assigned to the medical subspecialties, cardiology, hematology, and infectious diseases as morning introductory rotations four days a week. He signed up for a full week of medical neurology.

He started out on cardiology and learned read ECG's. The associate professor of medicine in charge of the division of cardiology insisted that the initials for electrocardiogram be expressed as 'ECG', the English way, and not 'EKG', the Germanic way. He was the paragon of the virtue of attending to details. Garven was constantly grilled on the need to measure 'P' waves and 'QRSs', to listen to the neck pulsations as well as the chest, and to get a detailed description of the family history of heart disease and diabetes and of the personal history of smoking, eating, and lack of exercise—the risk factors of heart disease. The professors quizzed Garven about his examination, especially about whether or not the patient had a murmur. Garven figured he was partly deaf because he could not detect a murmur even after the professor announced its presence. That did not keep him from describing a murmur in detail in his own exam once he read or heard that someone had heard a murmur. It was like describing a normal ovary in a gyn exam despite having fingers to short to palpate one. Garven had become a consummate practiced liar on both subjects.

While on cardiology, one of the geriatric arrhythmia patients fell out of bed, a common enough occurrence in hospitals despite every precaution. He was groggy and somewhat disoriented the next morning. The intern thought he was being oversedated by the nighttime sleeper given by the other intern, and the resident presumed it was due to toxicity from his anti-arrhythmia drug, quinidine. Without asking permission, Garven called in a neurosurgery consult. He thought the behavior change came from the head injury.

Dr. Harralsen came on the ward that afternoon; and when the interns and residents learned that it was Garven who had sent in the consult sheet, they suggested to the young man from Cipher that he was an overzealous med student and that this was embarrassing to the service. They were perfectly capable of caring for their own patients' diagnostic needs.

"Acute subdural hematoma," diagnosed the neurosurgeon.

The associate professor of medicine disagreed.

"Not somnolent enough, no neurological deficit, no Babinski, no dilated pupil, Dr. Harralsen," he said, working to keep the note of internist condescension for the surgeon out of his voice, but not altogether successfully.

"Bet you a beer," Harralsen said, smiling good naturedly.

He was not going to back down.

"Oh, well, if it will make you feel better," the cardiologist said.

"I'll set up a one-shot carotid angio as soon as I can. Okay if your med student comes and watches?"

"Sure. Be good for him. He might learn to appreciate the value of a good physical exam instead of invasive contrast x-rays at the drop of a hat," the internist replied.

Dr. Harralsen and Garven accompanied the old man to the x-ray department. As they rode down on the elevator, Dr. Harralsen commented on the cardiologist's statement about physical examination.

"An ounce of contrast is worth a dozen internists, Garven. That's the pearl for today," he said.

The patient was placed supine on the fluoroscope table with the back of his neck supported by a small sandbag; so, it was extended. Four x-ray techs held the man's arms and legs while Dr. Harralsen instilled local anesthetic under the skin and inserted a long Potts-Cournand needle into the right carotid artery in the neck. The needle had a hollow center plugged with a solid metal cannula. The cannula was removed, blood spurted in rhythm with the heart beat, and a syringe of iodine contrast was attached. Dr. Harralsen pushed on the syringe's plunger and instilled the contrast. Serial x-rays were taken at half second intervals from directly over head—AP—and from the side—Lat.

When the x-rays were ready and determined to be of good quality, Dr. Harralsen removed the needle from the neck and pressed on the site for ten minutes. Then he went with Garven to look at the pictures.

"See, Garven," the neurosurgeon said, pointing to the same relative area on the Antero-Posterior and the Lateral films. "The dye fills out all the way to the left skull, but there's a quarter moon shaped indentation on the right. What's your diagnosis?"

With Dr. Harralsen pointing to the abnormality, it was clear, even to the uninitiated medical student.

"Acute blood clot," he answered.

"Acute subdural hematoma," Dr. Harralsen corrected. "Might as well talk the lingo if you're going to join the club."

"Right. Do I get to tell the internists, Dr. Harralsen?"

Garven had a look of one-upmanship on his face that the neurosurgeon appreciated.

"Be my guest, and enjoy every minute of it."

He called the OR to prepare for the operative and curative removal of the dangerous blood clot.

The second time Garven encountered neurosurgery during the winter quarter was on a late Friday afternoon. It was not his patient this time, but he was the student on call for the night. The neurology service was very busy that week, by their own reckoning of what it meant to be busy. They worked about half as hard as the internists and less than a fourth as hard as the average surgery house staff man in a given week. The worst of sacrifices would have been to go home later than five o'clock on a Friday night.

In his week on neurology, Garven learned that it was a practice on that medical service to save their lumbar punctures until late afternoon on Friday with an ulterior motive. They believed, wrongly, that it was of diagnostic value to do spinal taps on patients who were suspected of having masses, like tumors or blood clots, inside their heads. That way they could measure the spinal fluid pressure; and if it was high, they had evidence of an intracranial mass. Although they would never admit it, they secretly knew that about two percent of the people with masses who had an LP would develop severe neurological symptoms requiring transfer to the neurosurgery service and immediate surgery. The practice helped to clear out their beds.

Garven had a date with Elizabeth Fletcher that night. He was beginning to develop a real relationship with her despite the fact that he could not bring himself to overlook her homeliness or to be able to put up with her nervous, quirky personality. His pursuit of the heiress was on track despite those minor impediments. She was beginning to show an obvious and increasing romantic interest in Garven. It was Garven's plan that night to kiss her for the first time. He had spent his last few dollars on roses, an investment not to be disdained on his meager income.

The lumbar punctures were done by the ardent neurology residents, a total of six. Garven was not allowed to do one because it was considered to be a procedure beyond his capacity. He was amused at the fact that every one of the punctures required several painful jabs. He knew that he could get into the spinal canal in one puncture most of the time. He knew also that he had to make allowances for the 'lice and fleas' of medicine, currently the neurologists, without making derogatory comments.

At five thirty p.m., one of the lumbar puncture patients crashed. He went from alert and headachy before the LP to sleepy, to semistuporous, and on to stuporous, in an hour following the procedure.

"Get the head crackers, stat!" yelled the resident on call.

Garven put in a call to the neurosurgery ward.

When Garven announced who he was and from which ward he was calling, the neurosurgery resident said, "Let me guess; they just did an LP, and the patient is herniating."

His reference was to transtentorial herniation of the brainstem. When pressure from above the opening in the tough connective tissue partition between the cerebrum on top and the cerebellum and brainstem below exceeds that in the lower part of the cranial cavity, there is trouble. The upper brainstem herniates through the Opening—the tentorial notch—and presses against the rigid sharp sides of the connective tissue, the dura mater. This crimps the major columns of nerves passing to the body, including those that control the vital functions.

"You are clairvoyant," Garven said.

"This gripes my butt," said the neurosurgery resident. "Happens every Friday at just about this time. I think they do it on purpose. So, let this be a lesson to you. Don't ever, ever, ever do a spinal tap on a patient with a suspected intracranial mass. I'll be right over."

The neurosurgery resident gave the standard lecture to the neurology resident about when and when not to do LPs in a fashion not designed to cement friendships. The neurology resident made it elaborately clear that he was ignoring him. They left each other with mutual curses, and the patient was transferred to the surgical service. Garven left the neurology service with the feeling that they were doctors with impeccable taste in cuisine and music, all the finer things, with a fantastic mastery of arcane and unnecessary trivia, and that it was a specialty whose only value was to take care of the strokes, FLKs—Funny Looking Kids—and dements that would otherwise have cluttered the neurosurgery service.

The date with Elizabeth was more successful that Garven might have hoped. That night she seemed free of all the restraints heaped on her from her station in life as a rich heiress. She appeared to have suspended all suspicions about the intentions of the young medical student who was shorter than she, poorer than she, and no more physically attractive. Elizabeth loved the roses, and she loved the kisses more. The first kiss, given in his dilapidated old car, was tentative and chaste. Elizabeth leaned forward for another with her lips pursed and her eyes closed.

Garven found it best to close his eyes as well. He thought of Rita Hayworth with conscious effort and gave his date another sweet, closed mouth kiss. Elizabeth had never been kissed on the mouth before that night, and she liked it a very great deal. In a few moments the two of them were kissing away with the ardor of athletes. Garven found that the ploy of fantasizing about Rita Hayworth was very effective, and he was able to do his part quite admirably.

It was Garven who broke it off.

"Elizabeth. I care for you too much to let this go any further," he said.

It was the first time he had been in an impassioned situation with a nice girl, and he was not quite sure how to proceed himself.

"You're right, Garven. You are absolutely right," she said.

Her cheeks were glowing pink in the semi-darkness of the interior of the car. Her breath was choppy, and her pulse was racing. It was an effort for her to get control of herself.

"I love it that you didn't try to compromise me. I might have let you do it, you know. Thank you. Thank you."

Garven knew she was referring to the 'It' with a capital 'I'. He now worked to get Rita Hayworth's picture out of his head; so, he could think again.

They had been going together for a month. Now they saw each other almost daily, if only for lunch in the horrible hospital cafeteria. Garven reviewed his life of want and sacrifice, carried on the debate within himself over whether he should make this girl deliriously happy, and contemplated a future of financial ease for himself or if he should wait for another and marry for love. The ruminating thought process took about a minute. He took a leap into the great void.

"I didn't do any more because I...I think, I mean, I think I am in love with you," he stammered.

The stammer was not all put on. It had been hard to push the committal words out.

Elizabeth looked earnestly at Garven's face searching for the slightest hint of doubt, insincerity, or hypocrisy. The pink tinge to all she saw through her state of arousal would have obscured anything but the most flagrant deceit.

"Oh, Garven, you can't know how long I have waited for someone to say that to me. Someone who wasn't just after my money. I don't care two hoots about all that money, and I am thrilled to know that I have finally found someone that feels the way I do. Someone who cares for me, not the money, for me."

That might have been a trifle bit of an overstatement of Garven's attitude, but he did nothing to dissuade her of her illusions.

"I know we could live just fine on what you make when you are a great brain surgeon. My daddy can't protest if he knows that we plan to live on what you make!" she said, her enthusiasm bounding beyond the confines of anything Garven had ever suggested.

"*Whoa,*" he thought. "*In a pig's eye we can live on what I make. Starvation is overrated. This is getting out of hand.*"

Then he ran it through his rational brain again. His moment of passion had passed, and he was able to think clearly again.

He made a fateful decision.

"Look, Elizabeth," he said after a few moments. "I have been thinking about this for a long time."

It had been a couple of minutes.

"What, Garven?"

Her voice had a yearning quality.

"I had wanted to wait, to give you time. But my feelings are too strong. Please forgive me if this seems like rushing into something."

He paused.

"What is it?"

She could not contain her excitement. If he had wanted, she could have given his lines in this little play. She had been practicing them all her life, like every other girl.

"I had planned for a more fancy setting, more formal, but here goes," Garven said. "Will you marry me? Could we get married before I have to go to my internship, do you think?"

"Yes. Yes. Yes. I will, I will, I will. I want to be your wife. Yes," Elizabeth effused.

There was nothing left to interpretation, no coyness. Elizabeth Fletcher wanted to get married. If she were able to tell herself the truth, which she was not, she would have realized that she wanted to get married to anyone who treated her nicely, had no readily apparent major deformities or infectious diseases, and wasn't just an obvious fortune hunter.

"I don't have a ring," Garven said, embarrassed.

Not only had he not had the slightest plan to pop the fateful question that particular night, but he could not have come up with the money for the plastic ring that came as a prize in a Cracker Jack's box.

"It doesn't matter the tiniest little bit to me," she said.

And it didn't. She had made an irrevocable commitment, and no little symbol, however expensive, could make any difference.

"I guess that means we're engaged," Garven said.

"What on earth have I just done?" he thought.

His superego was working overtime, and he had to make a definite effort to get rid of the cautionary voice from his psyche.

"Now all we have to do is to take you home to meet mommy and daddy," Elizabeth said.

She was already deep into her plans for the nuptials and the whole vista of joy that was opening up to her. Elizabeth Fletcher had not had such a happy day in her entire twenty-eight years thus far. She could hardly wait to get home to tell everybody.

"You will come to dinner next Saturday night. I would take you there tonight if they were in town. Daddy is in Chicago for some beef growers' convention or something like that."

Garven had his suspicions about a grown woman who called her parents 'mommy' and 'daddy', but all he said was, "Yes, dear."

He suddenly realized with that note of acquiescence that he sounded for all the world like an old married man. His visions of the future again flashed before his mind's eye, slightly altered from his earlier picture of unrestrained acquisitiveness and uninterrupted pleasure seeking.

On Friday, Garven bought a diamond engagement ring. The diamond was so minuscule that the ring had to be held in an oblique light to be sure that it was present. He had to hawk his Burton-Cagle graduation watch and his spare tire to get that much. He was embarrassed by the tiny chip on the gold band, but it would have to do. He planned to give it to Elizabeth to formalize their engagement immediately before the dinner with her parents on Saturday.

The home of Arthur Fletcher was by all odds the most magnificent dwelling he had ever entered. It was bigger, richer, and more elegant even than the Sutton mansion in San Francisco where he had been a guest when the fraternity was giving him the rush. The house was completely out of harmony with the desert surroundings of Phoenix and, in being so, was also completely out of synch with the neighboring mansions, each separated by several acres of shaven lawn from the others. It was as if an outsized Tudor mansion or the London Bridge had been lifted out of London and set down unaltered in the middle of the Arizona wasteland. The house was made of the most beautiful dark woods, held the most delicate Queen Anne furniture, and boasted the most precious hand knotted Persian, Afghanistanian, Indian, Kashmiri, and Chinese rugs and the finest Parisian silk wall coverings.

The main incongruity with the English character of the house, besides its setting, was the presence of huge swimming pools and a yard ornamented with miniature palm trees. Garven arrived at the front door at the precise hour of the invitation, a full hour before dinner. The door was opened by the butler. His name was Jeeves. Garven was almost inclined to think the name was a joke of stereotypy, but there was little about the mansion or its butler to hint of a sense of humor.

Elizabeth bounded down the circular staircase and across the parquet floor to greet her fiancée.

"Come in, come in!"

Everything about her demeanor was inviting and showed her genuine pleasure at his arrival. Her usual drab looks were improved by the high natural color in her cheeks and the glow of her eyes and her unstoppable smile.

"Hi," Garven said.

Jeeves escorted Garven and Elizabeth to a sitting room off the main hall, asked if they were in need of anything, which they declined, then departed.

As soon as he was gone, Elizabeth jumped on Garven and covered his face with kisses. He was very uncomfortable with her demonstrative affections, fearing that her father would come in and disapprove.

"Hey, let me up for breath," Garven said with a big smile.

His voice lowered several decibels into a conspiratorial hush.

"I have something for you."

"Whatever could it be?" giggled Elizabeth.

She was beside herself with anticipation. Her very excitement made Garven all the more nervous. He knew the ring was a two-bit one. He did not relish disappointing her at that moment.

"Sit over here," Garven instructed.

He led her to a stiff backed chair with a hand made petit point seat cover. He knelt on one knee.

"Will you do me the honor of being my wife, Miss Elizabeth Fletcher?"

He was completely sober and formal.

Elizabeth looked at him, tried to speak, then gave up and simply cried.

The best she could do was to nod an enthusiastic "yes."

Garven slipped the ring on her finger. Luckily, her eyes were so full of tears that she could not really make out how miserly the ring looked. She rubbed it with profound affection. Garven guessed it was good enough.

Garven met the parents an hour later. They were polite, correct, and cool. From what he had imagined, that was a plus. The dinner was sedate and full of questions about his education, background, and his plans. The questions about his ability to make a living, and about his intentions towards Elizabeth were embarrassingly pointed. Garven resented the interrogatory, particularly as posed by her father. The questions carried an accusatory, ironic, condescending edge; and Garven was beginning to feel insulted. Although he was elaborately careful not to betray his feelings, he was frankly angry by the time the desert and coffee had come and gone.

"Perhaps we can retire to my den for a chat, young man," ordered Arthur Fletcher.

There was that 'young man' condescension that Garven so despised. As usual, it set his teeth on edge. He waited for Mr. Fletcher to call him 'son' which he hated even worse. Elizabeth gave him a look of encouragement as she and her mother left for someplace else.

The den was dark and important. Everything about it was important—big strong dark woods, deep green and brown leathers, a huge antique desk made of Honduran mahogany fit for a prince, carpets an inch deep, and original oil paintings of important ancestors on the Louis XIV paisley wall papered walls.

"Sit over there, son," Mr. Fletcher said.

There was no mistake who was in charge in that important room. And there was the inevitable, 'son'.

Garven's initial shyness and trepidation was giving way to something else, more akin to affront or even anger. He had the feeling that he was being talked down to, and he did not like it a bit. He also had a sense of foreboding even though Mr. Fletcher had said nothing that could be interpreted as threatening.

"Thank you, Sir," he said.

As a matter of minor stubbornness, Garven took as much time as possible to do so.

"I know something about you, Garven, from our conversation at dinner. But, you and my daughter seem to have become serious about one another; and I want to know a great deal more."

"There isn't much more to know," Garven said.

"Tell me who your people are. Who are the Wilsonhulmes?"

"My father is a doctor up in Emmett. He no longer practices. The people on my father's side are from Providence."

"The Wilsonhulmes—the banking Wilsonhulmes ?"

"Yes."

There was something about being grilled that really annoyed Garven. It bothered him that his family should be held up for inspection and judgment. He felt like telling Mr. Fletcher about his real father. That would set him on his ear. The result of his annoyance was that Garven was no more than polite, well short of communicative.

Arthur Fletcher filled in the awkward silence. He had had enough of sparring. He was not very good at it anyway. He did better when he gave orders, and his hirelings responded promptly and efficiently.

"I'll come right to the point, young man. I am not entirely uninformed about you and your family. Your father is practically a pauper. Your relatives regard your father as the black sheep and you as nothing more than a mercenary interloper. I have spoken to old Regis myself."

His words were calculated to sting, and they did. The only thing Garven could not figure out quite was why. He decided to listen.

"I have had many the fortune hunter face me across this desk, young man... "

The 'young man' descriptor had worn very thin. Garven chewed his lip.

"And before we were done, every one of them finally admitted the truth. They all left pleased with their efforts, but none of them married Elizabeth, as you can, no doubt deduce."

Now, Garven had been frankly insulted. He was angry; it showed in his face; and he no longer cared.

"And I take it that you fit me into the 'fortune hunter' category. Is that about it, Mr. Fletcher?"

"If the shoe fits, son."

His face was not unkind, just resigned. The older man had been in this position before, and the end result was predictable. The only thing to be determined was the price.

"I am not going to make a fool out of myself protesting that I am no gold digger. I will just say it once and for all, I'm not," Garven said quietly and with obvious emphasis by the way he enunciated every word lest there be a misunderstanding.

He was so adamant that he almost convinced himself of his boundless good intentions.

"That is subject to proof, young man. Had you given that idea any thought?"

"No, Sir."

"Are you familiar with the legal entity of a prenuptual agreement, Garven?"

"I've heard of it, but I don't really know what it means."

"I will enlighten you, then. It is really very simple. You say that you and Elizabeth are going to be married. And you say that you are not interested in her money. Well, you prove that by signing an agreement that you will reject all claim to her money should you divorce."

Garven thought about that idea and decided that he did not like it. He searched for a face saving way to refuse to sign such a binding document that was so inimitable to his real desires. He was angry enough simply to be defiant.

"I love your daughter, and I am going to marry her with or without your blessing or money. I would never sign such an anti-marriage paper. That agreement all but guarantees a divorce to my way of thinking. It would say that we are never to be equal in the marriage, that we have things to separate us. No, thanks. Keep your agreement. If Elizabeth agrees with you that the agreement is a necessary pre-condition, then there will be no wedding. But I doubt that she will."

"Well, young man, that answers that fundamental question."

Mr. Fletcher had entertained the fleeting notion that this one might be different from the rest.

"*Now, I know,*" he thought to himself.

His face was impassive. It was business.

"Now all we have left is to settle on a figure," he said out loud.

Garven was shocked. He knew that Mr. Fletcher was something less than thrilled with him as a fiancé for his precious daughter, but he could not have expected such a brazen declaration of the older man's contempt for him. He fought not to show it, but Garven was furious. He became silent. He began to think of a way to get back at Mr. Fletcher.

"What are you suggesting?" Garven said, looking directly into the rich man's hard eyes.

"Let me ask you, Garven; what kind of debts have you racked up. Must be pretty expensive to go to medical school these days. And they pay a pittance in training beyond med school, isn't that so?"

"It is so," Garven responded.

Mr. Fletcher was sure he had the young man hooked in his weak spot.

"Looking long term, I have the greatest concern for my daughter's feelings, for her happiness. I don't think you ever really intended to marry the girl. Man to man, isn't that about the truth?" the CEO of the food conglomerate asked.

When Garven did not answer, even with a betraying facial expression, Arthur Fletcher considered his question to have been rhetorical.

"Let's get down to cases. How would this figure sound?"

He passed a note pad sheet with the number 100,000 written on it. It was as if he regarded it as ungentlemanly to say it out loud.

Garven almost gasped. He could not imagine himself in possession of such a sum. $100,000 would answer his every need until he could start making a handsome living as a brain surgeon. He looked at the gloating expression on his adversary's face. The man had a look of triumph. To Garven it seemed that he had become engaged in a social poker game with, for him, stupendous consequences riding on how he played his hand. He could take the sure figure and run or ask for more. In either case he would crush the innocent pawn in all of this, Elizabeth. That was a secondary consideration, he had to admit to himself. Or he could do the 'right thing' and turn the man down indignantly and marry his daughter and live happily ever after—in relative poverty. Garven rallied his thoughts very carefully in the pause while he handled the slip of paper. He had a knack of being able to think his most clearly when the stakes were the highest and the pressure was the greatest. He intentionally made his face unreadable. He took out his pen, put a line through the "$100,000", and wrote in his own hand, "$250,000", and passed the slip back across the desk.

Mr. Fletcher's face became a sneer. He looked at Garven with the uttermost contempt.

"Well, my boy, you value yourself highly," he said. "What if I just drop the whole offer? Where will that leave you?"

"I don't think my feelings are the issue," stated Garven flatly.

He was totally poker faced now, looking every bit the hard bargaining negotiator, the coyote.

"The issue is how your daughter is going to react. In the end, that is the only question."

Arthur Fletcher gave in. It was a cheap buy out when he looked at the situation long term. He would have gone double.

"Then there is a condition," he said as he took out his check book and scribbled in the figures and his signature. "You walk out of here tonight, send my Elizabeth a note telling her that you have reconsidered and that you do not love her and that you don't want to marry her—ever. You never say squat about this deal between you and me. That agreed, Wilsonhulme?"

"If I accept the check, I will do just that."

Garven had now placed all of his cards on the table. It was time to pay.

Mr. Fletcher pushed over the check. Garven glanced at the dollar number and gave a slight nod.

"Now, go. Leave by the back entrance. Just turn left as soon as you walk out the door. Good-bye, and good riddance."

He looked down at his desk as if he were going to take up other business now. He caught only a glimpse of what Garven was doing. The young man was writing something on the check.

"What is that, young man?" he bellowed.

He felt the first dart of doubt in the whole evening.

Garven showed the man the check. Across the face he had written "V-O-I-D."

"What kind of tomfoolery is this?" Mr. Fletcher demanded angrily.

"Elizabeth would never have believed me about this conversation. She would have had to think that I was just another jerk you bought off, another fortune hunter. But not with this," he waggled the disfigured check in front of his opponent's face.

Mr. Fletcher made a half-hearted attempt to grab it, but Garven anticipated his gesture and easily foiled his effort.

"I will tell Elizabeth all about this. She will have a choice. Marry me and never set foot in this house, and never see you again, or reject my offer of marriage. Which do you think she'll pick, big shot? You and your money, or me?"

It was a colossal bluff, the most audacious of his young life. Emotionally, Garven was somewhere in a place of limbo between heaven and hell.

-The End-

Synopsis of Book Four: *The Long Climb*

"David Stark is the best there is. He's not real big on publishing papers; nobody is at this place. But Dr. Stark has the best hands and the best judgment of anybody you'll ever see. He runs a very tight ship. I mean he is from the old SOB school of neurosurgery. Everybody hates him. He is as mean as a cornered snake, but he is fair; and he can make you into the best neuro guy there is. If you survive it."

"Boy, it really sounds like a lot of fun," Garven said.

"Forget about fun for the next four or five years, if you come here. But you will do ten times more surgery than you would ever think of doing at a place like the Mayo Brothers. That's the main tradeoff. You have to make a decision early on about the kind of education you want. You can get into a nice clean university hospital or especially into a private hospital. You won't work all that hard, and you'll know the literature like nobody's business. You'll probably even publish a few articles. That's the way to go if you are interested in academics. 'Them as can, cuts; and them as can't goes into academics' is the way the expression goes. You won't do much surgery in one of those clean places, but you will get a little time off. You might even think of yourself as having a life.

"Here, you will work your butt off from the day you arrive until the day you leave. You will learn to operate, and you will do boo-coo surgery. You won't have to worry about the 'publish or perish' bull; you will be too busy cutting. Believe me, you will see everything here--every disease, every complication, every kind of strange character; and I don't mean just the patients. Got to choose, Garven. Give it a lot of thought. This is not the place for everyone. You have to have leather balls to work here."

Heaven and Hell author, Carl Douglass, is a former neurosurgeon turned author who writes with gripping realism. Carl Douglass is the author of multiple novels and two nonfiction works, all of which have grown out of his extensive experience as a student, scholar, researcher, academician, general surgeon, and finally a neurosurgeon. His contemporaries were all raconteurs and commentators on the human condition, and Douglass learned to hold his own. Heaven and Hell, and the other novels in his Saga of a Neurosurgeon series, give the reader a glimpse into an extraordinarily rich and diverse career and life's experience. He now enjoys a bountiful life with his wife of fifty years. They live in a beautiful mountain valley in the Rockies.

HONORS, AWARDS, AND MEMBERSHIPS
Phi Kappa Phi University Honor Society
Alpha Omega Alpha Medical Honor Society
BS (Medical Biology) degree—magna cum laude
MD—magna cum laude
CDR/MC/USN

American Medical Association
American Association of Neurosurgeons
Congress of Neurological Surgeons
Fellow of the American College of Surgeons
The Association of Military Surgeons of the United States
Life Member of the Medical Society of Vienna
Diplomate of the American Board of Neurological Surgery

Past President, Our Community Foundation, Wasatch County, Utah
Past Medical Liaison Officer, Deseret International Foundation
Past Chief of Surgery,
Antelope Valley Regional Medical Center, Lancaster, California
Past Member-at-Large, Central Medical Committee,
Utah Valley Regional Medical Center, Provo, Utah
Past Member, Utah State Foster Care Review Committee